CHARM

BILLIONAIRE BUCK BOYS SERIES

DEBORAH BLADON

FIRST ORIGINAL EDITION, 2025

Copyright © 2025 by Deborah Bladon

All rights reserved. No parts of this book may be reproduced in any form or by any means without written consent from the author.

This is a work of fiction. Names, characters, places and incidents either are the product of the author's imagination or are used fictitiously. Any resemblance to actual person's, living or dead, events, or locales are entirely coincidental.

eBook ISBN: 9781926440804
ISBN: 9798293655281

Book & cover design by Wolf & Eagle Media

deborahbladon.com

CHAPTER ONE

Greer

"GREER LAUREL IRWIN, are you seriously not going to tell me where you are?" Krista Bellard, one of my oldest and sometimes dearest friends, whines over the phone.

I smile at the sound of my full name. She only uses it when she really wants something from me. In this case, it's information about my current whereabouts, but that's top secret. Krista can't stand being out of the loop, and right now, her curiosity is getting the better of her.

"You know you always have more fun when I'm with you," she says.

I'd amend that statement with an *almost* right before the always because things haven't been as rosy as they could be when we've been together over the past few months.

Krista's upcoming wedding has taken its toll on her and our friendship. I can't blame her for any of it, though. She's trying to balance the requests of her mom and her future mother-in-law with her fiancé's vision for the wedding. Add the demands of our shared business to that, and Krista's plate is full.

I feel a slight pang of guilt for keeping my destination a secret, but it vanishes as I step inside the house that will be my home for the next three days.

East Hampton is a dream this time of year. When I realized I had the opportunity to stay here for an entire weekend, I jumped at the chance. I was tempted to cartwheel at the chance, but I left those days behind when I gave up cheerleading after high school.

That was fourteen years ago. I shake my head at the thought of the girl I was on the day I graduated as a senior with an eye on the future.

My life hasn't conformed to the script I thought it would, but I'm not complaining.

"I'm in a safe place," I say to Krista as I drop my overnight bag and purse on the white tile floor in the entryway. "It's very safe here."

"That's a shitty clue, Greer." She laughs. The sound is so warm and comforting that I can't help but smile. Krista's laughs have always been the best.

"I prefer to remain clueless." I sit with that for a second before I chuckle. "You know what I mean."

"I know that you needed a break from Manhattan." She sighs. "My big break is coming up, so how can I fault you for wanting one, too?"

She can't.

She's set to jet off to Hawaii in just a few months for her honeymoon. Since it's her favorite place on earth, I'm over the moon happy for her.

East Hampton may not be Honolulu, but it's the perfect place for me to relax. I have three days to do that, and I plan on taking advantage of every second.

"If you run into any issues with..."

"Stop," Krista jumps in to interrupt me. "You're off the clock in every way. I vow not to disturb you for any reason. In fact, I'll forget your phone number until Monday at nine a.m. sharp."

I don't bother reminding her that I'll be back in Manhattan by six p.m. sharp on Sunday night. "What is my phone number, Krista?"

Silence greets me before she laughs again. "Very funny. I admit I don't know it off the top of my head, but I'll ignore your name in my contact list until Monday morning. How's that?"

I'm all in since it's just past seven p.m. on Thursday. I have all day Friday, Saturday, and most of Sunday to lose myself in the fresh air and the breeze coming off the water since this gorgeous gem of a house is beachfront with a perfect ocean view.

"Deal," I whisper, knowing I'll be the first person she calls if there's an emergency. I always am.

"I love you, Greer," she says. "In case I don't say it often enough."

We promised years ago that we'd never end a conversation without those three words, so I repeat them, "I love you."

"I hope this weekend gives you everything you need." Her voice softens. "Get a little sun if possible, and some sex wouldn't hurt you, although some of the best sex I've ever had hurt a little."

I'm not about to open a discussion about my non-existent sex life, so I avoid it altogether. "Don't stress about the wedding plans. You've got this."

"I sure do," she says, but doubt taints each word. "I'll see you on Monday, Greer."

Before I can tell her goodbye, she ends the call. I toss my

phone on a table next to where I'm standing. The vase filled with wildflowers that is sitting on it is an added bonus. I make a mental note to thank the owner of the house for her hospitality with a card and a fresh fruit bouquet.

Like a moth to a flame, I'm drawn to the wall of windows that beckon from across the expansive space. I dart around the large, comfy-looking furniture and a tall lamp set up next to a chair. I'll put that to good use later when I sit down to open a thriller novel for the first time in years.

I notice something isn't right as soon as I reach the windows.

The ocean is visible in the distance, but that's not the view that demands my attention.

I can't take my eyes off what is in the pool…or, rather, *who*.

I'm not sharing this house with anyone this weekend, so the man standing in the waist-deep water with his back to me is trespassing.

This wasn't how I thought my weekend getaway would kick off, but I'm an expert at solving problems, and that's all this guy is.

It's time for me to get rid of him.

CHAPTER TWO

Greer

I'M TEMPTED to call the local police, but I know I can handle this, or at least I think I can, unless the trespasser proves to be dangerous. I glance around the room and stop when I notice a black umbrella leaning against a wall not more than a foot from where I'm standing.

I have no idea why it's there and not in the umbrella stand by the front door, but who am I to question a gift when it presents itself to me?

I grab the handle before I flip open the lock on one of the sliding glass doors and step outside.

The man in the pool is still oblivious to the fact that he has an audience, so I clear my throat and take a deep breath. "Who the hell are you?"

My voice doesn't sound nearly as menacing as I want it to, and the fact that I'm wearing a pink tank top and denim cut-offs doesn't help with the *I'm-a-total-bad-ass* vibe I'm going for.

The flip-flops on my feet aren't doing me any favors, either. Still, I try to own it because the umbrella in my hand can easily transform into a pokey weapon in a pinch.

He glances over his shoulder at me before his left hand darts in the air in greeting. "Hey!"

Hey?

That's it? He's a trespasser, and his response to getting caught is a nonchalant *hey*?

"Who the hell are you?" I repeat my question, backing it up with a jab of the umbrella's tip in the air.

"Who are you?" He chuckles. "And what's with the umbrella?"

"I'm the one asking the questions," I say. "You're in my pool."

He turns to face me, and it's an instant feast of visual delights. His wet, dark hair is pushed back from his forehead, revealing a face that is a treat to behold. A square jawline covered with a late-day shadow, chiseled features, and a smile that weakens my knees aren't all there is to savor.

My gaze drifts to his broad shoulders, muscular arms, and bare chest before it drops to his abs. The water laps around his waist, so that's where the free show ends.

I shake my head to get back into the moment. I shouldn't be ogling the trespasser. I need him out of the pool now, so I step closer, holding the umbrella handle tightly in my fist.

"I'm in my neighbor's pool," he comments before he stretches. His arms rise in the air, proving just how fit this guy is.

Is he for real?

I don't just mean the whole Adonis thing he has going on. His answer seems super suspicious, given that the woman who owns the house I'm staying in specifically told me that all of her neighbors have pools. That came up during one of our many text exchanges on the vacation home rental app that I used to find this place. After she initially asked how many people would be staying the weekend, and I responded that it would just be me, she seemed intent on setting me up with someone during my stay.

I brushed off her suggestion that I seek out a chef who owns a bistro nearby, so she brought up 'the pool man,' as she referred to him.

Apparently, every homeowner on this stretch of the beach employs him for pool maintenance and repairs. She even gave me his phone number in case I have a pool emergency. I responded that I'd contact her directly if that happens, but she replied that the pool guy is good-looking and single, so I should feel free to reach out to him if need be.

Is that who this guy is? Is he taking a dip on the job and trying to cover it up?

"Are you the pool guy?" I ask, stabbing the umbrella in the air toward him.

It can't hurt to remind him I'm armed and semi-dangerous.

"The pool guy?" he questions back with a light laugh. "I told you I'm the neighbor."

"If that's the case, you have your own pool," I say in my best 'gotcha' tone. "The owner of this house told me that all of her neighbors have pools. If you have one, what are you doing here?"

He takes two steps toward me, causing the water around him to lap against his midriff again. It takes all of my self-control to keep my eyes on his face.

"The pump in my pool died," he tells me. "They're coming in the morning to fix it. I spoke to the pool guy myself, as you call him. I call him Martin because that's his name."

"Aha!" I snap that off my tongue. "I know for a fact the pool guy is named Paulie, so you're busted. Get out of here now before I call the police."

He cocks one eyebrow. "Martin is Paulie's dad."

"Yeah, right." I point the umbrella right at him. "Out now, mister, or I'm calling the police."

He holds both hands up as if he's surrendering. "No need to call the police, but you might want to turn around before I get out."

I gesture to the right with the umbrella, hoping he takes the hint to make his exit right now. "So you can tackle me? No way."

"Tackle you?" He huffs out a deep laugh. "Why would I tackle you?"

"I. Don't. Know," I say each word with purpose. "Why do you swim in random people's pools?"

"For the third time, I'm the neighbor." He rakes a hand through his hair, and *holy bicep,* that thing is huge when it flexes. This man could have me up and over his shoulder in no time flat if he wanted to. He could cart me off to his kidnapper's lair, and I'd never be seen or heard from again.

I take two steps back to get closer to the sliding glass door. I kick off my flip-flops, too, so I can bolt back inside if he charges at me. "Get out of the pool now, or I will call the police. That's the last time I'm saying it."

"I warned you," he says before he walks toward me.

I inch back again. "Warned me about what?"

"This." He moves toward the pool's edge before he starts to make his way up the ramp that leads out of the water.

With each step he takes, more of him is revealed, until... *oh, my God.*

He's completely nude.

He does nothing to hide anything, and I can't stop myself from staring.

Everything below his waist is just as impressive as everything above.

I've seen a few naked men in my life, but this guy puts every one of them to shame. Speaking of shame, I should not be staring at him right now.

I drop the umbrella and cover both of my eyes with my hands. "Grab a towel or something."

His laughter flows around me before I hear movement, and then, "Feel free to look."

I inch my fingers apart so I can peek. A white towel is wrapped around his waist, so all the good parts are covered. Impressive parts better describes what I saw...*no*, magnificent parts.

"I'm going home." He jerks a thumb toward the left. "Because I am, in fact, the neighbor."

"Okay," I say, because what else is there? He's not making a move to knock me out cold, so maybe he really is who he says he is.

"Don't trip over that umbrella." He tilts his head toward where I dropped it. "Maybe I'll see you around."

"Maybe you will."

He shoots me a brilliant smile before he crosses the lush green lawn as he heads toward the sprawling grounds next door.

"Maybe I'll run out of sugar, neighbor," I whisper as he disappears from view. "Scratch the maybe. I will run out of sugar."

CHAPTER THREE

Holden

"PUT MORGAN ON THE PHONE," I demand of my younger brother.

"To do what?" He chuckles. "Drool all over it?"

I stifle a laugh. "To hear my voice, Jameson. You know how much he loves his Uncle Holden's voice."

My nephew is barely three months old, but the little guy has a penchant for smiling whenever I talk to him. I admit it's become an ego booster for me. If work feels like hell, I'll play one of the many video clips I have on my phone of baby Morgan.

I can't help but favor the ones where he's listening to me talk to him.

"He loves your face," he corrects me. "I have no fucking idea why."

"You bastard." I laugh. "When you grow up, you'll realize how great-looking I am."

"I'm twenty-six, old man," he tosses out his preferred

nickname for me, even though I'm only seven years his senior. "You're a five out of a ten on a good day. I, on the other hand...I'm a ten every day."

I won't argue his ranking for himself, but I have a few things to say about where I land on that scale. "I'm so good-looking the woman staying next door couldn't take her eyes off of me just now."

I don't add that I was nude when the woman spotted me in the pool. If Jameson got wind of that, he'd never let me live it down.

"Mrs. Frye has to be raking in a bundle renting out her house all summer," he comments. "You must be making new friends since you're there every other weekend."

I come here often because this house holds a lot of memories for me. It belonged to my late grandparents before it was willed to me. The deed may be in my name, but I've made it clear to my brother and his wife, Sinclair, that they're welcome any time they please. The same is true for my best friends. Declan Wells and Rook Thorsen know they will always have a place they can call home in East Hampton. Since Declan and his wife are expecting their first baby, they've taken a couple of weekend 'babymoons' here. Rook, his fiancée, Carrie, and their daughter have only made one trip so far this year, but they have more planned.

I didn't make the trip this weekend just to catch some sun and enjoy the view. I have an ulterior motive, but I'll share that with my brother in due time.

"I've met a few people," I tell him. "None as memorable as the one I met an hour ago."

"That's the woman you said couldn't take her eyes off of you?" He chuckles. "She needs glasses, doesn't she?"

Smiling, I shake my head. "Go to hell."

"What's so memorable about her?"

Where do I start?

Long curly red hair, curves in all the right places, and a fearlessness that set me on fire are what come to mind first when I think about the woman next door.

Suddenly, my nephew's cries fill the air. It's loud enough that I know Jameson is holding his son.

"It's okay, Morgan," he whispers. "Daddy's got you."

My heart swells with that because I'm damn proud of my brother. He has grown into a remarkable man over the past few years. I'm honored to call him not only my sibling, but also my friend.

It hasn't always been easy between us, but we've repaired the fractures in our relationship. We went from not speaking to one another to him asking me to be his best man when he got married a few weeks ago.

It was one of the greatest honors of my life to stand beside him as he vowed to love his wife forever while she cradled their son in her arms.

"I have to go, Holden," he says. "Enjoy the time away, but don't stay gone too long. I need you at the office."

I may be the CEO of our grandparents' candy company, but Jameson is right there with me in his role as COO. I never worry when I leave Carden Confectionaries in his very capable hands.

"I'll be back on Sunday," I remind him. "You can handle anything that pops up before that."

"You know it," he says. "Later."

He ends the call, leaving me to think about my next move. I glance at the expansive kitchen where I've cooked many meals. I haven't baked anything, though, but there's no time like the present.

I stalk toward the kitchen to see what I can whip together

to take over to my temporary neighbor as a peace offering since I plunged into her pool without her permission.

Mrs. Frye told me I could use the pool whenever I please, but still, I should make amends with the beautiful redhead.

I stop just short of the kitchen island because I know exactly what I need to do to get in front of the umbrella-wielding woman again as soon as possible.

I sprint toward the main bedroom to get dressed since I'm fresh out of the shower and only wearing black boxer briefs.

She got an eyeful of me already today, so I'll cover up since I plan on heading over to see her now.

CHAPTER FOUR

Holden

THE PINK TANK top and denim cutoffs my temporary neighbor was wearing earlier have been replaced with white shorts and a matching T-shirt with the word '*Summer*' printed across the front of it in a rainbow of colors.

Her fiery red hair is now tied up in a messy top knot. Freckles dot her nose, but it's her eyes that I can't stop staring at. They're cobalt blue and bordered with long lashes.

She's so fucking enchanting that I lose my ability to speak.

"Can I help you?" she asks as if I interrupted the most important meeting of her life.

I nod like a bobble head doll as I try to keep my gaze locked on her face, but with her toned, tanned legs on display, that's not an easy task.

"Summer," I read her shirt. "Is that your name or an homage to the season?"

The corners of her lips quirk up a touch, but I don't quite get a smile. "My name?"

"Is that a question?" I push. "Or a confirmation?"

She studies me carefully, her eyes drifting from my face down to the light blue T-shirt I'm wearing and beyond to the faded jeans I put on before I left my house to come here. "Are you asking if my name is Summer?"

"Is it?" I push, expecting her to offer her actual name to me.

"Sure," she says with a grin.

I try to put her on the spot with my next question. "What's your last name, Summer?"

"Time," she answers quickly, and that comes with a smile.

Jesus, that smile could make men forget everything but her.

I can't help but chuckle because my roundabout attempt to get her to tell me her name just went off the rails. "Your name is Summer Time?"

"For all you know, it is. What's your name?"

It's been a long time since I've used an alias with a woman. I used to do it because of my family's wealth and my grandmother's constant reminder that with money comes curiosity. She wanted me to protect myself, so I resorted to using a fake name for one-night stands. I haven't done that in years, though.

The last time I hooked up with a woman I had just met was a few months ago when I was in Philadelphia for business. I introduced myself as Holden Sheppard before I took her to my hotel room for the night. A week later, she was at my office in Manhattan with her resume in hand, expecting a high paying position within my organization.

She was certainly qualified, but I had nothing to offer her other than a polite and unequivocal *no*. Mixing business with pleasure is something I try to avoid. I had no interest in partaking in more pleasure with her, but that didn't mean I wanted her anywhere near my business dealings.

Many people stopped their work to stare when she stormed away after I handed her resume back to her. I blame that on the fact that she announced to everyone within earshot that when we fucked I promised her a corner office and a six figure salary.

Neither was true, but that didn't stop my employees from gossiping about it for weeks. Things have finally settled down in that regard. I don't want a repeat, so I revert back to the alias I used for hook ups in college.

It's unimaginative since it's a name I pulled out of a hat. I literally pulled it out of a baseball cap when I was nineteen. The guy I was sharing a dorm room with scribbled a dozen first names and an equal number of surnames on scraps of paper. He dumped them into the cap, and we pulled out our fake names.

I ended up being Joe Campbell.

His alias was Bard Sanderson.

I still call him that whenever we connect over dinner or drinks.

"I'm Joe," I say with the ease that comes with using the name on and off for years. "Joe Campbell."

"Joe Campbell," she says, repeating it as though she's testing it on her tongue. "It's nice to meet you, Joe."

"You too, Summer."

A curt nod of her head closes that part of our conversation. "You didn't answer my question. Can I help you?"

The glass measuring cup in my right hand is a reminder of my bullshit excuse to see her again as soon as possible. I hold it up. "Can I borrow a cup of sugar?"

She glances at the cup before her gaze is right back on my face. "That's used for measuring wet ingredients."

I cock an eyebrow. "That matters?"

She nods slowly. "In my business, it does."

"So you're a baker?" I deduce.

She leaves that unanswered as she smiles again. "Follow me, Joe, and I'll get you exactly what you need."

CHAPTER FIVE

GREER

WHY DID *that sound so sexual?*

I didn't mean for it to, but it sure as hell came out as an invitation to come inside for a lot more than a cup of sugar. I don't know if he had the same idea in mind as I did when I came up with a plan to ask him if I could borrow some sugar.

All I do know is he beat me to the punch, but I'm not about to complain about it.

The man following me into the kitchen is even more attractive than I thought he was when I first saw him in the pool. That's saying a lot because I silently rated him a twenty out of ten as he stepped out of the water.

He's way beyond a fifty now.

His blue eyes are piercing, and as soon as I opened the door, they were locked on me. His hair is thick, dark brown, and peppered with a few strands of gray that make him second-glance worthy.

If I were being completely honest, I'd do a triple-take if I passed him on a sidewalk or saw him in the grocery store.

Since I have no idea where anything is in this kitchen, I open and close numerous cupboard doors before I find a set of sleek silver measuring cups. I know enough about culinary science to understand the importance of using the correct tool for the job, so I grab the largest cup and head over to the pantry.

It takes all of twenty seconds for me to spot a ceramic canister marked sugar.

"I can help," Joe says from the entrance to the kitchen.

I instantly conjure up a mental image of him standing directly behind me with his arms wrapped around mine as we scoop sugar out of the canister together.

That's what not getting laid in months does to a woman.

I shake off the thought and his offer to help. "It's okay. I can handle it."

"I know you can." He chuckles. "You were ready to stab me with an umbrella. I have no doubt you can handle anything, Summer."

There's a hint of amusement in his voice as he says my fake name. I can't help but smile. "Thanks, Joe."

"What's your real name?" he questions as he steps closer to where I'm standing.

"Does it matter?"

This weekend is a gift to myself. In a way, it's a short break from the pressures of life back home. What better way to escape the day-to-day than to pretend to be someone else?

"It doesn't," he acquiesces. "I hope we can spend some time together before you go back to…"

"The place I came from," I fill in the blank.

"Right." His lips curl into a grin. "Right now, you're

Summer from a mysterious place who showed up here to make my Friday a whole hell of a lot brighter."

"Is that what I'm doing?" I play coy. "I'm making your Friday brighter?"

He runs his gaze over me slowly. "You are. If you give me a chance, I'll make your Friday unforgettable."

I offer him the cup of sugar. "You've already done that. I'll never forget what happened at the pool."

"I'll take that as a compliment." He grabs the measuring cup, being sure to brush his fingers over mine.

Heat rolls through me, stoked by the intensity in his gaze. This stranger is seducing me, and I'm not going to stop him.

Maybe Krista is right. Maybe good sex is what I need. I have no doubt this man can supply that.

"You should," I say boldly. "I meant it as a compliment."

"In that case, you're stunning." He sets the measuring cup on the counter. "Fucking beautiful."

Hearing *that* word fall from his lips sends a wave of desire through me. I bow my head because I'm scared I'll blush like I did back in high school when a boy flirted with me.

"How would you feel about a night swim?" he asks, his voice low and thick. It's peppered with the same need that is enveloping me.

I tilt my chin up until our eyes meet. He towers over me by at least five inches. If I had to wager a guess, I'd say he's just over six feet tall. "Make it at midnight and I'll be there."

His gaze lowers to my T-shirt before settling on my shorts. "Suits or no suits?"

That's a subtle way of telling me that I'm setting the pace for our midnight encounter. "Unwrapping the gift is at least half of the pleasure of receiving it, right?"

"I much prefer giving," he says with a tempting smile. "But, I certainly won't say no to seeing you in a swimsuit."

"Bikini," I clarify.

His eyes darken. "This is pure torture. You know that, don't you?"

I glance at the time display on the microwave less than a foot from where we're standing. "Midnight isn't that far away, Joe."

"It's hours from now." He bites the words out, each slower than the last.

"You'll survive." I look into his eyes. "You came over to borrow a cup of sugar, so you must have plans to make something with that."

"Fuck no." He laughs. "That was so I could see you again."

My pulse beats faster. "You'll see me again at midnight."

"I'll think about you until then," he says in a voice that is deep, dark, and filled with unspoken promises. "I'll bring a bottle of wine?"

I like that he's asking, not assuming that I partake. "Red, please."

His right hand jumps up. I sense he's about to touch my face, but it drops back to his side in a fist as if he's fighting the temptation. "Midnight can't come soon enough."

I can't come soon enough, but I'll forgo my planned bubble bath orgasm and save it for him.

He arches a brow. "Is there anything else I can bring for you, Summer?"

I haven't had sex with a stranger in...*well,* never, so I don't know the protocol if there is one, but I ask for what I want because it's too important not to. "Protection. You'll bring a condom, right? I'm on birth control, but condoms are a must for me."

"And for me," he adds. "I'll take care of it."

"Thank you," I whisper.

"No, thank you." His voice lowers a little. "You came out of nowhere to make this night one I won't soon forget."

"This weekend," I say boldly. "I'm here until Sunday."

It's presumptuous to assume he'll want more of me after tonight, but I toss that out there because I already know I'll want more of him.

His eyes close briefly before they hone in on mine. "Whoever you are and wherever you came from, I'm so fucking glad you ended up here."

"Me too," I whisper. "I'm glad I'm here, too."

I ache to be kissed by him, but he doesn't give me that. Instead, he rakes me from head to toe like he wants nothing more than to devour me before he turns and walks out of the house.

CHAPTER SIX

Holden

FILLING the time since I walked out of Mrs. Frye's home hasn't been easy.

I thought I could focus on work since there's never a shortage of things that require my attention. As the CEO of Carden Confectionaries, I'm the guy who makes the last call on almost everything that matters. I take my brother's opinion into consideration, but at the end of the day, I have to decide what is best for the company that mattered so much to my grandparents.

Carden began as a shared dream for them and has since morphed into a billion dollar empire.

The weight of that is always on my shoulders, but I'll never complain about it. I consider it an honor to sit at the helm of the company, even when I'm faced with the task of working out deals to take over enterprises that are struggling or those that have an owner who has checked out of the business.

That happens more often than most people realize. The idea of launching a candy company can seem like an easy route to riches, but it's a damn hard climb even to get noticed.

Such is the case with a few businesses based in New York that my brother has recently reached out to . Jameson makes the initial contact, and then I swoop in to work on the finer details of a deal that will expand Carden's empire.

That's what our grandmother wanted before her death, so Jameson and I are intent on following through on her wishes.

I glance down when my phone indicates an incoming video call. It's almost eleven. That should narrow the options of who is calling, but it doesn't. My brother, my sister-in-law, and my friends all know that I'm available for them twenty-four seven. If at all possible, I'm never out of reach, although I plan on leaving my phone behind when I go to see Summer in just over an hour.

"Declan," I greet my friend as the call connects. "Why aren't you asleep?"

I know the answer to that question, but I ask it anyway. Like Jameson and me, Declan and his brother run a business whose sales rival those of Carden's. They're not in the candy business, though. Wells, their brand, is all about underwear.

His hair is a mess, and he's sporting a light growth of beard. Impending fatherhood looks good on my old friend, but I don't tell him that. He owns a mirror, so he's well aware of what he looks like at the moment.

"I can't sleep," he says before he yawns. "How hard do you think fatherhood is?"

"Your brother is the guy to ask that question to," I point out, since Declan's brother, Sean, is already a dad. I add on our shared best friend as a great resource, "Rook has been doing the dad thing for five years, Declan. Call him."

"So he can tease me about how fucking scared I am?" He

chuckles. "No way. You've been watching Jameson navigate fatherhood. Does it look easy or hard?"

"Both," I answer as I settle into a spot on the sectional in the living room. I prop my bare feet up on the coffee table. "As with anything worth having in life, some bad always comes with the good."

"I'm pretty sure you're quoting the birthday card I gave you last year. I thought it was perfect since you're getting grayer by the day. The bad being the gray. The good being... hell, I don't know, with age comes wisdom, so the good is wisdom."

That's enough bullshit nonsense to force a question out of me. "When's the last time you slept?"

"I sleep," he insists. "I fall asleep fine, but wake up in the middle of the night with a million thoughts racing through my mind. All I want is to be a good father to my son."

His son.

Gilbert Stetson Wells is due to arrive in just a few short weeks. I'm already madly in love with the kid. The pile of gifts I have at my apartment in Manhattan is proof of that.

"You're going to be a great father," I tell him what I truly believe. "Don't doubt yourself, Declan. You're one of the best men I know, and you've read a hell of a lot of books about babies. You could teach a class."

He chuckles. I sense some of the weight is being lifted off his shoulders. "Maybe by the time you have a kid, I'll be in a position to teach you the basics of being a dad."

I want that, but I've yet to admit it to anyone other than myself. Having a child is the brass ring for me. Even though my marriage ended in a bitter divorce, it hasn't soured me to the idea of taking the plunge again and starting a family.

I'm not in any rush, but it's something I see on the horizon.

"I'm going to try and sleep," he says through another yawn. "What about you? Are you hitting the hay soon?"

"Not yet." I shake my head as I watch him rub a hand over his jaw. "I'm going for a swim right away."

"Of course, you are." He laughs. "You're in East Hampton with a heated pool at your disposal. Why wouldn't you swim as much as you can?"

I don't bother mentioning my pool is out of commission, or that I plan on swimming with a beautiful woman.

"Are you free for lunch on Monday?" he questions, his gaze shifting to something beyond his phone.

"Are you asking me that or your beautiful wife?"

His lips split into a smile. "I hear Abby stirring in our bedroom, so I'm off to check on her. You and I are having lunch on Monday. Bring your credit card."

Before I can say anything, he ends the call.

"Bastard," I whisper as I drop my phone next to me. "It's his turn to buy lunch."

I push up to my feet and head toward the primary bedroom. I need to put on a pair of board shorts and grab a couple of condoms to tuck into one of the pockets. Then, I'll visit the private wine cellar in the basement to choose a bottle of red that my grandparents stocked there.

They saved hundreds of bottles of the best vintages for special occasions. My midnight swim with the neighbor falls into that category because I sense tonight is going to be one for the record books.

CHAPTER SEVEN

GREER

I DIDN'T HAVE a lot to choose from when it came to bikinis. I only brought three with me because that's all I own.

The one I finally decided on is red and fits like a second skin. The thin strings that hold the top up are tied tightly at the base of my neck and not as tightly behind my back. The strings on the sides of the bikini bottoms are secured in loosely knotted bows.

I don't want Joe to struggle getting me out of it.

I laugh to myself as I gather up two towels and head toward the main living area. I've imagined everything that will happen tonight, right down to him removing my bikini.

In my mind's eye, it's a slow pull on the strings to reveal everything that's underneath the material. For all I know, Joe will want me so desperately that he'll rip the suit from my body.

The laugh shifts into a soft smile on my lips.

I should be nervous, but all I'm feeling is excitement. It's been a while since I've slept with a man, but this feels right.

It'll be a fun adventure, and I'll leave East Hampton feeling satisfied and relaxed.

A soft rap at the front door tells me my neighbor is a few minutes early. I can't say I'm surprised. I'm anxious to get the night started, too.

I swing open the door to find him smiling at me. He's shirtless and wearing a pair of striped navy blue and white board shorts. When I saw him naked in the pool earlier, I got a glimpse of his bare chest, but up close, it's hard not to stare. He's all muscle and tanned skin. I feel like I hit the lover lottery this weekend.

"Summer," he says my fake name in a voice edged with intensity. "You're incredible."

A slow smile spreads over my lips. "Forgive me if it takes a minute for me to get used to you calling me that."

"Forgiven," he says with a smile of his own. "For the record, if you want to share your real name with me, I'm all ears."

I'm keeping that to myself. When I leave here on Sunday, I can do it knowing this tryst won't follow me back home. My life is too full for a man at the moment. "For the record, that won't happen."

A deep chuckle flows from him. "Understood."

I move aside to let him in. His bare feet pad across the tile floor as he heads toward the kitchen. "I'll open the wine."

"I'm not sure where the corkscrew is," I say as I trail him. "Or the wine glasses."

"I know where to find them."

I tap his shoulder right before he reaches the entrance to the kitchen. Just that light touch sends a pulse of awareness through me. It's enough to make me freeze in place.

He glances back at me with one eyebrow perched in silent query.

"I...um, I..." I stammer through that before I take a deep breath so I don't sound like a blubbering fool. "I wasn't aware that you knew where things were in the kitchen. Did you know where the measuring cups were when I was looking through the cupboards earlier?"

He turns to face me. "Yes, but in my defense, I was enjoying watching you search for them. You tapped your chin every time you opened a cupboard and they weren't there."

I hold back a smile. "I didn't do that."

He taps his chin with his pointer finger. "Like this. When you do it, it's fucking adorable."

"I don't do that," I argue playfully.

"You sure as hell do, Summer."

I drop the subject for one that fascinates me. "So, you know your way around the kitchen here?"

"I do." He acknowledges with a brisk nod. "Mrs. Frye cooks dinner for me sometimes. Technically, she sits and sips wine while she instructs me on how to cook us dinner just the way she likes."

Surprised by that, I smile. I only know the owner from our message exchanges on the vacation home rental app. She was incredibly friendly. I could have done without her trying to set me up, but I stepped right into that when I mentioned I'm divorced and traveling alone.

"I told you I was the neighbor," he reminds me. "I'm a damn good neighbor."

"I'll be the judge of that."

He rakes me from head to toe. "You'll judge me a ten out of ten."

Shaking my head, I laugh. "You're a little too sure of yourself, Joe."

"I know what I have to offer." He steps closer to me. "You're about to have a weekend you won't soon forget."

The assurance in his words is matched by the promise in his gaze. I know he's speaking the truth. This man exudes a raw sensuality that I've never experienced before.

"But first, wine." He flashes me a smile. "I'll pour two glasses."

I nod, suddenly struck with the overwhelming urge to ask him a question. "Are you single?"

His gaze finds mine again. "I am, but I'm not looking for anything…"

"Oh, no!" My hand jumps in the air to ward off what I know he's about to say. "I'm not looking for anything either other than some weekend fun. I don't want to overstep a line drawn by someone else. That's all."

"A line drawn by another woman?" he questions. "If you're asking if I'm married or involved, I'm not. I'm happily divorced."

"Me too," I blurt out without taking a second to consider whether I want to share that with him.

His gaze drops to my bikini top. "Your ex-husband is an idiot of the highest caliber."

Biting the corner of my bottom lip, I nod. "You have no idea."

I could say the same to him about his ex-wife, but I don't know what tore them apart. I don't want to know. Dealing with my divorce has caused me enough misery to last a lifetime.

"We're both available, so let's take advantage of it." He motions toward the wine bottle. "If I don't open this soon, so we can savor the taste, I'll be tempted to pass it over to taste you."

"Who needs wine?" I tease.

"Not me," he says, but there's not a hint of amusement in his tone. "If you're willing to let me dive right in, I'm more than ready."

"Dive right in?" I question because I want to hear him say the words.

"I'll spell it out for you." He moves toward the large dining table to set the bottle down. "I'm going to strip that bikini off of you in the next ten seconds and dive between your legs because I've been craving you since I first saw you."

To accentuate the point, he slides two foil packages from his pocket and tosses them onto the table near the wine bottle. "We'll need these later. For now, I want you to come on my tongue."

His words echo through me as I glance at the condom packages. This is happening. I'm about to give myself to a complete stranger. That's something I never thought I'd do, but yet, in this moment, it's the only thing I want to do.

"I want that, too," I whisper so softly that it's barely audible.

I know he hears it because a slow smile glides over his lips. "Let's start with a kiss."

CHAPTER EIGHT

Greer

JOE'S HANDS jump to my face. The touch of his skin against mine is electric. Heat ignites deep within me, coursing through my veins. I feel as though I'm lit up, aching for more, and we haven't even started our exploration of one another yet.

His gaze pierces me. He looks into my eyes as though he's searching for a secret I'll only share with him.

"You want me," he states. It's not a question because there isn't one to ask. My body is aching for him. I know he can sense it.

"More than you know," I whisper because it's the truth.

Everything about him screams sheet-clawing sex. It's the type of sex I've never had but always longed for.

I've settled when it comes to intimacy. I know that now. The hunger in his gaze is telling me I've missed out on something I'm on the precipice of experiencing.

Never in a million years did I think I'd end up in bed with

a handsome stranger this weekend, but I know if I don't take this leap, regret will haunt me for the rest of my life.

With a brush of his thumb over my bottom lip, he finally lowers his mouth to mine.

The kiss is gentle at first. It's soft and speaks of how tender he can be, but it shifts quickly. The aggression in it is matched by the movement of his hand as it drops to my shoulder and then beyond.

He traces a path with his tongue over my bottom lip as his fingers do the same on their journey to my bikini top. He slides the material aside so he can circle my nipple with the faintest touch before he pinches it.

That draws a gasp from me. "Ouch."

"It felt good," he whispers because he knows. "You liked it."

"So much," I confess with a purr, my hands dropping to the bare skin of his waist. "More."

It's one word that encompasses everything I want.

He steps back to shift his gaze to my exposed breast. "Pretty."

Normally, I'd feel compelled to cover up, but I want him to see me. I want him to see all of me.

Another pinch on my nipple earns him a low moan.

His gaze locks on mine. "I love that sound. I want to hear it again and again."

I'm tempted to tell him he will, but I want to show him. I need him to lure it from me.

He drops his head, capturing my nipple between his lips.

It's so sudden that I gasp. "Joe."

He flicks it with his tongue before he drags his teeth across it. It feels like so much, but at the same time, every part of me is craving more. I let out another moan. It's loud enough to steal his attention from my breast back to my face.

"You want more?" he asks, even though my body is answering that question with the way I'm responding to him.

I nod.

His gaze trails around the room, stopping at the dining room table we're next to. "Where? I'm good with laying you out on this table so I can feast on your pussy."

A shiver runs through me. "Really?"

His hands jump to my waist. "Give me the word and I'll be between your legs in the next thirty seconds."

"A bedroom," I say, because that will give me a few seconds to find my bearings.

I'm already overwhelmed in the best possible way.

"I think we can find one of those." Smiling, he reaches to scoop the condom packages back up.

I'm not sure why I do it, but I tug the material of my bikini top back into place, shielding my nipple from his view.

That draws a wickedly sexy grin to his lips. "You're beautiful. I can't wait to get that suit completely off of you."

"In the bedroom," I reiterate because I don't think I'm ready for table sex.

"Yes." He runs a fingertip over my wrist. The sensation of his touch is barely there, yet I feel it everywhere. "Are you nervous?"

"Are you?" I ask to shift the focus to him.

"No," he says with conviction. "Not at all."

I envy him. All of the excitement I'm feeling is edged with nervous anticipation.

"I'll be gentle," he assures me.

"Don't be."

"Then I won't be." His gaze sears through me. "Take me to bed. Now."

CHAPTER NINE

Greer

"I HAD no fucking idea when I woke up this morning that this was in store for me." Joe's breath coasts over my thigh just as his fingertip glides across my clit.

I'm hyper sensitive, so my back bows off the bed. "Please."

It's the same word I've been silently chanting since he followed me into this guest room and tugged on the strings of my bikini. They gave way with the same ease I had imagined when I put on the bikini.

His eyes widened as the material fell to the floor, and I stood exposed before him.

It took all of five seconds for him to haul me up by my waist and toss me onto the bed as if I weighed nothing.

His board shorts ended up on the floor, too, before he crawled onto the bed next to me.

"Please," he repeats my plea. "Please lick you?"

It's all I've wanted since he settled between my legs. He

gently lifted one over his shoulder to part my thighs so he could blow a breath over my core. I shuddered not only from the desire it fueled within me, but because I felt so vulnerable.

"One taste of you will ruin me." He chuckles, but that's gone as quickly as it came. "Why do I feel like you're about to change me forever?"

"Stop with the sweet talk." I half-tease. "I'm close."

He runs his finger over me again, stopping at my entrance. "I can tell. You're so fucking wet."

As if to demonstrate, he glides his fingertip over his bottom lip, leaving it glistening with my arousal.

I close my eyes, trying to stop the need from being so intense. I'm scared that as soon as his tongue is on my pussy, I'll scream from the orgasm that is already bearing down on me.

"You're beautiful," he whispers, his lips brushing against my inner thigh. "Every fucking inch of you is beautiful."

I raise my hips slightly. "Joe."

I can feel his lips curve into a smile as he presses a soft kiss on my skin. "Summer."

Before I can beg him one last time, he flattens his tongue and glides it over my cleft. Then it's on my clit, light flutters against it as the pressure builds within me.

I push up, wanting to experience more of his tongue, his mouth...more of him.

He growls against me as he slides a hand under my ass to tilt me up. "Jesus, yes," he whispers. "This is so damn good."

My hands ache to touch him, so I do. I weave my fingers into the soft strands of his hair. I tug a little, push down, and cry out when I feel one of his fingers glide into my channel.

"Oh, God," I say to myself, but it's too loud.

He laughs slightly, the vibration of that echoing through my core. "Come for me."

Unable to contain myself, I unravel. The orgasm hits me hard, sending pulses through me that drive my hips up and off the bed as I push his head down so he'll suck my clit between his lips.

Words that I don't recognize flow from me. They're woven into broken noises and cries that should embarrass me, but only fuel me more.

"Yes," he hisses, his voice hoarse. "Like that."

I go limp, my hands dropping from his hair to the bed. My legs fall open even more, leaving me shamelessly exposed.

The lightest brush of his finger over my already throbbing clit sends a shiver through me. "I'm going to fuck you, Summer. You're going to watch."

He flips me over with ease until I'm on my stomach. With a gentle swat of his hand against my ass cheek, he directs me. "Get on your knees."

I do. I have no choice. I've never wanted anything more than to be fucked by this man.

"Look at yourself," he orders as he slides off the bed.

A gasp escapes me as I look straight ahead to see my reflection in an arched full-length mirror leaning against the wall a few feet from the foot of the bed. My gaze shifts to his reflection as he sheathes his cock in a condom.

I'm mesmerized by all of it. The flush that's taken over my skin, the wild mess that is my hair, and the movement of his hand as he trails it over his dick.

I hadn't stepped foot into this room until I brought him here. I didn't take him to the bedroom I'm staying in. That felt too intimate. Almost as though it was too much, but this is even more.

My gaze never leaves his body as he gets on the bed, yanks me back, and lines himself up to my pussy.

I shudder when he guides the crown of his thick cock over my tender flesh. I'm already so sensitive. I'm so needy that I moan when he slides the tip in.

He grips my hips as he buries himself deep in me with one solid thrust.

I scramble forward, unable to contain the burst of pain and the immense amount of pleasure I feel. "Oh, please."

"Shh," he soothes with his voice as his hand does the same on my skin. He circles his palm on my hip. "We'll take it slow."

I push back slightly, feeling his cock stretch me fully. "It's so much," I whisper.

"It's everything," he growls as he pumps slowly into me. "So damn good."

Our eyes meet in the mirror as I watch him fuck me. He lets out an animalistic groan before he ups the pace.

I can't tear my gaze away because I've never felt this connected to a man before.

His hand glides over my skin, diving between my legs so he can circle a finger over my clit. I cry out because it's all so intense.

"You'll come for me again," he whispers into my ear. "Then I'll take you the way I want."

That's enough to push me over the edge. I come with a blinding intensity that I've never experienced before. I call out his name, not caring if it's loud enough that anyone on the beach can hear it through the open window.

His thrusts slow as I ride his cock through my orgasm.

As I still, he peppers my shoulder with kisses. Each feels like a gift to me.

"I want to see your face when I come," he whispers against my neck. "I'm flipping you over."

I should thank him for the warning, but it's over as soon as the words leave his lips.

I settle on my back, staring up at him. He leans over me, threading his fingers through mine so he can pin my hands to the bed above my head.

"I won't be gentle this time," he promises with a wicked grin.

"Don't be," I manage to say through staggered breaths. "Please don't be."

His cock slides over my slick pussy before he pushes inside. A tortured sound escapes him as he fucks me hard. His hips move with relentless precision, each rock hard inch of him taking me to a place I've never been before.

Every part of me aches, yet all I want is more of him.

I feel myself coming apart again as heat builds with me. Tears sting my eyes as I climax for a third time.

"Ah, Summer." His voice is dark and filled with need.

Each of his thrusts are more forceful than the last until he loosens his grip on my hands and takes my mouth in a lush kiss.

"Jesus," he breathes the word out against my lips. "I'm so close."

His hands drop to my waist, and he rears back to drive into me as he comes with a roar.

CHAPTER TEN

Holden

BY THE TIME I've exited the bathroom after discarding the used condom in the trash, Summer is wearing a short royal blue silk robe. I can only assume that she snuck out of this room and into another bedroom to retrieve that.

I can't say I'm surprised that she left while I splashed water on my face to try and center myself. I know I wasn't quick about it. That's because I stared into the ornate mirror hanging above the sink in the bathroom that's attached to this bedroom. I swear I look different after that experience, but it's likely just good sex messing with my mind.

Scratch that.

It was great sex. In fact, it's the best I've ever had.

"You're smiling," Summer points out as I tug my board shorts back on.

"Thank yourself for that," I say, dragging a hand through my hair. "You're something else."

Her hand drops to the front of her robe. She pulls on the

end of the sash as if she's tightening it. "You are. I'm sore in places I've never been sore before."

"Another compliment?"

A light burst of laughter falls from her as she stalks toward me. "You know you're good in bed."

Chuckling, I grab her around the waist to tug her close so I can kiss her. I do it softly, taking the time to breathe in the soft floral scent of her skin. "I know you're an incredible woman."

She leans back slightly so our eyes lock. "Hungry?"

"For you?" I ask because all I want is another taste of her.

Studying my face, she shakes her head. "For food. I can make you a sandwich."

I won't turn down anything from this woman. Eating a sandwich with her will give me more time to stare at her. I consider that a win. "I'd like that."

She tilts her chin slightly. The only light in the room is from a small lamp on the nightstand. Summer must have turned it on before she left the room. It's casting a warm glow over her face that makes her eyes dance. "I hope you're adventurous. I had my rideshare driver stop at this cute little market so I could pick up a bunch of fresh ingredients for the weekend. How does a grilled fig, apple, and brie sandwich sound?"

I'm impressed. I was thinking peanut butter and jelly were on the menu.

"It sounds like my new favorite sandwich." I smile. "You work in the culinary world, don't you?"

I'm pressing for more information because I'm damn curious about her. Beyond what we just did in bed, all I know about Summer is that she's divorced and not afraid to arm herself with an umbrella when she feels threatened.

"I took a few cooking classes." She huffs out a laugh.

"I'm trying to improve my skills in the kitchen. The sandwich was the first thing the instructor taught us to make."

"Let me guess." I brush my lips over hers for a kiss. "You got an A plus."

She leans closer for another, deeper kiss. "You can grade me after your first taste."

I know she's talking about sandwiches, but my first taste of her will linger with me for a hell of a long time, and it tops any ranking system in existence.

"I want you to be brutally honest about the sandwich, Joe."

I raise a hand in the air as if I'm making a vow. "I'll tell it like it is. You have my word."

"THAT WAS FUCKING AMAZING," I say as I place both of our plates into the dishwasher. "Your culinary instructor would be proud of you."

Summer brushes a hand over her shoulder. "I agree. I did a mighty fine job."

She did. The sandwich was delicious. The best part was watching her savor her creation. The way she licked her bottom lip was mesmerizing. As I ate my sandwich, I had to remind myself not to stare at her.

"How about an after sandwich swim?" I ask even though it's inching close to three a.m. and I can tell she's tired.

She's yawned a few times since we sat down to enjoy our snack.

"Isn't there a rule about not swimming after eating?" she questions, a sly smile spreading over her lips.

I take the bait and answer the question in a way I hope

gets me what I want. "Probably, but I know for a fact there is no rule about eating after eating."

Her brow furrows. "Don't you mean there's no rule about eating after swimming?"

"No," I answer succinctly as I close the distance between where I'm standing and the stool she's sitting on next to the large kitchen island. "I meant what I said. There's no rule about eating you after eating."

To drive my point home, I trail my pointer finger over the smooth skin of her thigh. I caught a glimpse of white lace beneath the robe, so I know she took the time to slide on a pair of panties when she put on the robe.

Her gaze leaves my hand to focus on my face. "If we do that, neither of us will get any sleep tonight."

"Is that a problem?"

She laughs, but a yawn takes over. "For me, yes. I've been up since five this morning...or is it yesterday morning?"

"That's almost twenty-four hours."

Nodding, she places her hand over mine before it can reach its final destination. I want to touch her again. Ripping the panties off of her and burying my tongue in her pussy seems like the perfect after sandwich treat.

"I need to sleep, Joe," she whispers. "Can we pick this up tomorrow?"

"It is tomorrow," I point out as I lift her hand to my lips for a soft kiss on her palm.

That pulls more laughter from her. "Later today, then?"

"Later today," I agree with a nod. "I'll take off."

She leans closer to wrap a hand around the back of my neck as she pulls me in for a kiss. It's soft yet raw in its intensity. My cock throbs as she bites the corner of my bottom lip slightly. The pinch of pain is enough to send my feet forward until I'm standing between her legs.

The kiss breaks when she sighs. "I'm already looking forward to later."

I steal one last kiss from her. I'd say it's almost chaste, but that would be a lie. There's nothing innocent about how I feel when I touch her.

"Later, as in an hour from now?" I tease while brushing a strand of her hair from her forehead.

"Around noon would work," she says, placing a hand in the center of my bare chest. "I need some time to catch my breath. Don't you?"

I can't hold back a smile as I avoid answering the question because I'd have to admit that I've been breathless since I walked into this house hours ago. "I'll be back then."

"It's a date." She runs a fingertip over her bottom lip.

Fuck me if that's not one of the sexiest things I've ever seen. I stare at her, saving the image to memory. "It's a date."

CHAPTER ELEVEN

GREER

I RAKE a hand through my hair as I settle on a leather bench beneath one of the windows in a bedroom I haven't been in before. I stepped in here because I know that I'll get a bird's eye view of what is proving to be a breathtaking sunrise.

The last time I was in East Hampton was years ago, and the small condo I stayed in didn't have a view of anything other than my ex-husband. At the time, I thought I could see forever in his eyes, but now, I realize that was hope. I hoped the relationship would last until one of us died, but instead it crashed into a million pieces on a day that was both the worst and best of my life.

The warm air filtering into the room from the open window is scented not only by the rose bush that sits below it, but also by the ocean. I could breathe it in all day and never get enough of it.

I glance down at the pool. The water is still now. The beach is deserted except for a couple walking hand in hand in the distance. I know if I took a leap and dove into the pool for a very early morning swim, no one would notice.

This property sits on a gentle hill. It's far enough from the beach that curious onlookers can't see much more than a row of lush, leafy trees that border the pool. I suspect that's why Joe felt emboldened enough to skinny dip when it was still light out.

I skim a hand over the front of my robe. Unlike earlier, I'm nude beneath it since I took a quick shower right after Joe said goodnight to me.

Laughing softly, I whisper to myself, "Joe did it. You can, too."

I take off in a run toward the staircase that will take me down to the first floor and beyond that to the pool.

I promised myself I'd experience at least one first this weekend. Since I've never had a one-night stand, that box is now ticked off. I've also never skinny-dipped, but I'm about to. That's two firsts for me, and I haven't even been here for twenty-four hours.

"There's no time like the present," I say as I slide open one of the glass doors that look onto the pool deck.

I hurry outside, dropping my robe on a lounge chair before I dive into the warm water just as the sun starts to rise. I swim the length of the pool beneath the water before I pop my head out and squint as my eyes adjust to my surroundings.

"Summer." The gruffness in that voice has been echoing in my ears since he left me less than two hours ago.

I look to the left and see Joe standing at the edge of the pool, a dark gray towel wrapped around his waist.

I skim a hand over my face to chase away any extra drops of water. "What are you doing here?"

"What do you think?" He drops the towel, revealing that he's nude. "I'm here for a swim."

I rake him from head to toe. I've seen it all before, yet I can't stop staring. "Just a swim?"

A wicked grin settles over his full lips. "Are you offering more?"

I stand tall, revealing more of myself to him as I rise out of the water until it's lapping below my naked breasts. "What do you think?"

MY FINGERS DIG into his shoulder as he plumps one of my breasts in his hand. I whimper from the need that has been building within me since he dove into the pool. He teased me then, kissing me hard before he pulled back to study my face in the light that is being cast on us from the sunrise.

"You want more," he assumes as I try to close the small amount of distance between us.

I'm pressed against the side of the pool. Joe is just a few inches in front of me. It's not close enough for me, though. I want to feel his body against mine.

"I do," I confess. "I want you."

Normally, a declaration like that would make me feel shameless, but all of my shame has already been tossed aside, because this man knows how to fuck.

"I don't have a condom," he growls. "But, there are so many ways to make you come for me, Summer."

I both hate and love that he calls me by a name that doesn't resemble my own. I'll always wonder what my real name would have sounded like coming from him.

"Tell me one," I plead.

His lips part in a soft smile. "With my tongue, but I'm saving that for later since you've already experienced it."

Disappointment rolls through me, but it's gone as soon as he lowers his head to take one of my nipples in his mouth. He drags his teeth across it. The bite of pain is so exquisite that I let out a moan.

"Every time I do that, you like it more," he says in a gritty tone.

I can't argue because my fingers are threaded through his hair as I try to push him forward so he can take my breast into his mouth again.

He does, but this time it's a lash of his tongue against my throbbing nipple. I toss my head back in pleasure, but that all changes the second I feel a hand between my thighs.

"Legs apart," he orders in a deep tone. "I'm going to watch you come apart for me."

I don't hesitate to do what he asks. Locking eyes with him, I let out a slow breath.

"You are so fucking beautiful," he whispers as his fingers glide over my pussy. "I can't wait to hear you come for me again."

CHAPTER TWELVE

Holden

I FINISH the last bite of the banana foster pancakes in front of me. When I finally look up, Summer is staring at me with her top teeth raking over her bottom lip.

As she was preparing our breakfast, I made her another promise that I'd be honest in my rating of it. This food is off the fucking charts. If she's not working in a restaurant kitchen at the moment, she needs to be.

"You outdid yourself. This was even better than the sandwich." I push the plate aside and grab the glass of freshly squeezed orange juice.

I can take credit for that, but it's only because Summer asked me to handle it. After watching her orgasm in the pool, I felt indebted to her. The look on her face as she came was filled with both wonder and pure vulnerability. Witnessing it was a gift. Playing a part in it was a true honor.

"Flattery will get you everywhere, Joe."

I swallow the orange juice in my mouth before I bark out a laugh. "Good to know."

She drags her fork through a puddle of maple syrup on her plate. "You already knew that. Between your love of skinny dipping and your charm, you're kind of irresistible."

A slow smile spreads over my lips. "Am I?"

She stares at my face before her gaze wanders down my bare chest. "Don't act like you don't know that."

My hand drops to the waistband of my jeans. After I kissed her senseless in the pool, I went home. That happened immediately after she came on my hand.

As we exited the pool, she glanced over her shoulder to tell me I should get dressed because there was a breakfast invitation with my name on it.

I would have been fine to eat in the nude, but I could tell she wanted a few minutes to collect herself, so I gave her almost thirty. I used the time to take a shower and put on the jeans.

When I came back here and knocked on the edge of the open sliding glass door that overlooks the pool, she greeted me in a pale blue off the shoulder dress. Her hair is in a ponytail. She looks fresh-faced and happy. Or at least I think that's what happiness looks like on her.

"How often do you skinny dip in Mrs. Frye's pool?" A light laugh accompanies the question.

"Rarely," I answer honestly. "Yesterday was the first time I've ever been caught."

Skepticism knits her brow as she considers my answer. "Seriously?"

"Seriously," I accentuate each syllable. "I'm damn glad it was you who caught me and not Mrs. Frye."

Her hand leaps to her mouth as she tries to conceal a laugh. "I think it would have made her day."

"Just her day?" My arms cross my chest. "Not her week, or her month, or…"

"Her year?" she finishes what I started. "I can't speak for her, but it certainly made my weekend a lot more interesting."

"And climactic?" I ask with a wicked grin on my lips.

"Very climactic," she agrees. "There have been so many climactic moments already."

I want to add to that total. Witnessing her climax has fulfilled me in a way I've never experienced before. I want more of that. If I didn't have to leave, I'd have her over my shoulder and headed to the bedroom right now.

"I want you," I say, because it feels impossible not to express it vocally. "Now, obviously."

Her gaze drops to my jeans again and the unmistakable bulge I'm not trying to hide. I'm semi-hard just from thinking about fucking her again. "I want you, too, Joe."

Those words will have to sustain me until I can get my hands on her again. That can't happen right now because I have to go home. Booking Martin for a last minute repair call isn't easy, and I need to sort out the pool issue before I go back to Manhattan on Sunday.

She sighs heavily, which expresses exactly what I'm feeling. "I'd love to crawl back into bed with you, Joe, but I need to handle a few things this morning. I have to make some calls."

I admit I'm curious about that, but this is a weekend fling. Details about her life back in the place she calls home don't matter. "Understood. Martin is going to show up to fix my pool soon, so I need to head back."

Her eyes light up. "The pump in your pool really is broken? You didn't make that up?"

I slide off the stool I've been sitting on and walk toward where she's standing. "Why the fuck would I make that up?"

The smile on my face draws one to hers as she shrugs a shoulder. "I assumed you just preferred the pool here, so you made up a story about your pump being broken."

"I prefer mine. You will, too," I tell her, knowing I want, *no,* I need to have this woman in my home, and in my bed.

"What's so special about it?" She inches closer to me, tilting her chin up as if she's offering herself to me for a kiss.

I make the move, cupping my hand over her cheek before lowering my mouth to hers. I part her lips with my tongue, tasting the sweetness of the maple syrup and her.

She smiles against my lips. "If your pool is as impressive as that kiss, I can't wait to dive in."

I lean back slightly so I can look into her eyes. I'm completely captivated by her. "Meet me there for a drink this afternoon."

She nods slowly. "Around four?"

"Sure," I say, even though that feels like an eternity from now.

Her fingertips tap dance over my bare shoulder. "Why do I get the feeling that bikinis are optional in your pool?"

"They are," I answer swiftly. "Swimming trunks are, too."

"They're always optional in your world, aren't they?"

I don't bother telling her that I was behind on laundry when I arrived from New York City yesterday, so I tossed both pairs of board shorts I brought with me into the washing machine along with a handful of T-shirts and some boxer briefs. It was a glaring reminder that I need to bring extra clothes with me on my next visit so I can leave them here.

I never imagined that during my brief swim, I'd be caught buck naked in Mrs. Frye's pool. I'm glad I was, but swimming in the nude isn't something I've done more than a handful of times in all of my thirty-three years.

"You're not complaining, are you?" I answer her question with one of my own.

Her laughter fills the air around us. "You know I'm not. I'm all for you being naked as often as possible."

"If I didn't have to deal with Martin, I'd drop my jeans right now," I tell her.

Her hands slide down my shoulders until they settle on my forearms. "Save that thought until later. I'll be at your house at four o'clock sharp."

"I'm counting on it," I groan, frustrated that I have to wait hours to see her again. "Don't be late."

"I won't be," she promises before she seals her lips over mine for a final kiss before I leave.

CHAPTER THIRTEEN

Greer

I SCOOT around a hedge that separates Mrs. Frye's property from Joe's. I'm taking the same path he did after I found him in the pool yesterday. I didn't realize I was paying attention to exactly where he disappeared to since I was still in shock from seeing a naked, hot-as-hell stranger within the first few minutes of my weekend getaway.

I debated going down the winding driveway of the home I'm staying in and then up Joe's driveway, but I took the shortcut route, and I'm glad I did.

My eyes widen as I gaze at what can only be described as a slice of East Coast paradise.

The grounds of Joe's home are meticulously taken care of. The lush green lawn is cut to the perfect height. Beds of brightly colored flowers border trimmed hedges. A large pool is the centerpiece. It's surrounded by what look like very comfortable light blue lounge chairs. A matching sectional is off to the side under a trio of large white umbrellas.

Not too far off in the distance, I see a tennis court. Judging by the line of leafy green trees that frame the edge of it, it's set on Joe's property.

In addition to all of that, a spectacular home is the crown jewel.

Painted shades of white and blue with too many windows to count, it has to be at least twice, if not three times, the size of Mrs. Frye's house. To say it's breathtaking is an understatement.

"You're here!" Joe calls out to me from a spot on the lawn. I hadn't noticed him standing there, but my excuse is that with this much beauty in front of me, I was temporarily distracted.

He's wearing a pair of white board shorts and a light blue, short-sleeved button-down shirt that's hanging open. Sunglasses shield his eyes from my view, but I know he's staring straight at me.

For all of two seconds, I thought about walking over here with only my white string bikini and sunglasses on. I couldn't summon the bravery to do that because I wasn't sure if the pool repairman might still be lurking. The wispy white cover-up I'm wearing helped tame my reservations.

"Hi, Joe." I wave to him. "Is the pool fixed?"

He curls a finger in the air to lure me closer to him. I pad across the gray porcelain tile decking toward him. Before leaving Mrs. Frye's house, I slipped my feet into a comfortable pair of white sandals that have seen me through a few summers of walking the sidewalks in Manhattan. They're not stylish by any means, but I intend to kick them off when I get rid of my cover-up in the next minute or two.

As soon as I'm within his reach, Joe's hands are on me. He tugs me into him, giving me a full dose of the intoxicating smell of his skin. There's a hint of cologne, but the underlying scent is just him. If given the chance, I'd breathe it in for hours.

With a brush of his lips over mine in a soft kiss, he groans. "I've been waiting all afternoon for that."

Me too, but I don't admit it. I'm becoming addicted to him, but the spell has to break the day after tomorrow. My life in Manhattan doesn't have room for weekly jaunts to the beach for fun and fucking.

"Should we take a dip?" I try to mask the eagerness in my tone.

I want to get back into the pool with him because the way he touched me early this morning still has me spinning. I've never come that hard from a man using just his hand on me, but Joe has proven he's talented in many ways.

"Soon," he promises as he glides a finger over my forearm. "I made some snacks. I want you to try them."

Surprised that he went to the trouble to prepare something for us, I smile. "You made us food?"

His hands glide up my arms to circle my biceps. "Good food. You'll like it, Summer."

Something tells me I will, since I like him a lot. "I'm game to try."

He gestures toward his home. Unlike Mrs. Frye's house, it appears that the floor-to-ceiling glass doors that lead out to the pool area slide completely to the side, giving way to a wide path indoors from here. My view of the main living area of Joe's home is unobstructed. It's a warm and welcoming space with striking wood beams on the ceiling. Area rugs cover the hardwood floors. Shelves filled with books line one wall. A grand fireplace is on the opposite end of the room.

I take a tentative step toward the interior. I feel like a dozen butterflies have taken flight in my stomach. I thought our time together would be restricted to the pool area and perhaps his bedroom. I didn't contemplate what it would feel like to enter his home to share a quiet moment like this with him.

"What are you thinking about?" Joe asks as he falls in step beside me. "I sense there's a question waiting to be asked."

My feet stall as I look up at his face. "Your house is gorgeous. It's magazine-worthy."

His gaze leaves my face to trail around the room before it settles back on me. "I'm not sure I agree with the magazine worthy designation, but I like it here."

I want to ask if he lives here full-time, but that's more information I don't need. If I leave East Hampton with the knowledge that I can rent the house next door whenever it's available, that will signal I want more than a weekend with him. Right now, the thought of this man being my occasional weekend lover is warming me from the inside out, but that situation is too ripe with potential consequences for it to work.

"I can see why." I slide my right foot forward an inch before pulling it back. "It's the ultimate East Hampton home."

He looks into my eyes. "You seem nervous? Are you unsure about coming inside? Do you want me to get you an umbrella?"

I crack a smile at the reminder of my makeshift weapon.

"You're safe with me," he assures me. "You have my word that you'll walk out of my house in one piece when I'm done with you."

The words and the tone of his voice promise an afternoon I won't soon forget. "When you're done with me?"

He nods slowly, his eyes never leaving mine. "When I'm

done feeding and fucking you. You'll leave here completely satisfied. I guarantee it."

I don't question that because I sense he's right. Regardless of how the food he prepared tastes, he's so skilled in other ways that I could be starving and not notice my hunger pangs as long as his focus was on me in a bed, or a pool, for that matter.

"I'll prove it." He chuckles. "Food first, though. Come with me."

He holds out a hand. I drop mine into it without hesitation, knowing that when I do walk away from this house, I'll do it with a smile on my face because I'll be satisfied in ways I've never been before.

CHAPTER FOURTEEN

Holden

I'M NOT the worst cook in the world, but I'd certainly never label myself as a great one. When it comes to my skills in the kitchen, I'm mediocre at best.

Through a hell of a lot of trial and error, I've learned how to prepare an array of foods that appeal to the palate of an almost six-year-old. Rook's daughter, Kirby, has been the inspiration for my recent interest in cooking, or rather, preparing food.

I can make a peanut butter and jelly sandwich with my eyes closed, and scrambled eggs with cheese sprinkled on top are a necessity when Kirby stays at my apartment in Manhattan for a rare sleepover.

That's only happened a handful of times when Rook's been bombarded with work, or when he's wanted to treat his fiancée to an overnight getaway.

After Martin fixed my pool and fucked off, I jumped into

my car and headed to my favorite market in the nearest town. I filled up a basket with an array of cheese, meats, and crackers. To add to the charcuterie board I was picturing in my mind, I tossed a jar of pickles into the mix, along with a few different types of nuts and four fresh figs. The final touch was a container of the olive tapenade that the market stocks from a local vendor.

Arranging it on one of the cutting boards I found tucked in the back of a cupboard took the most time. I'm not an expert when it comes to displaying anything, but judging by the look on Summer's face, she's mildly impressed.

"Did you buy it like this, or is this one of those build-it-yourself situations?"

I laugh. "Does it really matter?"

She gives me a playful smile. "It matters a lot."

Rubbing the back of my neck, I study her like the puzzle she is. I can tell she's got a playful streak and teasing someone is something she enjoys, so I play along. "Why?"

Her gaze leaves the food to land back on my face. "If you created that masterpiece on your own, I'm very impressed."

"It's not like I prepared the tapenade," I admit. "But, yeah, I arranged it all."

"Are you a food artist?"

"Hell no." I shake my head for good measure. "I'm a guy who plopped some savory stuff on an old cutting board so he could feed the woman he wants to fuck for the next few hours."

"No one could ever accuse you of being subtle, Joe."

"I want to make you come again," I say it slowly enough that there's no room for misunderstanding. "So, start eating, Summer."

She grabs a salty cracker, puts it between her front teeth, and clamps down. I feel that right down to my cock. She has yet to take my dick between her pretty lips. I hope that happens today and doesn't involve any biting as aggressive as what she just did to the cracker.

"Your mind just went to a dirty place," she accuses as she finishes the cracker with a final bite. "I see it in your eyes."

"I feel it in my cock."

That sends her head back in laughter. "As I said, subtly is not your strong suit."

"You like that about me," I say with zero doubt.

"I appreciate that about you." She taps my shoulder. "If more people were as direct as you are, the world would be a lot less confusing."

Something tells me that she's talking about someone in particular. Her ex-husband, perhaps? That's a maze I don't want to wander into since my focus this weekend is great sex with some good food thrown in the mix to keep us fueled.

"Let me be very direct then," I start. "After we eat, I want to fuck you."

Her gaze takes a slow trip over my face, studying me carefully. "Are you open to a compromise?"

"It depends," I answer succinctly since I'm curious about what she has in mind.

"I'm not going to ask what it depends on because I already know you'll agree to my compromise," she says like the vixen she is.

Her confidence is hot as fuck because this woman knows how desperate I am to be inside of her again.

Before I can say anything, she's laying out her proposal, "I propose that after we eat, I suck you off before we fuck."

I lean forward to claim her mouth in a deep kiss.

A smile blooms on her lips as she leans back to catch her breath. "I take it you're open to my compromise, Joe?"

"Is that a real question?"

She kisses me again, nipping my bottom lip with her teeth. "Let's eat, so we can get to the good stuff."

CHAPTER FIFTEEN

Greer

I GLANCE down at the charcuterie board and what's left of our late afternoon snack. We spent the last hour eating our way through most of it while talking about books, movies, and everything else two strangers might discuss while desperately trying not to strip naked to fall into bed together.

It's not that I preferred the food over what I'd promised Joe, but we agreed to enjoy the spread he had prepared for us.

I did. I know he did, too, but just as we were finishing up, his phone rang three times. He ignored it the first two times it happened, but as it started up again, he cursed under his breath and told me he had to take the call.

Naturally, he bolted out of the room before he answered. I would have done the same if mine had started ringing. Fortunately, it hasn't, but I've kept it close. It was in my hand until we sat down at the kitchen island to enjoy our food. Now, it's screen side down next to me because I stole a peek at it once Joe was out of view.

"Sorry about that, Summer." His deep, growly voice fills the silence in the room as he comes back into view around the corner. "It was a pressing work matter."

Normally, this is where I'd ask what he does for work, but I don't want to know. That knowledge would open a door that could tell me a lot more about him than I need to know.

When we say goodbye on Sunday, that's a forever goodbye in my eyes.

"So, you're not retired at thirty-five?" I tease.

His hand jumps to his hair. He rakes it with a push of his fingers through it. "I'm thirty-three, but I get it. The gray adds a sort of maturity to my look that I can't say I mind."

"I'm thirty-two," I admit. "I've yet to find my first gray."

He walks up to where I'm sitting before placing his phone next to mine. "You'd be just as striking with gray hair as you are with red."

For the first twenty years of my life, I had a love hate relationship with my hair. I wanted to shave my head bald when I was a kid because of the nicknames my friends would bestow on me.

Red.

Fire engine.

Stop sign.

At some point before I graduated from elementary school, I was known by all of those.

Just as I was about to leave my college years behind, I began to appreciate the beauty in my hair. It speaks to how fierce I am. It's bold in a way that reflects who I am as a woman.

I love it now. I wouldn't trade it for any other color in the rainbow.

I tuck a strand behind my ear. "Thanks, Joe. The salt and little bit of pepper look you have going on suits you."

"Little bit of pepper?" he parrots. "You're being kind."

"That's not kindness. It's honesty," I correct him. "Your hair is more brown than gray."

"My brother would argue that point with you," he says, giving away a detail about his life.

I skip past the urge to ask if his brother is older or younger than him, because, again, this is not a *'getting to know you'* weekend. My goal for the next two days is to be fucked senseless as often as I can.

He gestures toward the almost bare cutting board. "You enjoyed my creative endeavor."

"It hit the spot," I acknowledge with a nod toward my stomach. "I'm all filled up."

"More wine?" he asks as he picks up the half empty bottle he opened when we first sat down.

I wave my hand over the rim of my glass to chase away his intention to pour more for me. "I don't want to get tipsy."

"You had half a glass," he points out as he tops up his glass. "Are you a lightweight, Summer?"

"A lightweight drinker?" I ask even though I know full well that's what he means.

He answers with a brisk nod and a smile.

"I'm not," I confess, although it's been years since I drank more than one glass of wine or one cocktail in a sitting.

"That's another little sliver of information I can file away in my memory about the mysterious woman who I spent an unforgettable weekend with."

I lean forward and tilt my chin up. "What other information have you filed away about me?"

He brushes his lips over my cheek. "Wouldn't you like to know?"

I would, but his perception of me is his alone. I'll leave East Hampton on Sunday with memories of him, too. Maybe they'll line up with who he is in his real life...maybe they won't. It doesn't really matter because this weekend feels like the best dream I've ever had.

"I'd like to move ahead with what I proposed earlier," I effortlessly change the subject to one I know he's been waiting for.

He backs up a touch. "I'm ready whenever you are."

I glance toward the main living area and what looks like a very comfortable armchair. "Strip and go sit in that chair."

His gaze trails mine. "Now?"

I tug the cover up I'm wearing over my head. "Now, Joe."

Our eyes lock as he moves swiftly to undress. The second his board shorts are down around his thighs, his cock is in view. It's hard as stone, and a drop of his arousal on the tip beckons me.

I don't want to waste my first taste of him, so I run my hand over his cock, scooping up the drop of pre-cum with my fingertip before smoothing it over my bottom lip. My tongue follows the same path as he stares at me.

"Jesus," he whispers, pushing his shorts to the floor. "You're so fucking hot."

I lean forward to kiss him softly. "I'm just getting started."

CHAPTER SIXTEEN

Holden

LAST NIGHT SHOULD BE a blur given the copious amount of wine I drank and how little sleep I had, but I remember every glorious fucking moment of it, and I do mean glorious fucking.

I've had my fair share of lovers, but none are as memorable as Summer.

She blew me, I ate her sweet pussy, and we fucked twice. The first time was in the chair in the main living area. It was moments after I came down her throat, but the need for her was so great that I had to have a taste of her. As soon as she came apart on my tongue, she wanted to feel me inside of her. I sheathed my cock in a condom before I ordered her to ride me.

We couldn't take our hands off each other in the pool after the sun set. We kissed for what felt like just short of forever, I got her off with my hand again, and after we showered together, I took her into my bed.

That fuck was slow and I'd say sweet, but there was nothing sweet about it. It was intense, mind-numbing and after it was over, I fell into a deep sleep sometime around six a.m. with her next to me.

She must have left, because it's now nearing noon, and she hasn't emerged from Mrs. Frye's house. I don't have her number, so I can't send her endless text messages asking if she wants to hang out today.

I feel like a college kid who had a night he'll never forget. I'm in the middle of a weekend I know will linger with me for a hell of a long time.

I needed this more than I realized.

A knock at the front door sends me in that direction in a sprint. I was planning on a walk on the beach soon, so if it's Summer waiting behind the door, I'll invite her to join me.

I swing it open with a flourish and a wide grin on my face.

A pair of paws land in the center of my bare chest as a loud bark fills the air.

"Copper," I say the dog's name while I pat his furry head. "Hey, buddy."

"Hi, Holden," Wally, one of my neighbors, greets me as he clings to his dog's leash.

"Wally." I toss him a smile. "How are you?"

"Good." He nods so briskly that the straw hat on his head inches forward. "I was wondering if I could borrow something."

"Sure." I give Copper one final pat before he lands back on the floor on all four paws. "What do you need?"

"Your expertise."

I know where this is headed. Wally doesn't own a car. In fact, he has never had a driver's license. Mrs. Frye is his usual go-to when he wants something from town, but since she's not here, and my BMW is sitting in the driveway, Wally sees me as his ticket to wherever he's headed.

The expertise part of it is a ruse that always works on me. He'll tell me that he needs a second opinion on what fresh fish he should buy to grill tonight, or what dessert at the bakery would be my first choice.

A journey with Wally is a guaranteed hours-long adventure, and I'd much rather spend that time waiting around to see if Summer strolls out of the house next door and wanders over here.

Before I can let him down easy, he tosses more information in my direction, "I had a nice conversation earlier with the young lady staying at Mrs. Frye's house this weekend. She was getting into a car with a driver. They were headed to town. She offered to pick up a few necessities for me. What a sweet angel she is."

I smile at his description of Summer.

If she's already in town, maybe a trip there wouldn't be such a bad idea. "Did you forget to ask her to grab something you need? I can drive you into town to get it."

The offer may be genuine, but my motives aren't. I'm not going to slide behind the wheel of my car just to take Wally to get one ingredient he may have forgotten for his regular Saturday grill night. I'm aiming to get more time with Summer, and if I have to head into town to make that happen, I'm all for it.

"No need." He laughs off my suggestion. "I was hoping to peruse your library so I'd have something to occupy my time this afternoon. You must be an expert on what's good to read. Do you have any suggestions?"

Leave it to my grandmother to create a library in this house that the locals swarm to. Wally isn't the only one who stops in randomly when I'm around to pluck a book off the shelves. I can't complain since the books are always returned in pristine condition with a hearty thank you.

"Come on in." I step aside to give him and Copper the room they need to enter. "I can't lend a hand with suggestions, but as you know, there's plenty to choose from."

"Don't I know it."

I give the dog another pat on the head. "I'll find those treats I bought Copper the last time I was here."

"He'll love that." Wally flashes me a toothy grin. "I promise I won't be long."

That's a promise he's guaranteed to break. Wally is notoriously slow when it comes to browsing the books in my late grandmother's extensive library.

It looks like I'll need to wait at least a few more hours to see Summer again.

CHAPTER SEVENTEEN

GREER

I'M EXHAUSTED, but it's in the best possible way.

After I went into town and grabbed a few essentials and non-essentials, I came back to my weekend retreat with the intention of settling in for a nap that I hoped would last at least two hours.

That never happened.

Instead, I spent almost ninety minutes talking on the phone. I took two very important personal calls, and when those were done, I focused on business for only twenty minutes.

Three quick calls took care of an issue that had popped up that Krista was ignoring. It wasn't crucial, but I'd definitely label it as important.

Now that it's all smoothed over, I'm finally ready to enjoy my Saturday night.

A series of quick knocks at the door brings a soft smile to my face. It has to be Joe. In anticipation of seeing him tonight, I showered after my calls and put on a maxi dress. It's a perfect shade of green for me, and the fabric is so lightweight and breezy it feels like I'm wearing almost nothing.

In a sense, that's true since the only thing I have on other than the dress is a pair of black panties.

I take my time walking across the tiled floor to reach the door.

I've been nothing but eager since I met the man. I'm way past the point of playing hard to get with him, but it can't hurt to make him ache for me for an extra few seconds.

I swing open the door, and there he is. The dark-rimmed eyeglasses he's wearing are new to me, and a very nice touch. "I like your glasses."

He pushes them up the bridge of his nose. "You do?"

"Very much." I nod in appreciation, my gaze tracking over the black V-neck sweater he's wearing. He's paired that with charcoal gray pants and shiny black wingtip shoes. "You've got a naughty professor vibe going on."

His head falls back in laughter. "Why does that sound so hot coming from you?"

"Why do you look so hot dressed like that?" I counter, smiling brightly.

"I am hot." He pinches the neckline of the sweater to tug it away from his skin. "It's too fucking hot out for me to be wearing this many clothes, but I have big plans tonight."

Trying to shield my disappointment, I nod. "Big plans?"

I almost laugh at myself. What the hell kind of question is that?

He tilts his chin up. "Work plans."

"So, you do work from here." I jerk a thumb in the direction of his house. "You live here full-time, don't you?"

His gaze skims my face, but before he can answer, his phone starts ringing.

"Dammit," he whispers. "I need to go, Summer, but I wanted to check in."

"Check in?" I question as his phone quiets.

He nods. "I wanted to make sure you have everything you need until we hang out again tomorrow."

Smiling, I tap a finger against my lower lip. "I have absolutely everything I need for tonight."

"Good. So, about tomorrow…"

"What time were you thinking of getting together?" I interrupt before he can finish.

Call it eagerness, or a lack of patience, but I want to see him again as soon as possible since I need to head back to Manhattan tomorrow.

"Martin mentioned swinging by in the morning to double-check that the pump in the pool is working as it should." He chuckles. "I told him three times that it is, but Martin never takes my word for it."

"Come here for breakfast as soon as he leaves," I blurt out.

I really want to tell him to stop by tonight on his way home, but he's the one who brought up getting together tomorrow. I take that to mean he's not interested or available to spend time with me tonight. Naturally, I'm disappointed, but this weekend has already been a dream.

He nods. "Should I bring anything?"

"Condoms," I say with my gaze locked to his. "Don't forget those."

He leans forward to kiss me softly on the mouth. As he pulls back, a groan escapes him. "If this meeting weren't as important as it is, I'd cancel it in a heartbeat."

As if on cue, his phone starts ringing again, luring him back a step.

"You need to go," I remind him.

"I need to quit my fucking job." He laughs.

"I'll see you tomorrow, Joe."

"You can bank on that," he says before he kisses my cheek and darts off down the driveway in a sprint.

MY MOONLIT WALK DOWN the beach was everything I imagined it would be. The water was warm as it washed over my feet. I collected a few white rocks to take home with me, and I stood looking up at the moon, grateful for the life I have.

I take one last look at the almost deserted beach before I step back onto Mrs. Frye's property. The scent of white lilacs fills the air. As soon as I glance to the right, my breath catches.

A smile slides over my lips as tears prick my eyes. I bend down to breathe in the unmistakable smell of the lilac bush that's next to me. The angel white lilacs move softly with the light wind that's blowing my hair back.

Their fragrance fills the air, reminding me of summers past, and one late winter day, I thought I'd never recover from.

Closing my eyes, I tilt my chin up as tears flow down my cheeks.

A loud bark in the distance pulls me from my memories.

I look toward the beach to see Wally and Copper walking under the moonlight.

It's a peaceful sight, and although I'm tempted to join them, sleep is calling my name.

I have a lunch date tomorrow that I need to be rested up for, because I have a feeling Joe considers me his dessert.

CHAPTER EIGHTEEN

Holden

I EASE BACK on the padded chair I've been sitting in for the past two and a half hours. That's how long it took me to make one of my brother's recent dreams a reality.

With a smug smile on my face, I wave goodbye to the man who sat across from me, eating a perfectly grilled steak while I convinced him to sell his company to me.

He's the reason I'm in East Hampton this weekend, so it seems fitting that I toast to my accomplishment. I wave the server over. He practically sprints across the crowded restaurant to get to me.

"What can I get for you, Mr. Sheppard?" he asks, eagerness edging his tone.

I've been in this establishment enough times in the past few months that he knows how well I tip. He's been nothing but attentive and helpful during this business dinner, so I'll reward him handsomely for that.

"Get me a glass of your best champagne." I stop to consider my request before I amend it. "Actually, pack up a slice of that chocolate cake thing I had for dessert. I'll take that to go."

"No champagne, sir?" he questions.

"Send a bottle to the table in the corner." I tilt my chin in that direction. "I sense they're celebrating something important."

The only reason I noticed is that the man at the table passed a small box to the woman just moments ago. She squealed in delight when she popped it open. She tugged a gold chain with a heart pendant hanging from it out of the box before he fastened it around her neck.

Maybe it's a birthday or an anniversary celebration. Whatever it is, the cheap wine they're drinking doesn't fit the occasion.

"I'll tell them it's courtesy of you," the waiter boasts, as if he's doing me a favor.

"Don't," I warn with a stern look. "It's the thought that counts, not the source."

He grins. "I'm going to steal that saying, sir."

"Steal away. Pack me up that dessert. I want to deliver it as soon as possible."

Just as he rushes away, my phone vibrates on the table. I turned off the ringer during dinner so I could focus solely on the man who just left this restaurant with a smile on his face that could light up the night sky.

"Jameson," I say as I answer the call. "What do you need?"

"Information," he says evenly. "Tim Lightell just sent me a cryptic text message."

Tim must have sent that text the moment he walked out of

the restaurant. James has been working his ass off trying to set up a meeting between Tim and us for months. When I heard that Tim would be in East Hampton for the weekend, I made sure I would be here, too.

I lured him to this restaurant with the promise that I'd make it worth his while. I did that and more since he left after shaking my hand on a deal that will put a seven figure payout in his bank account once the sale of his company is finalized.

"What did the message say?" I play along because making Jameson suffer is part of my job as his older brother.

"Nothing." He chuckles nervously. "Call your brother. That's it. Did you fuck up things with him, Holden? I've been trying to set up a meeting with him for a hell of a long time. I want his company. We need it."

We don't need it, and Jameson is the only one who wants Tim's company. One very short conversation with our grandmother years ago convinced James that she wanted Carden to take over Toffee Twist.

I wasn't part of that conversation, and I fucking hate toffee. As much as I wanted to, I couldn't ignore it when my brother suggested we make Tim, the owner, an offer to buy his business.

He tried to play hardball, but he lost that battle tonight when I tossed out a number that made him realize he could retire to a home near a golf course and leave the toffee business behind forever.

"It's good to know that your first thought is that I fucked things up, James." I keep my tone even so he can't tell I'm teasing him. "Your faith in me is inspiring."

I can tell he's taking a few extra seconds to craft a response. "You're my brother, Holden. I trust you. I have faith in you. Just tell me what Tim is talking about."

Putting him out of his misery right now serves me well in two ways. It'll make him happy, and I'll get this conversation over with so I can get out of here and surprise Summer.

"Toffee Twist is yours," I say bluntly.

"What the fuck?" he asks, laughing his way through the question. "What the hell are you talking about?"

I take a second to acknowledge the server with a nod when he drops off a small white box I know contains the treat I can't wait to put into Summer's hands. "Give me a minute," I whisper so I can finish my conversation with my brother before I settle up for the night.

He politely takes off, leaving me alone.

"Give you a minute for what?" James jumps to the conclusion that I was talking to him.

"That wasn't meant for you," I tell him succinctly, not bothering to explain where I am or who I was talking to.

"I'm bouncing off the walls here, Holden. Are you saying you worked out a deal with Tim?" The volume of his voice rises slightly. "Did you buy his company?"

"We shook on it," I explain, so he knows exactly where we're at in the buying process. "I don't foresee any issues, though. Toffee Twist is now part of the Carden empire."

"Jesus, Holden." His voice breaks. "Was this your plan all along? Did you go to East Hampton this weekend to work this out?"

If I dive into the details now, I'll be stuck talking to him for the next hour. That's time I'd much rather spend with Summer. "I'll stop by your place tomorrow night once I'm back in the city. I'll explain everything then."

"Fine. Good," he spits both words out quickly. "I'm over the fucking moon here. I've wanted this for a long time."

That's why I made it happen.

I don't tell him that as I wave the server back over. "I need to go, James. Kiss your boy for me and get some sleep."

"Will do," he says. "You're the best, Holden."

That's all the thanks I need. My brother's admiration was something I longed for when we were estranged from each other. I'll never take it for granted again.

CHAPTER NINETEEN

GREER

WRAPPING my short silk robe around me, I rush down the stairs toward the front door.

What I thought was a light knock less than a minute ago has now turned into an incessant press of someone's finger on the doorbell. Hoping that I'm right in my assumption that Joe is waiting for me on the other side of the door, I smile as I reach the bottom of the stairs.

A quick run of my palm over my hair is all I need to do before I race to the door and stop dead in my tracks. "Who is it?"

"You know who it is." Joe laughs. "Let me in. I have this chocolate dessert thing for you."

"You brought me dessert?" I ask as I lean against the door.

"Don't sound so surprised," he says in a tone I can barely make out. "You knew I'd come back tonight."

After unlocking the door, I open it swiftly. "I didn't know that."

His gaze travels up and down my body. "Tell me you're naked under that."

I do one better. I show him. With a quick tug, the sash of the robe gives way, and it falls open.

"Fuck," he groans. "You get cake later. I want you now."

Stunned by the need in his voice, I can only nod in acknowledgement.

In one effortless movement, he drops the box in his hand on the foyer table, deposits his eyeglasses next to it, and wraps his hands around my waist.

He gives the door a kick with his shoe, sending it flying shut with a thud. "I haven't stopped thinking about you since I left you earlier."

"But, you had work to do," I say coyly as he plants a trail of light kisses over my neck.

"I got done what needed to be done." His gaze finds mine. "Now, I get to do what I've wanted to all night."

"What's that?" I ask, knowing that whatever it is, I'm going to enjoy it a hell of a lot.

He pushes me back a step and then another. "What do you think?"

I stare at him as he continues marching me backward. I want to remember him forever, so I catalog the shape of his eyes and the slope of his forehead in my memory. I'll never forget the fullness of his lips or how it felt when he kissed me.

Suddenly, I feel the large dining table behind me. Before I can protest, he's hauled me up by my waist so I can sit on the table.

"Lean back," he orders, pushing a finger lightly into the center of my chest.

I sprawl my hands out as I carefully lower my back to the table.

His fingertip never leaves my skin. He runs it over my hardened left nipple before it glides down the center of my body toward my core.

With his gaze still locked on mine, he yanks my ass to the very edge of the table before he drops to his knees.

Not a word leaves him as he trails his tongue along the inside of my thigh. He draws a tight circle with the tip.

"Joe," I whisper his name. "Please."

"I promise I'm going to enjoy this a hell of a lot more than you will," he rasps.

I scream when he laps his tongue against my clit. Weaving my fingers in his hair to hold on to him, I glance down at this drop dead gorgeous man, fully clothed, eating me as he moans his way through it all.

I STARE at the wrinkled sheet where Joe fell asleep early this morning. He was next to me then, breathing heavily in an effort to catch his breath. I watched him sleep for more than an hour before I finally drifted off, too.

We couldn't keep our hands off each other for hours after he arrived. I practically tore his clothes off of him before we bolted for the bedroom.

When we finally came up for air, the sun was rising, and my heart felt an ache it hadn't experienced before. I knew what it was instantly. It wasn't regret or sadness. It was gratitude.

Joe Campbell gave me a gift that I desperately needed. I needed to let go and experience everything I haven't allowed myself to experience in the past seven years.

I'm leaving East Hampton as a better version of myself, and I know that going forward I'll make more time for myself. It won't be easy, and it doesn't have to be frequent, but it needs to happen.

"You're packing," Joe says from behind me. "I thought you were mine until tonight."

Those words pierce me, but it's in the best way possible. I was his for a short time, and I relished in that.

I turn to face him. Naturally, he's nude. He has no shame and he shouldn't given how striking he is.

I'm wearing a plain white T-shirt and leggings. It's more about comfort than style for me, because I need to do a quick tidy-up before I head back to Manhattan.

"That call you took earlier was really important," he says as if he can read my mind. "You need to go back to the place you came from now."

Nodding, I keep my destination to myself. "Someone super special needs to see me as soon as possible."

That's an understatement, but this man doesn't need any details about my life.

He scratches his upper lip. "You don't have time for one last nude swim?"

Since it's creeping up on noon now, and I made a vow that I'd be home before dinner, I shake my head. "I wish I did, but…"

"But your someone super special needs you." He crosses his arms over his chest. "You asked me if I was involved with anyone, Summer. Are you?"

The way his jaw is twitching tells me that if I were seeing someone else, he'd have a problem with us sleeping together. This man has been cheated on. I've never had to deal with that, but I've seen firsthand how that level of betrayal can impact someone. He doesn't want another man to experience that pain because of something he did.

"No," I answer with no hesitation. "I'm happily divorced, remember? I'm also very happily single."

Nodding, he takes a few measured steps toward me. The fact that his cock is hardening right before my eyes is making it hard to focus on anything but that.

"You're staring at my cock," he points out, laughing. "You're more than welcome to kiss it goodbye."

I kiss him instead, pressing my lips to his for a slow, sensual kiss.

"Jesus," he whispers. "You're something else."

"So are you, Joe."

"You'll think of me from time to time," he says in a low tone.

I narrow my eyes. "Is that a question?"

"No," he answers. "It's the truth. You'll think of me. I'll think of you."

Nodding, I kiss him again. "I will think of you."

He cups both hands around my face, kissing me again with more intensity. It stirs something deep within me.

"I need to tidy up," I say, trying to lessen the heaviness of the moment. "I arranged for a driver to pick me up in an hour."

"To take you to the airport?" he asks.

I tap my bottom lip with my finger. "I'll never tell."

He stares deeply into my eyes as though he's searching for something. His lips part, but before he can say anything, his phone chimes.

"That's got to be Martin." He laughs. "I texted him early this morning to tell him not to come around until this afternoon. Leave it to Martin to show up right at noon."

"Go," I say softly. "I'll clean up a bit and head home."

He bites the corner of his bottom lip. "Take care of yourself, Summer Time."

"You, too, Joe Campbell. " I smile. "If I didn't mention it before, I'm glad we met."

He drops his hands to my body, wrapping me in his strong arms. "I am, too. I'm also pretty damn grateful you didn't stab me with that umbrella."

Laughing, I tap the center of his chest with my hand. "Kiss me goodbye."

The kiss is tender as he holds me against him. I soak in the moment, and in his touch, knowing that this man is one in a million and I'm lucky that for one brief weekend I had him all to myself.

CHAPTER TWENTY

GREER

THE RIDE back to Manhattan from East Hampton felt like it took forever. In reality, it obviously didn't, but my impatience to get home made it torturous.

As soon as the SUV is parked next to the curb in front of my home, I'm launching myself out of the door of the vehicle so I can sprint up the concrete steps.

I glance back at my driver, who also happens to be my friend. Robby has been an integral part of my life for years. His job as an account executive with a clothing company was phased out several months ago, so he's been filling in his time as a rideshare driver.

When I mentioned to him over lunch last week that I was heading to East Hampton, he offered to drive me there and pick me up. We worked out a deal that compensated him not only for the cost of fuel but also put a few extra dollars in his pocket. Since he's set to start a new job a little over a week from now, I was grateful we had the uninterrupted time in the car to catch up.

"Go!" He directs me with his hand. "I'll bring your bag."

I blow him a kiss just as the front door of my house opens wide.

The one word that I've missed hearing all weekend fills the air. "Mommy!"

"Olive!" I yell back to my daughter.

Her brown hair bounces on her shoulders as she carefully descends the concrete steps. I fly toward her, taking the steps two at a time until we meet in the middle.

Her arms wrap around me as I lift her up until her feet are dangling in the air.

"I missed you, Mommy," she whispers.

Tears prick my eyes as I repeat those words back, "I missed you."

"I had the best time," she tells me. "Grandma and Grandpa held hands, and they kissed. Don't tell them I saw."

I set her down on her bare feet. My sweet girl's big blue eyes search my face.

I hold in my emotions. This is the first time we've been apart overnight since the day she was born seven years ago. I've clung to her so tightly because she's everything I treasure in this world.

Olive Celia Irwin is the reason I do most of the things I do.

"Are you okay, Mommy?" Her hand swipes my cheek. "You look like you might cry."

"Those are tears of joy, Olive," Martha Bergvall says from where she's standing near the open front door of my home.

Next to her is her husband, Bruce.

They are my family, and the people who pitched in to

help me raise my daughter. Our relationship is as complicated as it is clear.

Martha and Bruce are my ex-husband's parents. They're my daughter's grandparents, and yesterday, they took her to Coney Island, so she could ride a Ferris wheel for the first time and overindulge in lollipops and cotton candy.

"Did you have fun, Olive?" I ask even though I know the answer to that question.

Olive told me all about her adventures in a series of text messages sent from Bruce's phone. She also explained it all in a rush with joy wrapped around each word this morning when she called me just after I woke up.

Joe was still fast asleep, so I snuck out by the pool and listened to my little girl detail what a blast she had at the place she's wanted to visit for so long.

I intended to take her there myself next month, but Martha asked if they could take her now. I know why she did it. She recognized I needed a chance to sleep in, read, and think. She knew I needed time to rediscover myself.

"It was the best time ever," she stresses before her gaze jumps behind me. "Hi, Robby."

"Olive Irwin," he says her full name to lure a smile to her face. "I promised I'd bring your mom back to you, and I did just that."

Olive skirts around me to get down to Robby. She gifts him with a big hug. "Thank you, Robby."

His brown eyes latch onto mine. "I should take off."

Nodding, I smile. "I'll text you before you start the new job."

"New job?" Martha asks because her curiosity is a cornerstone of who she is. "That sounds exciting."

"It is," he affirms with a nod. "I'll stop by this week and tell you all about it."

"Good." She wipes her hands on the red apron tied around her waist. "Come inside. I'll pack up some dinner you can take with you."

"Seriously?" he asks, his eyes brightening.

"Grandma makes the best biscuits," Olive boasts, since they're her favorite. "There's soup, too, but those biscuits are the best."

Robby shrugs. "I can't say no to any of that."

He rushes past me with my bags in his hands and Olive on his heel. They both disappear into my townhouse behind Martha.

Bruce smiles down at me. "We missed you, sweetie, but I'm glad you had a break."

"Me too." I rush up toward his open arms.

Bruce gives the best hugs. He's a large man with bushy brown eyebrows and a crooked smile.

"Our girl had a great weekend, too," he whispers. "Thank you for letting us take her, Greer. Thank you for letting us love her."

A tear falls down my cheek as I look up and into his face. "Thank you for loving us both."

"We always will," he assures me with a tight hug. "We're family. Nothing on this earth can ever change that."

CHAPTER TWENTY-ONE

Holden

"YOU'VE BEEN WEARING your glasses full time for weeks now," my brother points out as he walks into my office, dressed like he's heading to a football game.

He's sporting a baseball jersey that his wife gave him shortly after she gave birth. Sinclair thought it would be funny to purchase the blue and red accented jersey with the word "Daddy" printed on the back, along with a bright red #1.

I've been out on the streets of Manhattan with James when he's been wearing the jersey, and the curious looks and propositions he's been getting from women and a few men have brought some joy to my life I didn't realize I needed.

"It's been two weeks," I correct him, since that's when I came back from East Hampton after spending the weekend with Summer.

He picks up a pencil from my desk and taps the point

against his palm. "Did you run your supply of contact lenses dry? Do you need bifocals, old man?"

A rush of hearty laughter falls from between my lips. "Fuck you."

"You will always be older than me, Holden." He scribbles a circle on the top of a pad of paper that I never use. "Hence, you're an old man compared to me."

I push my glasses up the bridge of my nose. "I have more than enough contact lenses, and my prescription is spot on. I just like wearing the glasses."

The truth is, they remind me of Summer. I've thought about her countless times since we said goodbye.

I have no doubt that a call to Mrs. Frye would end with me having Summer's real first name. I pay Mrs. Frye handsomely to watch over my Hampton house when I'm not around, but beyond that, we're friends.

The reason I haven't taken that step is that Summer made it clear that the one weekend was all she wanted. Tracking her down in the '*real world*' isn't going to happen.

I may not know her well, but I respect the hell out of her boundaries.

"Are you going to your meeting dressed like that?" I ask my brother before I turn my attention back to the screen of my laptop.

I've been running sales numbers on some of the new products we launched last quarter. I can already tell what needs to be cut from production.

"I'm meeting my wife and son for lunch." He shakes his head. "For some reason, known only to Sinclair, she asked me to invite you."

I push back from my desk and stand. "She knows how much her son loves his uncle."

"Morgan loves his daddy the most." Jameson jerks a

thumb behind him. "My shirt confirms I'm the number one daddy in the world."

"Your shirt is fucking hilarious." I scoop up my phone and tuck it into the inner pocket of my suit jacket. "You're changing out of that before your meeting this afternoon."

"Why?" He shrugs. "The owner of Sweet Indulgence will get a kick out of it."

I'll take his word for it because all I know about the company he's trying to acquire is that it's a small operation renting an expensive storefront in Chelsea. According to Jameson, the owner claims they are bleeding money, and she wants a deal in place as soon as possible so she can leave that chapter of her life and Manhattan behind for Los Angeles.

I won't get involved until Jameson is certain this company has the potential to generate revenue for us if we take it on.

"Whatever works." I grin. "Let's go see our boy."

A slow smile spreads over his lips as his blue eyes lock on mine. "You know that I love that you love my son as much as you do, right?"

I brush past him to head toward my open office door. "I know, James."

"When you have a kid, I'll love them, too," he says. "You're going to be a great dad one day, Holden."

That hits me hard. I turn back to face him. "Thanks."

"I mean it." He drops a hand on my shoulder to give it a firm squeeze. "Any kid of yours will be lucky to have you."

I don't press my luck because I know I'm one comment away from him teasing me with an insult. "Lunch is on me."

"There was never any doubt about that." He gestures to the door. "I'm starving, so get a move on, old man."

CHARM

LUNCH with my family was exactly what I needed. The food at my favorite diner, Crispy Biscuit, always hits the spot.

The fact that I watched my sister-in-law steal fries off my brother's plate was the icing on the cake. The owner of the diner knows Jameson well enough to anticipate what he'll want to eat. She told him she'd bring him a burger and fries before he even had a menu in his hands.

When she added, "with extra fries," to the statement, he tossed her a smile, and he got a wink back in return.

I opted for a sandwich that in no way compared to the one Summer prepared for me. I need to shake that woman straight out of my mind, but that's an almost impossible task since this city is filled with women with red hair.

I spot one across the street from me, but her hair is too short and not quite the same shade as Summer's.

The odds of her living in the same city as me are slim. I scrub a hand over my face and get my mind back into the game. The game being work.

"Holden!" A familiar voice calls to me from the left.

Without even turning, I know it's Rook. The added "Uncle Holden" that comes at me tells me that his daughter is with him.

I kneel on the crowded sidewalk so I can take Kirby in my arms for a hug. Our bond is special since I took on the role of being her tap dancing partner a few months ago.

"Hey, Kirbs." I hug her tightly. "What's happening with you today?"

"We're going to get ice cream!" she screams in my ear.

There's no way in hell I can be mad at her, even though I know I'll hear ringing in that ear for the next hour.

I glance up at Rook. As usual, he's wearing a three-piece suit that resembles the one I chose today. It's not uncommon for us to dress alike. It's always a coincidence, but his daughter gets a kick out of it.

"You're twinning again," Kirby declares with a smirk. "If my daddy didn't have black hair and a beard, you'd be impossible to tell apart."

That's a stretch since we don't resemble each other in the slightest, but I don't say a word because she's a girl with her own view of the world. I'll never do anything to try to change that.

I push up to stand and look Rook in the eye. "Ice cream in the middle of the work day?"

"Don't knock it until you try it." He laughs. "Come with us."

"Please!" Kirby tugs on my hand. "I need to tell you some stuff."

Since I had dinner with Rook and his family two nights ago, I can't imagine what Kirby has to tell me, but the life of a kid is never dull, so I nod. "I'm in."

"I'm getting strawberry," Kirby announces as she takes Rook's hand with her free hand. "Who's with me?"

Laughing, I smile down at her. "I am. Strawberry ice cream, it is."

CHAPTER TWENTY-TWO

Greer

I STARE at Krista from where I'm standing near a pallet that holds one of our best sellers. We're in the crowded stock room of our store. This business we've built together has been a labor of love, and now my *sometimes* best friend is telling me she wants to bail on me.

Crossing my arms over my chest, I look right at her. "Repeat that."

"Howie got a job offer in Los Angeles." She takes a breath. "He's going to take it. I'm going with him."

I heard that part just fine the first time she said it. I panicked slightly because I pictured longer working days and late nights devoted to fulfilling online orders. In addition, someone has to ensure our staff shows up to help cover the duties in our small storefront.

It's what she said after she announced that she's moving to California with her soon-to-be husband that knocked the wind out of me. "You said something else, Krista."

I want to believe that I misheard her, but it was clear as a bell. Still, I need to hear it again.

"We need to sell Sweet Indulgence, Greer." There's a tremor in her voice. "I already found a buyer."

It doesn't even matter that I'm not in a financial position to buy her out at the moment. Our business agreement is ironclad. One of us can't sell their half without the other agreeing to sell theirs as well. When we launched, we couldn't picture one of us running it without the other, so we put that sentiment into a legal document and signed it.

We started this business to honor our best friend. All Celia Edlund ever wanted was to run a candy business. It was her dream for years, but she didn't live long enough to make that a reality, so Krista and I did it.

Sweet Indulgence is built on our shared love for our late friend.

"You're thinking about Cels," she says the nickname I bestowed on Celia shortly after we met in third grade.

"Don't," I warn with a finger in the air. "Don't call her that."

Celia and I were a duo until we met Krista in middle school. From that point on, the three of us were inseparable until we lost Cels.

Her chance to enjoy this business was stolen from her before we even launched. We did that three years ago.

I had a stable and flourishing career in advertising at the time. Krista was floating from one job to another. When she came to me with the concept of our very own candy company, I was skeptical, but I couldn't shake Celia's words from my mind.

"*One day we'll work side by side at a candy counter, Greer,*" she said months before she died.

I took the leap but held onto my job. That only lasted six

months, and then I had no choice but to go all in. It was all too much for Krista, and I wanted nothing more than to make it a success.

"I can't sell," I whisper. "I just can't, Krista."

Her brown eyes well with tears. "Celia would want us to be happy. I'll be happy in Los Angeles. I'm under consideration for an internship with a fashion designer there. You know how much I've always wanted to design dresses."

I know that she's wanted many things over the years. Becoming a fashion designer is something I've never heard before, even though it's obvious she's been thinking about it for some time if she's applied for an internship in another state.

"I'll keep running it on my own," I say, hoping to reach a compromise. "You'll still reap the rewards financially."

"I need the lump sum this sale would give me." She swipes a tear from her cheek. "It will help us really get set up out west, and it'll allow me the financial freedom I need to focus on the internship. Please, Greer, just give it some thought."

I don't need to give it any thought. My answer won't change.

"You could go back to East Hampton to think it over," she suggests. "You were so happy after that weekend. You said the time away gave you clarity."

It did. It was clear to me after my weekend away that I'm a very lucky woman. I have an amazing daughter, great friends, and family that I love. Spending time with Joe helped me see that it's okay for me to carve out moments that are just for me, even though my primary focus for the foreseeable future is raising my daughter and growing this business.

I got back to Manhattan with more determination than ever to make Sweet Indulgence the best it can be.

Krista's grandma's candy recipes are what launched us, but our new creations are what have sustained us. Our online presence is growing by the day, thanks to an aggressive social media campaign I developed.

I can't let it go now. My gut tells me that if we stay on the path we're on, we'll see increased sales in no time.

"It's been over a month since you came back from your trip," she points out, sticking to the subject of my getaway. "Isn't it time to go back?"

It's been precisely thirty-six days since I last saw Joe, but I have no intention of going back to East Hampton. Besides, I have nothing to think about. I'm going to cling to Sweet Indulgence as tightly as I can.

"I set up a tentative meeting next week with the company that wants to buy us." Her voice cracks. "It's called…"

"I don't care what it's called." I stop her with a shake of my head. "We're not selling Sweet Indulgence to a company that won't honor what it truly means to us."

"Celia will always be with us." Tears roll down her cheeks as she pats the center of her chest. "I think it's okay to hand the reins of what we've built to someone else."

"It's not," I say with my own tears welling in my eyes. "I can't let it go."

"Please think about it," she pleads, her hands twisting in the material of the front of her dark green T-shirt.

It doesn't help that it's one of the branded shirts that I designed after countless attempts to come up with a logo for Sweet Indulgence. I glance down at the matching shirt I'm wearing.

I even had several made in Olive's size because my little girl is proud of what her mom has built.

"We can take the meeting without promising them

anything." She exhales loudly. "Can you at least give me that, Greer? If you hate the offer, I won't press it."

I don't believe her, but if this is what it takes to get her to drop the idea of selling our business for now, I nod. "What day and time is this meeting?"

"Next Wednesday morning at ten." A soft smile spreads over her lips. "Just meet me here at nine. I'll handle our transportation to and from the meeting. You don't have to do anything but show up."

"I won't agree to sell," I warn her with a stern look.

Nodding slowly, she tucks a strand of her blonde hair behind her ear. "You agreeing to go to this meeting means everything to me."

I glance at the floor and the worn sneakers on my feet. They once belonged to Celia. I borrowed them from her a few weeks before she died. I couldn't bear to donate them or throw them out, so I wear them to feel closer to her.

"I'm only agreeing to the meeting, Krista," I say, stressing each word. "I hope you understand that."

"I do." She scrubs both hands over her cheeks. "I need to get out to New Jersey."

Since that's where our production facilities are, I nod. She has a lot of work to tend to there today. All I hope is that she gives it the attention it needs.

"I love you, Greer," she whispers. "I truly do."

I cross the space to wrap my arms around her. "I love you, too."

CHAPTER TWENTY-THREE

Holden

I THANK the man working at the bodega around the corner from my office. He's one of the few people in this city who doesn't give me a perplexed look when I pick up a newspaper.

I'm well aware that the news of the day is just a swipe away on my phone, and I admit that's where I get the majority of my information. Still, I have an ulterior motive for carrying a newspaper folded under my arm on my way into the building that I spend the majority of my time in each day.

I remember fondly the vision of my grandfather arriving at Carden with a newspaper tucked under his arm. He always wore a sharp suit in a color I'd never be caught in. I'll never forget what he looked like in a canary yellow suit with a bright blue button-down shirt with a wide collar under the jacket. My favorite suit of his was mint green with white stitching.

My grandmother hated it. She literally cringed whenever he wore it, but Carrick Sheppard knew exactly how to make her smile even when he was dressed in a way she abhorred.

I'd never attempt to mimic his fashion sense, but the newspaper under my arm is a tribute to the man who started this business with his beloved wife. It's given me a life I never dreamed possible.

"Glasses again?" my brother asks as I near where he's standing outside the building.

I've worn my contact lenses multiple times since I left East Hampton, but glasses have their benefits. They always garner second looks from our employees when I pass them in the corridor or board the elevator with them.

I ignore the question and take the coffee he offers me. "Thanks, James."

"I should be upfront about that." He chuckles. "Consider the coffee a bribe. I want us to buy this company, Holden."

He's made his interest in Sweet Indulgence abundantly clear to me. It's so clear that I'm not going to fight him on this. I looked over the financials one of the owners provided to him. It's a solid investment for us, especially since the storefront on Chelsea is prime real estate and their lease for the next year and a half is part of the deal.

We'll rebrand it as a Carden location and make it work better for us than it has for the current owners.

With the right amount of attention and thoughtful marketing, acquiring this company can be a win for us. I can feel it, and my intuition is rarely wrong.

"Krista and Greer will be here at ten," he tells me.

"Krista and Greer?" I question.

He shoots me a look meant to convey his frustration with me, but it falls flat because he adds a smile to it. "The owners of Sweet Indulgence, Holden. Try to keep up."

"Right." I nod.

Other than the financials, I haven't conducted a thorough review of the files he sent me regarding the business he wants to acquire. He's the one who handled all the legwork. All I need to do is show up for this meeting.

"Let's get inside." He starts walking toward the lobby door of the building that houses our offices. "Drink the coffee. I don't want you falling asleep mid-meeting."

I punch his shoulder. It's hard enough to sting, but light enough to make him laugh. "Don't be an asshole, James."

"You love that about me."

I laugh, too. "True. It's true."

***

I GESTURE toward the rectangular conference table and the vacant chair at the head of it. "I'll flip you for it."

Jameson barks out a laugh. "What? No."

As CEO, I automatically take that seat and run our meetings, but it wouldn't hurt him to take control of this one.

"You're the one who shepherded this deal," I point out.

"You're the Sheppard in charge."

"So?" I take another sip of the coffee he got me. It's way too fucking strong for my liking, but I need the caffeine jolt it's providing, so I'll finish every last drop.

"So, sit your ass down." He rakes a hand through his hair, messing it up slightly. "Krista and Greer will be here soon."

"You're chomping at the bit." I sit while motioning to the chair next to me. "You need to calm down. We'll get this deal done."

As he takes his seat, I glance at the open doorway to see two members of our team file in.

"Gentlemen," Sasha Cardinal, one of our in-house lawyers, greets us both as she sits next to me.

Jameson's assistant, Marc, takes the chair beside him. Marc retired from Carden after a stellar career that spanned decades. My brother was able to lure him back to work as his right hand man. His knowledge is invaluable, so I'm glad to have him here.

Jameson's phone buzzes in his pocket. He tugs it out, scanning the screen before he looks in my direction. "Krista and Greer are here. They're on their way up."

"You're not going to greet them at reception?" I shake my head. "Rude, James. That's so fucking rude."

Sasha and Marc both laugh.

My brother pushes back from the table. "I'll wait for them at the elevator."

"I was kidding."

"You were right." He starts walking toward the door. "I want them to feel welcome."

As soon as he's out of the room, Marc glances at me. "He's killing it lately, Holden. That kid has really taken to the role of COO."

Leaning forward, I nod. "I'm damn proud of him. He's got the job under control. He's an incredible dad. He's not a half bad brother either."

Marc grins. "He wants this deal. He sees a lot of potential in it."

"As do I."

"Good." He slaps his hand on the table. "I wish your grandparents had lived to see this day. You two working this well together was all they ever wanted."

I take comfort in knowing that. Jameson and I are a solid team, and we'll prove that again today with this negotiation.

CHAPTER TWENTY-FOUR

Greer

I SUBTLY STUDY the face of the man who was waiting for us as we exited the elevator. There's something familiar about him, but I know we've never met before.

Jameson Sheppard introduced himself as the Chief Operating Officer of Carden Confectionaries. As he shook my hand, he explained how his grandparents launched the enterprise decades ago.

Krista nodded in response to everything he said. This is the most nervous she's ever been. I knew it as soon as I walked into our store and saw her shoving a fistful of jelly beans into her mouth.

A bright red one got away from her. It bounced down the front of the light blue dress she's wearing. Thankfully, it didn't leave a crimson trail behind.

I couldn't help but laugh. She joined in, and that immediately broke the tension that had been brewing between us for days now.

I glance down at the red blouse and matching pants I'm wearing. I even chose red heels.

There's no rhyme or reason behind it. I didn't want to appear too formal, but still wanted to look presentable, since I know this is important to Krista.

This meeting isn't going to end the way she wants, but I'm here, and that's what matters at the moment.

"My brother is waiting for us in our main conference room," Jameson says as he leads us down a corridor. "Holden is excited to meet you both."

Good for him. I have no interest in meeting the man.

"He's the CEO, right?" Krista asks excitedly. "I read all about both of you on the company website last night."

I, on the other hand, read a fairytale to my daughter last night before she fell asleep. The main character was a princess who fought a few dragons and broke down some barriers to find success. She did it alone without the help of a company whose sole focus was to steal her dream away.

I may have been the one who hastily typed that fairytale into the notes app on my phone while Olive was kissing her grandparents good night.

"He is." Jameson motions toward an open door at the end of the corridor. "We're meeting in there. I should warn you that the view is stunning. Most people who enter the room for the first time are awestruck by it."

I've seen New York City from every angle over the past thirty-two years. I'm wild about my beloved city, but it would take a view unlike anything I've ever seen to leave me awestruck.

Jameson steps aside to let Krista enter first. She doesn't make a sound.

I'm right on her heel, but my arrival is punctuated by an uncontrollable gasp leaving me.

It has nothing to do with the skyline of Manhattan that's visible through the bank of windows behind the large table.

It has everything to do with the man at the head of that table who is pushing to stand.

With a shocked expression on his face that has to mirror my own, Joe Campbell greets me with a curt nod.

"Well, hello there," he says in that deeply delicious voice of his. "I'm Holden Sheppard. It's nice to meet you."

I STARE AT HIM, completely confused about what the hell is happening.

"What did you say your name was?" I blurt out.

He rounds the table to approach me. I instinctively take a step back. I want to run out of here, but I don't think my feet can make it. That single step took all of the might I have at the moment.

Joe walks toward me with steady steps. He looks so different dressed in a tailored three-piece suit and an expensive tie. His hair is slightly longer than it was in East Hampton. The glasses framing his face are the same as the ones he was wearing the last time I saw him.

I know it's him. It has to be him, yet he called himself Holden.

As soon as he's close enough to reach me, he extends a hand. "Allow me to formally introduce myself. I'm Holden Sheppard. I'm the CEO of Carden Confectionaries."

"Son of a bitch," I mutter silently.

I know no one hears me because Krista drowned out my words with her own. "I'm Krista Bellard."

Her hand lands in his for a hearty shake.

Joe's gaze drops to it. He offers her a weak smile, all while keeping his blue-eyed gaze locked on my face.

As soon as he's able to tug his hand free, he pushes it toward me. "You must be Greer."

"She is." Krista nudges my arm, signaling she wants me to shake Joe's hand. "Greer Irwin."

"Greer Irwin," he repeats, still holding out his hand.

I finally reach to touch it, but the shake is so brief that it garners me another nudge from Krista. "Greer," she admonishes in a low tone. "You promised you'd be polite."

I promised no such thing because I am always polite. Well, normally I am, but I'm standing less than a foot away from a man who fucked me into bliss just six weeks ago.

Now, he's attempting to buy my company.

"Let's sit," Jameson suggests, motioning to the large conference table. "That's Sasha Cardinal. She's part of our legal team, and the handsome guy to our right is Marc. He's one of Carden's hidden treasures."

The room erupts in laughter, but Joe doesn't crack a smile.

I don't either. I can't since a million thoughts are running through my mind.

Did he know who I was in East Hampton? Was he already planning on buying out my company back then?

Krista tugs on my hand, so I follow her toward the table. As I do, I brush right past Joe.

I sit down in the first available chair. It just so happens to be at the head of the table as far away from Sasha and Marc as I can get. I grabbed this chair for two simple reasons. It's closest to the door, and I assume it's going to be farthest from where Joe will be sitting... or Holden. Whatever the hell his name is.

My assumption is proven correct as he walks to the other

end of the table and faces me directly. His gaze finds mine, and he perks a brow as if he's asking me a silent question.

Crossing my arms, I shake my head before I look to where Krista has taken the seat next to Jameson since Marc moved over one.

"You can join us down here, Greer!" Krista calls through her cupped hands, as if I'm a million miles away, and she needs her voice to carry over the distance.

"I'm fine right where I am," I say in defiance, glancing at her.

I shift my gaze back to the man who blew my world apart just six weeks ago. He lowers himself into his chair, keeping his eyes locked on me the entire time. "I'm eager to make a deal. Tell me what it's going to take to make that happen, Greer."

CHAPTER TWENTY-FIVE

Holden

I'VE TRIED REPEATEDLY to drag Greer into this conversation about the potential sale of her business, but her partner is doing all of the talking...and I do mean *all of the talking*.

It became apparent in the very early moments of this meeting that Greer has zero interest in selling Sweet Indulgence to me, or more precisely, to my company.

When I mentioned our vision for both the company and the storefront they now inhabit, Greer shook her head. She was essentially cutting each of our ideas down with a single shake of her head. Every time it happened, I moved on to the next idea that Jameson and our marketing team had jotted down for me.

Nothing impressed Greer, including the smile I tried to dazzle her with. That resulted in a frown from her and what I think was a slight eye roll.

She's pissed as hell.

I have no clue if it's because she wants to retain control of her company.

There's a damn good chance that she's fuming because I'm not Joe Campbell.

Either way, I plan on grabbing a moment alone with her once this disaster of a meeting concludes.

"We need to get back to work," Greer announces loudly.

"What?" Krista's head snaps in her business partner's direction. "We haven't accepted their offer yet."

Greer shoots her a look. "We're not accepting anything."

"Ever?" Krista jumps to her feet. "Please, Greer. Let's talk about this."

Greer stands, too, so I do the same. Jameson follows my lead.

"If you two need a moment to discuss the offer in private, we'll give you the room," my naïve brother says.

He has no idea I spent the better part of three days naked between Greer's legs, and her rush to run out of here likely has a lot more to do with that than the offer we presented.

"Thank you, but we're leaving." Greer's voice is strained. The frustration in her tone is unmistakable.

"Really?" Krista stomps her shoe against the floor.

The only response she gets from Greer is a blank stare.

Jameson looks to me for guidance, but I've got nothing to offer him other than a half-shrug of my shoulder. I have no fucking idea if this deal is salvageable or not, but my gut is telling me that approaching Greer right now is not what she needs.

"Thank you all for making time for us," Krista says as she hurries over to where Greer is now standing near the closed door. "I'll be in touch."

Greer doesn't back that up with anything other than a

glance in my direction. Seconds later, both women have left the room with my brother chasing after them.

"It seems someone isn't on board with selling their company to Carden." Marc chuckles. "Do you think Jameson can change Greer's mind?"

From what I just witnessed, I'd say no.

That doesn't mean I won't try to persuade her to give the offer more consideration. I'll do that in person because I want to see her again as soon as possible.

"I FUCKED UP." Jameson slaps the back of his phone against his palm as he enters my office.

It's been almost thirty minutes since Greer ran for the hills with Krista and Jameson chasing after her. That's not exactly how it happened, but I was able to get a clear view of them heading toward the elevator since I stepped out of the conference room mere moments after they did.

I watched my brother sprint after the two of them.

I know he was clinging to the slim hope that he'd pocket a deal with them today to purchase Sweet Indulgence, but he wasn't seeing any of it through the same lens I was.

Greer may not want to sell her company to us, but I don't believe that's what sent her bolting out of the room.

It was seeing me again.

"How so?" I motion for my brother to come into my office so he can take a seat in one of the guest chairs that face my desk.

"How so?" he parrots as he drops into the chair. "Um, Holden, were you asleep in that meeting? One of the partners in the business didn't want to be here. I think Greer would have rather had a wisdom tooth pulled than entertain the idea of selling to us."

I can tell he has more to say by the way his knee is bouncing up and down. I know my brother. Nervous anxiety has its grip on him.

"Krista mentioned that Greer had minor reservations about selling, but what we witnessed wasn't minor." He closes his eyes briefly. "That's on me. I should have had a sit-down with her before today to get a better sense of where she was in terms of selling. She obviously wants nothing to do with us."

I could allow this to continue until he thoroughly chews himself apart for not connecting with Greer before today, but I can't let that happen.

Being upfront and honest with my brother is important to me. I owe him that because since we put our issues behind us, he's only been truthful with me.

"Greer wants nothing to do with me," I correct him. "What happened in the conference room today was about me."

"You?" Confusion knits his brow. "How?"

"We know each other," I start, but stop to rethink where I want to go with this. "Or she knew me as Joe Campbell before she saw me today."

"You fucked her?" he asks, jumping to the logical conclusion since he knows the alias I've used to hook up with women in the past.

I see no reason not to own up to that, so I nod. "We spent time together in East Hampton."

"Wait!" He darts to his feet. "Are we talking a long-ago hook up or is this a more recent thing?"

"It's a six week ago thing."

Scrubbing his hands over his face, his head falls back.

"Jesus, Holden. She's the woman who stayed at Mrs. Frye's place the weekend you went there to secure the deal with Tim. It's her, isn't it?"

"Yes," I acknowledge with a brisk nod. "I met Greer then."

He drops back into the chair. "No wonder she wanted nothing to do with us. You gave her a fake name, took her to bed, and then dropped out of sight."

I tap a finger on the top of my glass desk. "It wasn't quite like that, James. She didn't give me her real name either, and she made it very clear that what happened in East Hampton that weekend stayed there."

"Talk about a coincidence." He takes a deep breath. "So, where does that leave us now? Krista is desperate to sell, and you fucked Greer over, so…"

"I didn't fuck her over," I spit out each word slowly.

"I want that company, Holden," he repeats what he's been telling me for weeks now. "They offer something unique. We need Sweet Indulgence to be under the Carden umbrella."

A mental image of Greer with the umbrella firmly in her grasp when she caught me in the pool pops into my mind. I can't help but chuckle.

Jameson's eyes narrow. "What the hell is so funny?"

I ignore the question and get back on the track I know he wants me to focus on. "I'll speak to Greer."

He tilts his head. "You think that's the solution? She couldn't get away from you fast enough today."

He's right about that, but I'm willing to risk being told off by the most beautiful woman I've ever met. "Tomorrow is another day. I'll reach out to her then."

"I can feel Sweet Indulgence slipping away from me."

If he weren't smiling right now, I'd feel like shit, but

we're in this together. Sometimes things go as planned. At other times, they shoot straight to hell at high speed.

"Do what you can," he says as he stands. "I trust you to do what's right for the company, Holden, but more importantly, what's right for you."

"What's right for me?"

"You like this woman." He tucks his hands into the front pocket of his pants. "Something tells me behind all that anger, she likes you, too."

"She likes Joe Campbell."

Jameson snorts, his hand jumping to cover his mouth to restrain his laughter. "That's such a bad fake name, Holden. You've been using that since you were what? Eighteen?"

"Nineteen," I correct him. "It's a solid name."

Agree to disagree on that." His head shakes. "Out of curiosity, what was Greer's fake name?"

"That's none of your business," I say because for some reason I want to keep it to myself.

"You do like her," he says. "Don't try, and deny it. Work out a deal with her. We can up the offer if need be."

I'm well aware of that, so I nod. "I'll talk to Greer tomorrow."

I don't bother adding on that I can't fucking wait to do that. I'll be counting the hours until I'm standing face-to-face with her again.

CHAPTER TWENTY-SIX

GREER

WE EXIT the building without one word passing between us. I know Krista is heartbroken. I hate that. Causing her pain is the last thing I want to do, but I felt as though I was tossed into a lion's cage when I walked into that meeting room.

"Krista." I grab her shoulder from behind before she can rush off. "Stop, please."

"Why?" Her voice carries over the late morning hum in the heart of Manhattan.

People mill about around us. Cars pass by on the street, and the constant noises of the city surround us, but none of it drowns out the pain in her tone.

"I have to talk to you," I say calmly. "Please turn around."

She does, and I'm met with bloodshot, reddened eyes. It's an instant reminder of the day Celia died. I was the one who broke the news to Krista. On that cold, rainy afternoon, she'd stared at me, trying to understand what I had just said. I was trying to do the same. I struggled to piece together how my vibrant best friend, who had so much to look forward to in life, was no longer laughing, planning, and gushing about everything the future had in store for her.

I pull Krista close, hugging her tightly. "I'm sorry, Krista."

Her arms circle me much the same way they did when we lost Cels. "I'm at a loss for what happened back there. The way you acted was so... it wasn't like you at all, Greer. I'm really confused."

The calmness in her voice gives me hope. Maybe we can get through this. Maybe there's a chance she'll give me the answers I need.

"I'm confused, too," I say.

"About what?" she asks, her eyes searching my face for something. Maybe it's a clue as to why I was so rude in the meeting or why I ended it so abruptly.

"When exactly did you connect with the Sheppards?" I ask tentatively because I don't want her to shut down on me.

"A few months ago, I guess." She looks toward a passing taxi. "Can we talk about all of this later? I feel overwhelmed right now. I don't know how I'll be able to make the move to LA work without this sale."

I don't know if that's an overt attempt to make me feel guilty, but that's exactly what's happening. Being responsible for Krista not chasing her dreams would leave me so guilt-ridden that I would come to resent the business.

I know that because I know myself.

I also know that I'm angry with her for not discussing a potential sale with me when she realized it was what she wanted and there was a possibility that it could happen.

"Did they approach you, or did you approach them?" I ask, ignoring her plea to talk about this later.

I can't give her time right now because I sense Holden

Sheppard is going to track me down before the end of the day.

She shakes her head in frustration. "Jameson came into the store one day. He introduced himself right away and asked about the business."

"What did he ask?"

Krista half-shrugs. "He was interested in a few of our products. Apparently, he'd been in the week before that and had picked up some of the passion fruit gummies, and the cinnamon poppers we introduced last fall. He loved them both."

Since I came up with those recipes, I should feel pride in knowing he liked them, but I don't. For all I know, Jameson hated everything, but wanted to gain the upper hand by pretending to love our offerings.

"Did he ask you straight out if you wanted to sell, Krista?"

"Not right away," she answers with her gaze locked on mine. "He said that he knew how hard of an industry we're in, and that the competition is fierce."

He's right about that. I debated jumping into the candy space, but my need to fulfill Celia's ambitions won out in the end. That's changed since we launched, though. I love the business, and the prospect of passing the torch to my daughter eventually leaves me teary-eyed.

"When exactly did the subject of selling Sweet Indulgence to Carden come up?" I try to keep my tone even.

I know I should be transparent and tell her about what happened in East Hampton between Holden and me, but I'm still trying to wrap my mind around it.

Her gaze drops to the sidewalk, so mine follows.

I watch silently as she kicks a gum wrapper with the toe

of her shoe before mumbling something about people who litter.

Just as I'm about to repeat my question, her hand dives into her purse. Her phone pops out. She taps the screen and exhales. "It was about two months ago. That's when Jameson first mentioned that Carden would be interested in buying the company."

"You're sure?" I ask because this is too important for her not to be certain.

She flips her phone around to show me something, but it's back facing her before I have a chance to see anything.

"Jameson sent me a text message exactly two months ago today asking if I had ever considered selling." She tilts her head slightly while looking at me. "I responded that I was."

Without asking me.

I want to point that out, but this is not the time to remind her of that. She set out on a path to get everything in place to sell our business without considering what I wanted.

"Anyways." She sighs heavily. "I'd like to go home, Greer. I have the worst headache. Can you handle the delivery this afternoon on your own?"

I tuck a strand of my hair behind my ear. "I can. I will."

"Should I tell Howie that we're not moving?"

The question stings because she's putting a burden on me that isn't only mine to shoulder. If she had given me more of a heads-up about everything going on in her life behind the scenes over the past few months, I would have been better prepared for today.

Although I can't blame her for the shock I felt walking into that conference room to see Joe standing there.

Holden...his name is Holden.

"I've had a lot thrown at me the past couple of weeks, Krista." I manage a small smile. "We need to discuss this more. Let's sit on things for a day or two, and talk again, okay?"

A grin spreads over her lips, instantly changing her expression. "I can't tell if that means there's still hope for the sale to go through, but I'm going to believe there is until you tell me otherwise."

I won't confirm or deny that there's hope because I feel numb right now. Making a decision that will alter so many lives requires a clear mind. My mind is cluttered with memories of East Hampton and thoughts of Celia at the moment.

"I'll go now." She reaches forward to hug me. "I love you, Greer."

"I love you," I whisper. "I always will."

CHAPTER TWENTY-SEVEN

Holden

IT'S BEEN twenty-seven hours since Greer stormed out of the meeting. I've spent nearly all of the time since thinking about what I want to say to her, yet I still have absolutely no fucking clue how this is going to play out.

This is my third time walking past the storefront of Sweet Indulgence today. The first time was four hours ago. I peered in the window, but felt like a creep since I caught the eye of a customer standing inside.

I didn't see Greer anywhere, so I took off to grab a cup of coffee.

My second attempt to see her was another epic fail. As I turned the corner to approach the store, I saw her leaving. Her back was to me, but I'd recognize her anywhere.

She wasn't alone, so I didn't approach her. The man she was with was making her laugh. I did get a brief glimpse of his profile when he turned to look at her. He's old enough to be her father, but I know better than to jump to any conclusion.

I hung around out front for over an hour, but she didn't reappear.

I'm back now as the clock ticks closer to mid-afternoon. As I pass the store, I look inside. I spot her instantly. She's standing in the middle of her store, gazing around at the customers filling the small space.

The research I did since I last saw her has helped me understand the business and their goal. What began as an online venture has evolved into this small storefront and a side hustle that involves setting up candy buffets at various events.

We've bought out a few companies that focused solely on that, but Sweet Indulgence seems to have approached that particular endeavor differently than others have.

They not only rent out the required tables, containers, and labels for the candy buffet, but they supply a multitude of premium candy choices.

The candy bar is manned for the entire event. The host or hostess sent by Sweet Indulgence prepares personalized candy bags on the spot. It's a step beyond what I've usually seen, so it makes sense that they are seeing substantial growth in that sector of their business.

I wait until two customers leave before I make my entrance.

I'm not surprised when a bell hanging over the door rings to signal my arrival.

"Welcome to Sweet Indulgence," Greer says in a cheerful tone as she turns to face me.

I can't say for sure, but I swear she mutters "*dammit*" under her breath as soon as she spots me.

I take a deep breath because seeing her again is enough to make my heart thunder inside my chest. This woman does something to me. I don't know if what I'm feeling is pure lust or a hard like. It doesn't matter either way. I just want more time with her.

"Mr. Sheppard," she snaps my name off her tongue as her arms cross her chest. "To what do I owe the displeasure?"

Holding in a laugh, I step closer to her. "Hello, Greer."

Her eyes widen as she steps back, retreating far enough that her ass bumps into a tall display of brightly wrapped candy bundles. It sways but stays upright.

She turns to the side to look at it, giving me the full view of her profile.

The faded jeans and branded dark green T-shirt she's wearing amplify her curves. Her hair is loose and in waves around her face.

She's as breathtaking as she was the first time I saw her.

"What do you want?"

I'm not offended by the hostility lacing her tone. I expected it. "To talk to you."

She glances at a customer who is filling a wire basket with an assortment of treats. "About what?"

"You, me, this business," I try to cover it all in one breath. "We need to discuss all of it."

The shopper glances our way. Greer reads the subtle clue when the woman's hand rises in the air.

"I need to help one of my customers," she tells me. "Besides, I'm very busy. I don't have time to talk about you, me, and this business right now."

"When then?" I push. "It needs to happen."

She shakes her head before setting off toward the small checkout counter. I watch in silence as she rings up the purchase, answering each question the woman has. Greer explains how one rolled candy treat came from a recipe passed down from generations. She takes credit for creating a fruit-flavored, tri-colored lollipop the woman claims her grandkids love.

The entire interaction is unrushed and has a friendly tone. It's far from a routine business transaction. As Greer hands the small pink bag with the candies to the woman, they wish each other well. That ends with a hug when Greer rounds the checkout counter.

There is a lot more to Sweet Indulgence than I realized. I'm not here to weigh the merits of what I just witnessed against the increased profit I know I would enjoy if Carden acquired this company.

I'm here to see if the possibility of a deal even exists at this point.

More importantly, I'm here to see Greer, because now that I know who she really is, I want to get to know her more.

Just as that customer exits the store, another two enter.

I curse under my breath, but if it takes all day to get a word or two with Greer, I'll wait.

I glance her way to see her walking toward me. She stops just short of where I am.

"I told you I'm busy." She scratches the side of her neck. "You should go."

"When should I come back?"

"Never." She smiles.

I can't help but smile, too. "What time are you done work?"

"Never," she repeats.

I amend my question. "Will there be a time later today when we can talk? It doesn't have to be here. I can buy you dinner so we can talk uninterrupted."

"I have dinner plans," she says in a rush.

Frustrated, but determined, I suggest an alternative. "What about dinner tomorrow?"

"I'm busy for dinner every night."

"This week?" I question.

"Forever," she answers. "I can meet you for a drink tonight after eight. It needs to be quick and close to here."

I'm familiar enough with the neighborhood that I know there's a Beaumont Hotel two blocks from here. "There's a bar in the lobby of the Beaumont…"

"Hotel?" she finishes my sentence. "Are you seriously suggesting we meet at a bar in a hotel?"

"Yes." I rub my chin. "I'm suggesting we meet at the hotel bar for a quick drink before I go my way and you go yours."

It's the last thing I want, but it's obvious she wants little to do with me, so I'll respect that boundary.

"There's a bar around the corner." She jerks her thumb to the right. "I've never stepped foot in it, but Krista has and recommended it. You can't miss it. There's a dragon sculpture near the entrance."

"I'll be there." I tuck a hand in the front pocket of my pants. "At eight, you said?"

"After eight," she clarifies. "Let's make it at nine. I can give you thirty minutes then."

I'll take it, so I nod. "I'll see you then, Greer."

CHAPTER TWENTY-EIGHT

Greer

I'D BE LYING if I said I didn't put any effort into how I look tonight. I showered when I got home from work before putting on a pair of white jeans and a simple short-sleeved light blue sweater. The flats on my feet are comfortable enough for me to walk blocks in. I'll do that after I meet with Holden. I already know I'll need to decompress before I head back to the Upper East Side where I live.

It's humid enough outside that I opted to pull my hair into a tight, high ponytail. It tends to curl with the humidity, and right now, it feels like it's one of the few things I can control in my life.

I swing open the door to the bar, smiling when I see the dragon statue next to it. Since the awning above the door clearly states the bar is called Regrets, I laugh aloud. Hopefully, I won't have too many of those when I leave in thirty minutes.

I'm barely inside when I spot the man I'm meeting. He's

standing next to a long wooden bar with a glass tumbler in one hand. It has a trace amount of amber liquid in it, which he swallows in a single gulp.

He places the empty glass on the bar, says something to the bartender, and then approaches me.

The jeans and gray T-shirt he's wearing are a far cry from the tailored suit he had on earlier. He looks more like Joe Campbell now, but Joe was never real. He was a relaxed version of Holden Sheppard. Or maybe he's the more calculated and cunning version. I still don't know if he recognized me as the co-owner of Sweet Indulgence when we met in East Hampton.

My personal information was supposed to stay between Mrs. Frye and me. It's not outside the realm of possibilities that she accidentally let my name slip to him, and he saw an opportunity to swoop in and seduce my company away from me.

I shake off that thought because, in a big picture way, Sweet Indulgence is a small company compared to most of the recent acquisitions of Carden Confectionaries. I know that because I spent part of my afternoon researching the company Holden owns.

"Hello, Greer," he greets me, but keeps his distance.

I appreciate that, but still, I have to wonder if he'll keep the discussion on a strictly business level tonight.

"Hi," I answer succinctly, not bothering to add his name to it because I'm still trying to get used to the fact that it's not Joe.

"Let's grab a table." He motions toward a trio of empty tables. "The bartender is bringing me another scotch. I didn't order for you because I wasn't sure what you'd like."

He knows I like red wine, but I'm glad to hear he didn't presume anything, because I rarely drink. I did in East

Hampton because apparently I was living my life without any inhibitions during that weekend.

I've snapped back into reality now.

I take a seat at the table that is closest to the corner. Holden sits directly across from me, but the table is circular and small, so the distance between us is only a few feet.

The bartender appears with Holden's drink in hand. When he asks me what I'd like, I make it clear. "Just water, please. Light ice. No lemon or lime."

"I'll get that for you," he says in a warm tone.

Holden stares at me as he sips from his glass. He places it down, still not saying anything. I can't tell if he's gathering his thoughts or waiting for me to launch this conversation.

Fortunately, the bartender shows up with my water. I down half in one gulp before he's back at the bar.

"I had no idea who you were in East Hampton, Greer."

My head pops up. "You didn't?"

"No fucking idea." Holden chuckles. "I knew your real name wasn't Summer Time."

I manage a small smile. "It doesn't take a detective to figure that out."

He smiles, too. "I've used the Joe Campbell name at different times over the past fourteen or so years."

"Why did you use it that weekend?" I ask, sipping another mouthful of water.

"There's no particular reason." He shrugs. "Things between us felt fun, and since you tossed out a fake name, I jumped on board and did it, too."

It makes sense, so I nod. "I had no idea who you were either then."

"I know." He chuckles. "Your reaction at the meeting gave that away."

"It was that obvious?" I ask as he drinks.

He places the glass down again, sliding a fingertip over the rim. "You looked as shocked as I felt. I could not fucking believe you walked into my conference room. I thought I'd never see you again."

"That was the plan," I whisper.

"Plans have changed," he points out the obvious. "We need to figure out how to handle it."

I stare at him. He's not wearing the eyeglasses he had on earlier. I suddenly wonder if they're a fashion statement and not a necessity. "No glasses tonight?"

I accentuate the point by circling a finger in the air around my right eye.

Shaking his head, he chuckles. "I typically wear contact lenses. I am now. Glasses are my last choice, but after you told me you liked the look weeks ago, I've been wearing them more frequently."

I almost repeat how much I like the look, but I refrain and keep my mouth shut. He doesn't need to hear how gorgeous I think he is, or that he's by far the best lover I've ever had.

"That bracelet is cute." He tilts his chin toward my left hand. "That's a friendship bracelet, right?"

Panic soars through me. I look down and I'm immediately grateful that all the letters on the colorful, beaded bracelet are turned inward and out of his view. I didn't do that on purpose since I'm not the one who slid it onto my wrist at dinner tonight.

Olive did that. She made it with Martha this afternoon as they sat on a bench in Central Park after buying the kit at a toy store. Martha had one with GRANDMA spelled out on it around her wrist. Bruce's was fashioned with bright blue beads in addition to the word GRANDPA.

Mine is almost all pink with the most precious word in the world at the center of it all.

MOMMY.

I place my hand over the bracelet, shielding it completely from Holden's view. "It is a friendship bracelet."

"Am I safe to assume your business partner didn't give you that?"

I almost laugh out loud as I drop my left hand to my lap, ensuring the bracelet is out of his view. "Krista's mad at me now, but we'll figure it out."

Nodding, he takes another small sip of his scotch. "She wants to sell. I take it you don't."

"I don't," I whisper. "But, we have a lot to talk about. We will. Krista and I are close."

"I'm open to negotiating the offer to terms that would suit you both," he effortlessly shifts into full business mode. "I can have an amendment to you by tomorrow at noon."

I glance at my lap and the bracelet. It's a reminder of why I want to hang onto Sweet Indulgence. I'm just not sure I can if Krista is ready to walk away from it. "Don't bother."

"For now?" he asks in a low tone. "Or are you closing the door to a deal completely?"

"I need to talk to Krista," I answer, ignoring his questions. "I need to do that first before I make any decisions."

His left eyebrow perks. "Even a decision about whether or not you should go to dinner with me the night after forever ends?"

I stare straight into his brilliant blue eyes. "I had fun, Holden. I had a lot of fun during our weekend together, but nothing has changed. I'm not interested in more. I never will be."

He leans back in his chair to finish his drink.

"I'll let you know about whether we're open to negotiating." I push to stand. "You'll hear from me soon."

He's on his feet before I can take one step away from the table.

I swing my left hand behind my back to hide my bracelet from him, but he doesn't notice. His gaze is pinned to my face.

"Never is a long time," he rasps. "I want you, Greer. That hasn't changed."

The words crawl inside of me, tempting me to throw all caution to the wind, but I stand strong. "I'll be in touch about my company. Thanks for the drink."

A slow smile spreads over his lips. "It was just water, but you're welcome. I'll wait to hear from you, Greer, or should I say, I can't wait to hear from you."

I turn and walk straight to the bar's exit. It takes every ounce of strength I have not to steal another glance at him.

As soon as I'm outside, I press my back against the brick exterior of the bar and draw as much fresh air as I can into my lungs.

My gaze drops to the beaded bracelet on my wrist. I'm a mom first and a businesswoman second. I can't be anything to Holden Sheppard but a memory of one weekend of his life because that's all he can ever be to me.

CHAPTER TWENTY-NINE

HOLDEN

I REACH my arms out as soon as Jameson walks into the main living room of his penthouse with his bundle of joy. "I want to hold him."

"Says the greedy uncle." He laughs. "Sinclair is fast asleep, or she'd be fighting you for holding rights to Morgan."

I've seen my sister-in-law with her son. She's as smitten with the kid as I am. James is right there with us, as is anyone else who has ever seen the angelic face I'm looking at now.

As my brother tenderly passes his baby over to me, I feel the same rush of emotions I do every time I'm near the little guy. This is the ultimate. I'm holding the newest member of my family who will grow every day until he's old enough for me to teach him how to throw a baseball and avoid getting caught when he breaks a window.

I did the same for James, so it only seems fitting that I school his son in the fine art of being a Sheppard, although I will definitely circle back to offer to pay for any windows Morgan might break.

The conscience I lacked when I was a pre-teen seems to have taken root within me now.

"Hey, buddy," I whisper to my nephew as he stares up at me. "It's me. Your favorite uncle."

"Berk and Keats would take issue with that," Jameson points out. "Sinclair's brothers love him just as much as you do."

"Impossible."

He chuckles. "You didn't show up here just to cuddle with Morgan, so what's up, Holden?"

I take one last look at the baby before I level my gaze on James. "I met Greer for a drink tonight. Technically, I was the only one drinking. I had scotch. She had water."

He takes a seat in a chair across from where I'm sitting on the couch. "Now, that we've established what you ordered, get to the good part. Was this meeting related to business or pleasure? Please say both."

"It was both."

"Let me guess." He tugs on the waistband of the sweatpants he's wearing. "She doesn't want to sell or sleep with you again."

My eyes narrow, but I can't disagree, so I shrug.

"I knew it." Raking a hand through his hair, he shakes his head. "Your weekend with her killed the deal before we could even properly present it."

"Not necessarily," I say, trying to salvage some hope to hand him.

"What the fuck does that mean?"

I pretend to cover Morgan's left ear. "Language, James. Your son is right here."

He lifts his ass off the couch by a few inches to get an unobstructed view of the baby's face before he sits back down. "He's so enamored with you, he didn't even react to my voice."

"He knows which one of us is better-looking." I smile. "Just admit it."

"Go to hell," he swears again, chuckling this time. "Is there a deal to be had with Sweet Indulgence or not? Is it time to walk away from them?"

"No," I blurt out way too fast.

He taps my shoulder lightly. "That answers my question about whether or not you're still interested in Greer."

Shaking my head, I adjust his son in my arms. "I'm very interested in her. She has zero interest in me."

"Tough luck, old man."

"She hasn't completely closed the door to a potential deal, though," I tell him. "She'll get back to me in a day or two regarding that."

He scratches his elbow. "Maybe I should take that call, seeing as how you're personally invested in the sale."

"I'm not," I argue. "I can separate what I'm feeling for Greer with what's best for Carden."

"Sure you can." Wiggling his fingers, he darts both hands in the air toward me. "Give me my boy. It's time for his hourly kisses on the forehead from his dad."

I hand over his son carefully and then watch as my brother gingerly trails kisses across his baby's forehead.

"I love you, Morgan," he whispers. "Daddy loves you more than you know."

I've never been envious of my brother until now. I rarely admit it to myself, but I want what he has. A woman I love with every part of me and a child of my own are what I long for.

I'm not sure if it's something I'll ever have, but a man can dream.

I STEP out into the cool evening air outside of Jameson's building and scan the sidewalk. It's nearing eleven now, and another drink could be on the agenda, but there's a much more productive way for me to spend the next hour or two until I call it a night.

I fish my phone out of the back pocket of my jeans and scan the screen.

As expected, at least a dozen unopened emails are waiting for me. The notification on my text message app tells me that just as many text messages have come in since I walked into Jameson's home.

I skim through those quickly, not expecting to find anything interesting.

There's one from Declan, another from Rook, and the rest are all business related.

"Excuse me, sir."

I glance up when I hear a feminine voice calling out. I have no idea if I'm the sir she's talking to, but as soon as I lock eyes with the brunette standing close to me, I realize I am.

"Yes?" I ask.

"I'm lost," she says with a slight tremor in her tone. "I'm visiting New York and I went to a club. I got turned around, I think. I can't find my way back to my hotel."

The short silver dress she's wearing and the matching heels back up her story. As does the state of her hair since it's obvious this woman either got caught up in a windstorm, was dancing the night away, or was fucked in that club.

Regardless of how she ended up in front of me with her hair a tousled mess, I'll offer my assistance.

"What hotel are you staying at?"

A slow smile spreads over her lips. "The Bishop Tribeca. Do you know where that is?"

The phone she's gripping tightly in her hand would tell her exactly where the hotel is. Any rideshare driver in this city could take her straight there as well, but she's asking me for a reason.

"I'll grab a taxi," I tell her.

Since an available one is about to speed past us on the street, I step to the edge of the sidewalk to flag them down. The driver pulls over almost immediately, just a few feet from where we are.

"I'm Veronica," she says. "But you can call me whatever you want tonight."

I swing open the back passenger door of the taxi and hold out my hand to help her slide onto the seat. Without any hesitation, she places her hand in mine.

"I'm going home." I smile at her before I bend down to look at the driver. "She's heading to Tribeca. The Bishop Hotel."

Veronica says something that gets lost behind the car door as I slam it shut.

I pat my stomach through the thin material of my T-shirt. I'll grab a slice of pizza and a large coffee on my way home, so I can be full of food and caffeine as I clear my email and text messages.

I turn in a circle, taking in this block of the city I love. The architecture never disappoints, the residents always surprise me, and you never know what tomorrow will bring.

In my case, I'm hoping it will bring a call from Greer

Irwin. She's somewhere in this city right now, and that in itself is enough to put a smile on my face.

CHAPTER THIRTY

GREER

"SO, this man you met for a drink last night, what's he like?" Martha asks as she piles scrambled eggs onto the plate in front of me.

I glance over my shoulder to be sure that Olive isn't within earshot. "He wants to buy Sweet Indulgence."

"He what?" she asks, dropping the spatula in her hand on the large wooden table we always gather around for meals.

I found the table at an estate sale shortly after I bought this townhouse. I wanted a piece of furniture that had history attached to it because the home does as well.

The previous owners left me a scrapbook filled with images and notes of their time in the house. It's a treasure I keep close by because I open it whenever I need a reminder of how amazing their life was.

They raised three children within the walls of my home, and eventually their six grandchildren would come here for sleepovers and Sunday dinners. None of the images in the scrapbook reveal who they are, but there's a sense of family in each picture, including food on the table, muddy shoes strewn about in the foyer, and holiday decorations hanging from every corner.

I can only hope that Olive will leave here one day with a heart filled with wonderful memories, too.

"Krista has been talking to a company about selling the business," I fill Martha in. "She's moving to Los Angeles with Howie after their wedding. She wants the funds from the sale to help her settle in there."

Martha sits next to me, grabbing my hands to cradle them in hers. "Greer, oh my. How are you feeling about that?"

"Numb," I answer honestly. "I don't want to hold Krista back, but I always thought the company's future was with us."

"You can buy her out," she suggests. "We can pitch in. Bruce has some retirement savings. I have that inheritance from my mom."

I shake my head. "Absolutely not."

Since Krista and I agreed a long time ago that we'd only sell the business together, that's not an option. Even if it were, I wouldn't allow Bruce and Martha to invest more in me than they already have. They gave up the lives they had in Montana to move here to help me raise Olive. Bruce handles all of the home repairs and maintenance of the small garden in the back. Martha declared herself the cook when I asked if they wanted to live with us. That's only a fraction of what she does for me. She's become a second mom to me, and I love her for that.

I love her and Bruce for everything they've brought into my life and my daughter's life.

"Maybe this man will only buy Krista's half?" She grins. "That could work, Greer."

"That can't work," I say with a sigh. "It's not possible for a number of reasons, but even if it were, I can't be business partners with that man."

She eyes me suspiciously. "Something tells me you're holding back a piece of the puzzle."

I know I can tell Martha anything. She's made that crystal clear to me over the years. I may have married her son once upon a time, but since Aaron and I divorced, she has proven that she's still part of my family.

"I met him before I realized he wanted to buy Sweet Indulgence."

Her eyes widen. "You met him or you *met* him?"

I bark out a laugh because the second '*met*' that left her lips was accompanied by a lot of eyelash batting on her part. Martha is asking if I hooked up with Holden.

"The second one," I whisper. "I met him when I was in East Hampton."

Her hand jumps to cover her mouth. "I knew there was a fellow involved in that trip. You were glowing when you got back, Greer. Glowing. I am so happy for you."

I hate to burst her bubble of happiness, but I have to. "It was just a weekend fling. We agreed not to meet up again. We didn't even know each other's real names."

"You didn't tell him your name?" She giggles. "What name did you give him, Greer?"

I cringe when I say it, "Summer Time."

She laughs so loud that Olive comes running into the kitchen with a kite shaped like an owl trailing behind her.

"What's so funny, Grandma?" She instantly goes to give her grandmother a big hug. "Tell me the joke."

Martha taps the tip of Olive's nose with her index finger. "It's a grown-up joke, so this one is just between Mommy and me."

Olive shifts her focus to me. "Grandpa and I are going to go fly my kite. Can you come, Mom?"

My gaze falls to the green T-shirt she's wearing. It's one of the Sweet Indulgence ones I had made just for her. Olive is old enough to choose her own clothes for the day, although I've had to step in a few times, including when she tried to sneak past me in a sundress in the dead of winter.

Sweet Indulgence is a big part of my life. Seeing my daughter wearing that shirt today feels like a sign. It's a sign that I need to have an honest and open discussion with Krista before I reach out to Holden again.

"Mommy has to work," Martha intervenes. "She's going to eat some of those eggs I gave her, finish her coffee, and go set the world on fire."

"Don't!" Olive screams. "Setting fires is illegal, Mom."

Bruce laughs from where he's standing behind her. "Grandma meant that your mom is going to make the most of today. She's going to take care of business the way she always does."

I lock eyes with him and nod. "That's exactly what it means."

CHAPTER THIRTY-ONE

Greer

KRISTA TAKES a tiny sip of the iced tea she ordered. At this rate, we'll be sitting here for three days before she finishes the glass.

I, on the other hand, polished off my water in one gulp. I'm halfway through my refill now.

Krista glances down at the lemon slice I discarded on the napkin in front of me. "You've never liked lemon or limes, have you, Greer?"

"I like them when they're in something... like cake, or candy, but I don't want a random one swimming in my drink."

She breaks out a wide smile. "I like them in mine."

That's obvious since she always orders extra for her iced tea whenever we come here. We do that often since our store is just a block away. We even started calling it "our place" a few months ago. Now that Krista wants to move across the country, it will just be another coffee spot to me.

I texted her as I was leaving my house this morning, asking if she could make time before heading to New Jersey to handle some business there today.

She agreed without question, suggesting a time.

I got here thirty minutes before she did. The extra alone time gave me a few minutes to think about how I want to handle this situation. I have a long list of reasons why I believe we can still make it work if Krista retains her interest in Sweet Indulgence after her move.

I know it's not what she prefers, but there has to be a compromise that works for both of us.

After another tiny sip, she pushes the glass away. "I can't drink this. It doesn't taste the same."

"The same as what?"

"Regular iced tea," she says, swiping her finger over the rim of the glass. "This is decaffeinated tea."

I glance past her to the counter where she ordered her drink. The woman who prepared it is busy making a pink colored concoction for a little girl and her mom.

"Do you want me to get you a regular one?" I ask even though I'm already halfway out of my chair because I already know the answer to that question.

Krista is very particular about what she drinks and eats. Just last month, she sent a sandwich back to the kitchen of a restaurant we were trying out for the first time because it had a speck of cilantro on it.

"No," she says, waving for me to sit back down. "It's fine."

I lower back onto my chair because this woman may look and sound like Krista, but that comment is not something my closest friend would say.

I envy the fact that Krista never settles for anything she

doesn't want, including improperly prepared iced tea, so this is completely out of character for her.

"What's wrong?" I ask in a rush. "What's going on with you?"

It could be related to the stress between us, but I have no doubt that Krista knows how much I love her, and I'm confident that we'll work out our business issues because our friendship is too important to both of us.

She bites the center of her bottom lip before her gaze drops to the front of the blue blouse she's wearing. "I'm pregnant, Greer. Howie and I are going to have a baby."

MY BIG PLANS TO talk about Krista's big plans for Sweet Indulgence were swept away in a sea of tears as soon as she announced she's pregnant.

We hugged as we cried, and as soon as we both settled down, we sat next to each other holding hands as she told me all about her morning sickness and the names they're considering for their baby.

They won't know the gender for a few weeks, but the names she shared with me are all perfect.

Her plan for Edlund to be her baby's middle name made me sob out loud since it was Celia's surname. Both of our children's names will honor our best friend, and I couldn't be happier about that.

I round the corner on my way back to Sweet Indulgence only to spot someone waiting for me.

It's a very handsome someone wearing glasses and a tailored three-piece dark gray suit. The light blue shirt underneath is the perfect color to accentuate his eyes.

I laugh inwardly because thinking about how hot Holden

Sheppard is won't help me in my quest to keep his hands off of my business and me.

"Greer!" he calls out when he spots me. "You look lovely today."

He may need to get his eyes rechecked because I'm not dressed to impress. I'm wearing one of my Sweet Indulgences T-shirts and a pair of white shorts since the temperature is supposed to skyrocket later this afternoon. To add to that, I look like I haven't slept in days. To be precise, it was only last night. I tossed and turned in bed last night thinking about his business proposition and our time in East Hampton.

I don't return the compliment because that's not the tone I want to set with him right now. I wasn't able to discuss business with Krista, so I'm no closer to knowing what I'm going to do than I was when I stormed out of Carden's offices.

"I have a hectic day, Holden," I say as I approach him. "I told you I'd reach out to talk when I'm ready."

"I know." He nods, tucking both hands in the front pockets of his pants. "I'm not here to pressure you. I come in peace."

I can't help but smile. "Do I want to know what that means?"

His face remains stoic. "I mentioned we wanted to present a new offer to you and Krista. I believe your response was 'don't bother,' but I bothered anyway and had it drawn up. I'll send it over to you via courier since I don't have any of your contact information."

This is the moment in time when I should offer my phone number to him, but I'm not about to do that. We've shared way too much time in bed. If he had my number, he could reach out to ask me out.

At least I think he'd do that, judging by what he said to me last night.

"I'm not in a position to make a final decision yet," I say.

I was set on not selling, but knowing that Krista is having a baby does change things. How could it not?

"No rush," he says in an even tone. "Take your time looking over the revised offer."

"Okay." I nod.

"Okay," he repeats, grinning slightly. "I'll take off. Unless you want me to stick around and stare at you for an hour or two."

I ward off a smile by biting the corner of my bottom lip. "Let's skip that."

"My loss." He sighs. "Have a good day, Summer."

"Greer," I correct him.

"I know." He leans close enough that I can feel his breath skirt over my cheek. "Forgive me if it takes me a minute to get used to calling you that."

The fact that he repeats almost verbatim what I said to him on the day we met hits me hard. I'm flooded with memories of being in his arms.

"Forgiven," I whisper, pulling back just far enough that I can look into his eyes. "I'll be in touch, Holden."

"I'll be waiting," he rasps. "Goodbye for now."

I don't echo his words. Instead, I watch as he walks away, keeping my gaze on him until he rounds the corner and disappears from view.

CHAPTER THIRTY-TWO

Holden

I SPRINT INTO THE HOSPITAL, sweat peppering my brow. Tugging on the knot in my tie, I'm able to loosen it just as I call out for the three people on the elevator to hold it.

One of them, a man dressed in scrubs, nods in acknowledgement.

As soon as I've boarded, I reach in front of him to press the button to head up to the sixth floor.

No one says a word to each other, as the elevator stops twice. More people stream on, buttons are pressed on the control panel, and when we finally make it to my floor, I'm out in a flash.

I was here the day Morgan was born, so I know my way around.

"Holden!" I hear my name coming at me from the right, so I glance in that direction.

Rook is there, dressed like he just rolled out of bed. There's a strong possibility that's the case because it's nearing two in the morning. I was at the office, mulling over some potential acquisitions that Jameson put in front of me before he called it a night hours ago. I also needed to carve out some time to update our shipping procedures, so tonight was the ideal night to focus on that.

It's been almost a week since Greer and I spoke inside her store. I anticipated hearing back from her by now regarding the new offer we presented, but her silence has been deafening.

James had suggested calling Krista on his own, but I told him to hold off. If this crawls into next week, I'll let him make that call.

I know how badly he wants to buy out Sweet Indulgence. I've done more research on the company, and I'm on the same page as him. It would be a solid investment for us and take us into a new space if we decide to continue with the candy buffet aspect of Greer and Krista's business model.

"Is he here yet?" I ask Rook. "Is Gilbert here?"

He slaps the center of my back while shoving a can of soda at me. "Not yet. Carrie is in with them now. Abby wanted a few minutes with her sister."

Leave it to my two best friends to fall in love with sisters. Declan's wife Abby and Rook's fiancée, Carrie, are as close as can be. The foursome has never made me feel like an outsider when I've hung out with them. They all treat me like family. It makes sense since that's how I view them.

"Did Declan wake you up?" I glance at Rook's messy hair. "You look exhausted."

"I'm a lawyer," he reminds me the way he always does. "Being exhausted all the fucking time is part of the job description."

"Who's watching Kirby?" I ask, although I think I already know the answer to that question.

"She's spending the night with Chesca and Brian," he confirms my assumption.

Chesca is Kirby's mom, and she's found the love of her life in a guy named Brian. Chesca and Rook's determination to put their daughter's needs first has paid off for them. The four adults in the equation all get along and even go so far as to have one meal together each month for Kirby.

I'm proud of Rook. He's always been a good man, but he's proving to be the kind of father I hope to be one day.

"Why are you dressed like it's two in the afternoon?" he questions as he pops the tab on his soda can. "You do realize no one gives a shit if you show up looking like a regular Joe."

That sets my head back in laughter, but not for the reason he thinks.

I'm reminded of the fake name I used with Greer when we met. For those three days, I was indeed a regular Joe, and not a guy trying to buy her company.

"It wasn't that funny." He takes a sip of soda. "I thought I grabbed a sugar free one for myself."

I glance down at the can in my hand and pass it off to him, taking his away. "I'll drink this. You take mine."

"That works because you're not as sweet as me."

I crack a smile. "You got that from Kirbs, didn't you?"

"It's part of a joke she made up," he says as we walk toward the waiting area in the maternity ward. "I'm too damn tired to remember the entire thing, but the punch line was something about her being sweeter than me."

"That's a truth, not a punch line." I sip from the soda, cringing at the sweet note of it. "Is this cherry flavored?"

He tilts his head to get a better look at the can. "So it is. It'll get you through the night. First babies are notoriously slow to arrive."

We round the corner of the waiting area to find Declan's

brother, Sean, his wife, Callie, and four very eager grandparents sitting in chairs.

"Uncle Holden has arrived," Rook tells the room. "Ignore the fact that he looks like he just stepped out of a boardroom. The bastard is always trying to one-up me."

I greet everyone present with hugs and fist bumps before I take a seat next to Rook.

I dig my phone out of the inner pocket of my suit jacket and check it again even though I glanced at it in the rideshare on my way here.

Unsurprisingly, there's nothing from Greer.

Why would there be? It's the middle of the night and she's likely tucked in a comfortable bed somewhere in this city. Hopefully she's alone.

CHAPTER THIRTY-THREE

Greer

"I HAD A NIGHTMARE, MOMMY," Olive pokes a finger into my cheek as I struggle to open my eyes.

"What time is it, sweetheart?" I whisper.

"Late," she snaps back with a giggle. "I looked out my bedroom window. It's dark out. I heard Grandpa snoring when I listened at the door of their room, so I let him sleep."

My eyes pop open. "Your grandparents are up on the third floor, Olive. You went up there?"

My sweet little princess yawns. "Grandpa told me if I ever had a bad dream, he'd tell me a good story. He said that balances it out in the brain."

She taps the center of her forehead to make her point.

I glance toward my bedroom window. It is indeed dark out, but there's light filtering in from the massive motion-activated light the neighbors installed on the fence. It's supposed to light up only their yard at night so their dog can find his way around after dusk. It's set to light up both yards.

I don't mind, though. It offers me an extra sense of security, and for that I'm grateful.

Olive looks at my phone on my nightstand next to where she's standing. She quickly taps the screen with her finger. "It's two fifteen. That's like late late."

"Super duper late," I add with a grin. "Let's get you back in bed."

"I think a piece of cake would make me forget my nightmare," she says with a fake sniffle.

My daughter knows my weaknesses, including when she pretends she's about to cry. I usually jump into action to ward off her tears, but this time, I pop up into a sitting position and watch her carefully.

There's not a tear in sight, but I do see a slow smile creep over her lips. "We're dressed the same, Mom."

I glance at her pink and white pajamas. The material is cotton, and it's a checkerboard pattern that Olive picked out herself. Martha made Olive a set first, and when I commented on how cute it was, she surprised me with a set, too. They match Olive's perfectly, right down to the pink buttons on the shirt.

"We are." I pat the spot next to me. "Sit and tell me about the dream."

She climbs onto the bed, dragging her purple elephant stuffed toy with her. Once she's comfortable, she runs her hand down my forearm. "I don't exactly remember it all, but I do know there was a scary pumpkin and a big zebra."

I scoop her hand into mine, giving it a light squeeze. "It sounds a little terrifying."

"It was more than a little." She sighs. "I think I need another night light."

I can't say that surprises me. She's had her eye on a stained glass cat-shaped night light for weeks now. It's displayed in the window of a vintage shop we pass by almost daily on our early evening walks.

"Maybe a cat shaped one would help?" I ask, holding in a smile.

"I do have enough allowance saved to buy one like that." She drags a hand through her shoulder-length dark brown hair. "I even made room on the table by my bed for it."

"Why don't we go pick it up tomorrow morning when they open?"

She bounces to her knees, almost falling off the side of the bed when she does. I reach out to circle her waist with my hands, pulling her close to me.

"You always save me, Mommy," she whispers. "You're my hero."

"You're mine," I say under my breath because she is.

"Grandma will want to come with us to the store." She snuggles up to me. "She likes looking in there for little treasures she says."

"We'll take Grandma with us."

"I think I can go back to my bed now." Her words get caught in a big yawn. "Will you tuck me in?"

I hold her hand as she slides off my bed before I swing both legs over to push to my feet. "You know it's one of my favorite things to do."

"You're the best mom in the world."

I glance down at her before I cup her small face in my hands and kiss the middle of her forehead. "You're the best daughter in the world, Olive."

"I know." She laughs. "I am pretty great."

"I WANT to wear my four-leaf clover today!" Olive yells as she enters the kitchen at warp speed. "Is that okay, Mom?"

Before Martha can get to where Olive is now standing, I'm there, taking the four-leaf clover charm from my daughter's hand. The small gold charm is unique in that there are two tiny diamonds on it. Each is in the center of two of the leaves. When I first gave it to Olive last year, she asked if I had lost the other two *"sparkly jewels."* I smiled and told her it was just like this when I got it.

It's a beautiful piece and just one of many charms that Olive now owns. It's been her favorite since I gave it to her, so whenever she asks if she can wear it, I never hesitate to say yes.

"It's more than okay," I tell her, glancing at Martha to see a broad smile on her face.

"Can I wear it on a chain around my neck like I did last time?" Olive asks with hope lacing her tone.

Since the charm can be easily strung on a gold chain or the gold charm bracelet Olive has, I nod. "Run back up to your room and get your chain."

She tugs it out of the front pocket of her denim overalls. "Ta da! It's magic. I have it."

Martha lets out a loud giggle.

Olive scoots around me to head right to her grandma to give her a big hug. "I knew you'd like that."

I turn and watch them embrace each other.

There was a time when I didn't know if I'd ever feel this level of happiness, but I'm grateful every day that I do now.

"I'll help you with the charm," Martha offers. "Mommy is going to drink her coffee and eat the waffle I made her."

I look at the table and the colorful plate that the waffle is sitting on. It's adorned with a dollop of fresh whipping cream and a mound of berries. Next to it is a cup of coffee made to perfection.

"Thank you, Martha."

"I like your pretty dress, Mom." Olive points at the pale green sundress I'm wearing. "You look like a fairytale princess today."

Smiling, I push my hair back over my shoulders. "I'm glad you think so."

"You're beautiful!" she shrieks. "So is Grandma. So am I."

"Carry that confidence with you always." Martha pats Olive's shoulders after clasping the chain holding the charm around her neck. "If you do that, no one can stop you."

"No one can stop me from eating my waffle." Olive jumps up and down. "Will you put extra strawberries on mine, Grandma?"

Tears well in my eyes as I watch them interact with each other.

Martha kisses the top of Olive's head. "Consider it done, my girl."

CHAPTER THIRTY-FOUR

Holden

I STROLL into Sweet Indulgence still wearing the same suit I was yesterday. Last night was one for the ages. Seeing Declan holding his newborn son is a memory that will stay with me until the day I die.

I watched one of my oldest friends stare at the face of the little boy who will change his life forever.

I glance around, noting that the brown-haired guy working the counter is wearing a blue button-down shirt and not a branded Sweet Indulgence T-shirt.

I can't help but wonder who he is.

He glances up and smiles. "Hey there. Do you need a hand finding something?"

"Someone," I say cautiously.

I know damn well that Greer told me she'd be in touch when she was ready, but I had a foolproof plan to get some face time with her today. Although my foolproof plan is proving to be full of holes since she doesn't seem to be around.

"Who?" he asks.

"The owner," I blurt out without clarifying which owner.

"The co-owners aren't here," he subtly points out the fact that two people do indeed own this operation. "Can I help you with something?"

"You can tell me when you expect Greer Irwin to get here."

His eyes narrow. "Are you a friend of hers?"

More like a frenemy that she enjoyed fucking, but none of that is knowledge this guy needs.

"Something like that," I answer evasively. "Do you know where I can find her?"

"I do, but I won't tell you." He chuckles. "No offence, dude, but you could be a stalker or something. I'm not going to give out her location just so you can go harass her."

"I'm not going to harass her," I say in an even tone. "I'd like to speak with her."

"You should come back tomorrow," he suggests. "Maybe in the afternoon."

That's not helpful at all, but it's obvious that in addition to working the counter, this guy views himself as Greer's private security detail.

I wish to fuck I had asked for her number the last time I saw her. Who am I kidding? There's a damn good chance she would have refused to share it.

There is another way for me to get it, but it requires going behind her back. I could ask Jameson to contact Krista to get Greer's number. The problem with that is I doubt like hell Greer will appreciate it.

"I'll come back," I say.

"You're not going to buy anything?" He points at a

display of brightly colored star-shaped lollipops on the counter next to where I'm standing. "Those are organic. They're made from all natural ingredients. Greer came up with the concept and had a hand in the recipe development."

I reach over and grab as many as I can fit in my fist. "I'll take these."

"All of them?"

"Sure. Ring them up."

He quickly shoves all eight lollipops in a bag and swipes my credit card. When he finally glances at it, he chuckles. "You're Holden Sheppard?"

Surprised that my name means anything to him, I nod.

"You should have led with that, dude." He shakes his head. "Greer and my sister are at the café around the corner having a coffee. Well, no coffee for Krista, but they're talking. They're talking about selling this sweet place to you."

AS SOON AS I round the corner, I see Krista on the approach headed in my direction. Apparently, the meeting hasn't started yet.

"Holden?" she calls out to me. "Is that you?"

I adjust my glasses and smile. "Sure is. How are you?"

"I'm good." She smiles. "I am so good."

"I'm happy to hear that."

Her gaze drops to the bag in my hand. "You bought something from our store? What did you get?"

I part the twine handles to give her a glimpse inside.

"Our star lollies." She laughs. "Those are fantastic. Greer designed them with a special someone in mind."

If the special someone has a dick, I already don't like him.

I don't bother asking who was behind the inspiration for the lollipops I'll pass off to my assistant to give to her daughters.

I glance into the coffee shop to see Greer sitting at a table. She's a vision dressed in green.

I'd give just about anything to walk in there, gather her in my arms, and kiss her senseless, but I resist the urge because we're not in a place where she would be open to that.

"I'm meeting Greer now to talk about selling Sweet Indulgence to Carden." She crosses two fingers on her right hand. "Wish me luck. I need this sale to happen more than ever."

I don't ask why because that's between her and her business partner.

"I'll call you and Jameson later if I have good news." She sighs. "I really hope I'll have good news."

I steal a parting glance at Greer. She's studying her phone's screen as she taps her chin.

"I'll tell Greer you said hi," Krista says.

"No." I wave the thought away with a flick of my hand in the air. "That's not necessary."

She lets out a string of short giggles. "You're right. You and Jameson aren't her favorite people right now."

I suspect Greer has no issues with my brother. I know for a fact, she doesn't feel that way about me.

"It was good to see you, Holden." She points to the door of the coffee shop. "Hopefully, this meeting will change all of our lives."

CHAPTER THIRTY-FIVE

Greer

KRISTA and I have been circling the same subject for the past thirty minutes. I've countered every argument she's made to sell Sweet Indulgence. I've been reviewing our financials, and with some tweaks I'm confident we can increase revenue. That would mean more money for Krista each month, and she wouldn't have to do anything to earn a dime of it.

I explained that all to her, but she's not on board.

A lump sum equivalent to her half of what Carden is offering us is the only thing that will make her happy at this point.

Even if we agreed to void the clause in our contract that states she can't sell her shares unless I sell mine, I don't have the money I'd need to buy her portion outright. My parents gave me a very generous down payment for my townhouse as a gift when my divorce was finalized. It came with a caveat. I can't use any of the equity to dump money into the business. My dad was adamant about that. He doesn't want me to end up with a failed business and no place to live.

Martha's offer to help is still on the table. Bruce has chimed in that he would be all in, too, but I can't risk their retirement nest egg to fuel my dreams. Besides, what they have offered would still leave me short by several hundred thousand dollars.

"Greer," Krista says my name with exasperation edging her tone. "I know how you feel about this, but I'm not going to change my mind."

She's made that abundantly clear.

I'd tell her that I won't either, but why state the obvious?

"Don't you ever feel the pull to jump back into the marketing trenches?" Her eyes light up. "You loved your job. I bet Heather would hire you back in a heartbeat."

My former boss has moved on to greener pastures. She's no longer employed at the tech company I used to work for. Besides, that chapter of my life is behind me now. It's closed.

"Carden will take Sweet Indulgence into its folds, Greer. It'll become a treasured part of its empire."

I almost bark out a laugh.

Holden Sheppard, his brother, and whoever else they have working at a high level with them will tear our company apart, bit by tiny bit, until all that's left are unrecognizable shreds.

As soon as the ink is dry on a deal with Carden, Sweet Indulgence will cease to exist.

Emotions bubble inside of me at the thought of that, but I take a breath to steady myself.

"Did you look over the offer they made the day after we met with them, Greer?"

Nodding, I take a sip of my now cold coffee. "I did."

"It's very generous." She glances at her tall glass of water. It's untouched. "It would set me up in Los Angeles, and it would give you a financial cushion until you talk to Heather about going back to work for her."

Again, I don't correct her about Heather because going back to my old job is not an option for a myriad of reasons.

"I want to have an answer for Jameson and Holden by the end of next week." She glances at the watch on her wrist. "I have a wedding cake tasting in a few minutes. I have to leave now if I hope to make that appointment."

I'm the maid of honor, but an invitation to join her at the appointment isn't there.

"You should go." I get up from my chair.

She does the same, grabbing her purse from the table as she does. "I love you, Greer."

I manage a small smile. "I love you, too."

"Please don't let this come between us," she whispers as she pulls me in for a hug. "You're like a sister to me."

A single tear falls onto my cheek. "I feel the same way about you. I always will."

I HAD PLANNED to go to the store after my meeting with Krista, but since her brother, Burt, is working the counter today, I headed to Riverside Park.

This place holds special memories for me. Most of them involve Celia, since we'd often meet up here to share a sandwich and talk about boys.

Eventually, those discussions focused on the men in our lives, and then what the future held for us.

Celia was my maid of honor when I married Aaron. The day of our wedding, she pulled me aside before we left for the ceremony and asked if I was sure I was doing the right thing.

Her intuition was rarely wrong. I shouldn't have ignored the nagging feeling inside of me that was indeed a red flag warning. Marrying the guy I had dated throughout high school and college seemed like a solid move, but it turned out to be a horrible mistake.

Our divorce stole a lot from me, including my self-esteem for a time.

I feel stronger now than I ever have before. I'm more confident and committed to the decisions I make, but I'm hung up on what to do with Sweet Indulgence.

I walk down a path that leads to my favorite spot in the park. It's one of the benches that are set under a row of trees. They directly face the Hudson River, so not only is the view spectacular, but it's calming in a sense.

I always come here when I need to think.

It seems that many other New Yorkers share the same sentiment. It's a bright and sunny afternoon, so I'm not surprised many people are sitting on the row of benches. Some are eating what is likely their lunch. Others are engrossed in conversation with the people next to them.

As I near the bench I've come to call my own, I notice a man sitting on it. He's wearing a suit, and like many of the other people here, his focus is on the phone in his hands. He does have what looks to be a white stick poking out from between his lips.

I smile to myself because I know exactly what it is. This businessman is enjoying a lollipop.

Sitting next to a stranger has never bothered me before, so I walk up to the bench, fully expecting to take the empty spot next to him.

That's the plan until he glances up and my breath catches.

Holden stares at me, his eyes widening as his gaze slides over my dress. He pulls a pink star-shaped lollipop out from between his lips. "Greer Irwin. I didn't expect to see you here."

CHAPTER THIRTY-SIX

Holden

THE SHOCKED EXPRESSION on Greer's face mirrors my own feelings. I didn't think I'd see her today, or any day in the near future.

After I left Krista outside the coffee shop, I took a walk, then a ride on the subway. I ended up here because this park has always offered me a sense of peace.

I move to stand since Greer seems stuck in place.

"You followed me here," she accuses with a finger pointed at my chest.

"I was here first," I say evenly. "I got here thirty minutes ago."

"He was here when I got here." A gray-haired woman sitting on the bench next to us looks up from her knitting project. "He offered me a lollipop, but sugar is not my friend."

Greer's gaze drops to the Sweet Indulgence bag on the

bench. "They're actually all organic. They're made from natural fruit juice. There's no added sugar."

"In that case." The woman's hand dives into the bag and comes out with a deep blue lollipop. "Look at this. It's so pretty."

A proud smile slides over Greer's lips. "I think so, too."

Her gaze drifts to my face, and I see a million questions there waiting to be asked, including one about why I'm carting a Sweet Indulgence bag filled with lollipops around with me.

"I stopped in the store earlier," I explain. "I was hoping you had something in particular, but the guy behind the counter suggested the lollipops. I'm glad he did."

"Burt," she blurts out a name. "You're talking about Burt."

"Sure," I agree. "He looked like a Burt."

"What does a Burt look like?" The woman sitting next to us asks as she unwraps the lollipop.

"Tall, brown hair, handsome," Greer says before I can get a word in.

"You think he's handsome?" I ask, jealousy driving the question out of me.

"He is handsome," she answers. "Everyone thinks Burt is handsome."

"I don't," I snap.

The woman now sucking on the lollipop turns her entire body to face us. "Oh, a lover's quarrel. This should be good."

Greer shakes her head. "We're not lovers."

"We were," I remind her. "One of us wants to be again."

"Is it you?" The woman next to us points at Greer. "If it is, I can't say I blame you."

Greer stifles a laugh. "It's him."

"Oh, dear, do it." The woman sighs. "Or do him. Either way, I don't think Burt has anything on this guy."

I glance at her. "Thank you."

"You're welcome." She shoves her knitting needles and yarn into a large purple tote bag next to her on the bench. "Can I take another lollipop for my grandson?"

"Take them all," Greer says, pushing past me to grab the twine handles of the bag to pass it to the woman. "We sell them at Sweet Indulgence in Chelsea."

"Sweet Indulgence," the woman repeats. "I'll stop by in the next few days."

"If I'm not there, tell them Greer sent you. They'll give you an automatic ten percent discount on anything you buy."

"I'll do that." The woman nods at both of us. "Don't let anger get in the way of the passion. There's fire between you two. I can feel it. Never let that slip away."

Greer sighs heavily as if she's pushing back the urge to respond.

I do it for both of us. "You're insightful. I've never met anyone like this woman. The passion and fire are real. It's undeniable."

Greer swats my forearm in what I suspect is an effort to get me to shut the hell up.

I catch her gaze and hold it. I need her to know that beyond the business deal we're trying to broker, what I felt in East Hampton has only intensified. I want her more than I've ever wanted another woman, and I need her to understand that.

"I'll leave you two to sort out whatever this situationship is." The woman waves her hand in the air. "Thank you for the candy and for reminding me why I love sitting in this park. This city is filled with interesting people, including both of you."

CHARM

"WHAT DO YOU WANT, HOLDEN?"

It's a direct question, but I'm unsure exactly how to answer it, so I go with what I want most. "You."

A pink blush creeps up her neck and invades both of her cheeks. It somehow makes her even more beautiful. "Don't do that."

"Don't do what?" I ask, stepping closer to her as two men on bikes speed past us on the path. "Tell the truth."

"Fine." She blows out a breath. "Let's start with why you really went to my store today."

"I was hoping to see you," I confess, because what's the purpose in lying about something so obvious? "I was also looking for chocolate cigars."

A smile blooms on her lips. "Chocolate cigars?"

I nod. "They look like regular cigars but are made of chocolate."

Laughing, she shakes her head. "I know what they are, Holden. I was asking why you're looking for them."

"One of my closest friends and his wife had a baby early this morning." I can't help but smile. "Sweetest little boy you've ever seen. Well, my nephew Morgan is also the sweetest baby boy, so..."

"Congratulations to your friend and his wife."

"They're happy," I state the obvious. "Super fucking happy."

"You are, too." She smiles. "Your friends matter a lot to you."

"I consider them family."

Her chin dips down. "You're lucky to have friends like that."

I ask a question that will tell me a hell of a lot. It's something I've been curious about since she walked into the conference room at Carden. "Do you consider Krista family, Greer?"

Her gaze drifts up to my face. She studies it carefully. "I do, yes."

I decide to go out on a limb because I sense I'm right about something. "That's why this is so hard for you. You love her and you love Sweet Indulgence. Choosing between the two is really fucking hard."

"It's torture," she whispers. "For a lot of reasons."

I'm desperate to know all of those reasons, and it's not because I want to buy out her company. I want to help her. I want to comfort her.

"Are you hungry?" I ask.

"Why?"

"I'm in the mood for another one of those charcuterie boards I put together in East Hampton." I glance at my watch. "I haven't eaten anything other than that lollipop since last night."

"Are you asking me to join you?" She eyes me skeptically. "Why do I sense that an invitation to go to your place is coming next?"

"Because it is." I glance toward a woman pushing a stroller headed in our direction. "We can stop on our way to grab everything for our snack, and then we'll pick up a bottle of champagne to toast to baby Gilbert Wells."

Greer looks at the woman with the stroller as she passes us. Scratching the back of her head, she exhales. "I'll come for the food and the champagne, but don't try and make a move on me."

"Maybe you'll feel the urge to make a move on me."

"You wish," she scoffs. "By the way, the best chocolate cigars in the city are at Wolf Candy."

I already know that, but we both know the real reason I went to Sweet Indulgence earlier was to see her.

"Thanks for the tip." I motion toward the path. "Are you ready to head to my place?"

She looks to the right before her gaze darts to the left. She laughs softly when she spots a woman in a suit walking down the path holding the handle of a black umbrella.

"You won't need one of those," I say, knowing exactly why she laughed. She remembers when we first met. "You already know you're safe with me."

She looks back at me with a wide smile on her face. "I know I'm safe with you. The jury is still out on whether my business will be if I do decide to sell it to you."

That's progress but I'm not going to pounce on the opportunity to discuss what she means.

This afternoon all shop talk is off the table. Good food and champagne are the only things I'm planning on focusing on besides her.

CHAPTER THIRTY-SEVEN

GREER

"WELCOME TO MY HOME." Holden drops his keys on a small desk in the foyer of what looks to be a lovely apartment.

From where I'm standing, it's impeccably decorated in rich, dark tones. The chocolate brown leather furniture looks incredibly comfortable. A massive couch faces a gas fireplace surrounded by gray tiles.

The entire space speaks not only to good taste, but also to a keen understanding of how to utilize each square foot to its maximum potential.

"Why do you look confused?" he asks. "Were you expecting something else?"

I take another step forward so he can shut the door behind me. "Your house in East Hampton looks nothing like this inside."

He glances around the room. "I had a hand in the design

decisions here. My grandmother handled that in the beach house. I inherited it from her after her death."

My heart feels like it clenches inside my chest because I've suffered loss, too. Celia's death was most difficult for me, but when my grandfather on my dad's side passed away, I was only fourteen. I cried myself to sleep for days. I still shed a tear when I remember my summers in Colorado.

He'd take me fishing and horseback riding. We'd have as many outdoor adventures as he could cram into the two weeks I got to spend with him and my grandmother.

After my folks retired, they headed west and bought a home there so my grandma could live with them.

There was a lot of debate after Olive was born about whether they should all relocate to New York, but they love the life they've built there. I take Olive there a few times a year to visit, and they video chat with her at least once a week.

"I'm sorry for your loss, Holden."

His gaze catches mine briefly before it drops to the floor. "Thanks, Greer."

He moves quickly through the space, holding tightly to the three shopping bags we picked up on our journey here. We went to a deli that Holden frequents. He's there often enough that they know him by his first name. After that, he bought a bottle of champagne that cost more than I'd ever spent on alcohol.

"I'm going to shower quickly if that's okay with you," he calls over his shoulder. "I need a refresh since I've been wearing this suit for over a day."

No one passing him on the street would suspect that. He smells as divinely masculine as he always does.

"Sure, of course," I call back. "Do you want me to get started on the charcuterie board?"

"I want you to help yourself to something cool to drink from the fridge." He gestures to the open doorway he's about to enter. "It's this way."

I start in that direction, taking in everything I pass with each step. Beautiful paintings hang on the walls. A framed drawing of a garden takes the center spot. It's obvious a child is responsible for it. I stop to read the name written in red crayon in the bottom right corner.

"Kirby," I whisper.

"Kirby is my friend Rook's daughter. She made that for me."

I turn to find Holden right behind me. "How old is she?"

"Almost six," he says. "She's an amazing kid. We're tap dancing partners."

That catches me so off guard that I let out a soft laugh. "What?"

He slides one of his black wingtip shoes slightly forward on the floor. "Sometimes Kirbs needs a hand to hold when she tries new things. She asked me if I'd take her to tap dancing lessons when her dad enrolled her. Somehow, from that, I ended up next to her in the dance recital."

There's a flutter in my chest when I imagine him tap dancing with a little girl not much younger than my Olive. Obviously there's a lot more to Holden Sheppard than I've realized.

"Before you ask, I'm damn good." His hands drop to his hips. "Play your cards right and I may give you a private show sometime."

I tuck my hair behind my ear. "A private show? That's not code for a naked show, is it?"

"Now it is."

I bow my chin to hide an uncontrollable smile.

"I know you're smiling, Greer," he whispers. "I also

know you wish you weren't, but there's something about me."

My head pops up until our eyes meet. "Don't flatter yourself."

"I'd much rather flatter you." His tone lowers dangerously. "You're beautiful, and it's not in that ordinary kind of way either. You're fucking gorgeous. You're breathtaking. There needs to be a new word to describe how captivating you are."

"Wow," I mutter.

"That's not the word I'm looking for." His hand darts up. It's headed toward my face, but he stops it short, dropping it before he touches me. "I'm going to take a shower before I say something that will earn me an umbrella poke."

"You told me I wouldn't need an umbrella today." I remind him. "Besides, I don't have one."

"There are three in the holder by the door." He jerks his chin up. "Keep your hands off of them. Get a drink, take a seat wherever the hell you want, and relax. I put the food in the fridge for now. We can work on it together when I'm done."

"Deal," I whisper, testing how the word feels on my tongue.

I may never agree to a business deal with this man, but being here with him like this feels right at this moment.

CHAPTER THIRTY-EIGHT

Holden

GREER POPS the last olive into her mouth, smiling as she chews. "This was delicious."

She's right about that. Usually, I pick up a sandwich and a coffee on my way home after pulling an all-nighter at the office, but today called for something different. Not only because I had Greer by my side when I walked into my apartment, but Declan is a dad, and that's put me in a feel good mood all day.

I may be exhausted, but I'm still awake, and the happiest I've been since I left East Hampton.

"I agree." I pour another splash of champagne into her flute before doing the same in mine. "We should toast."

"Again?" She picks up her glass. "I lost track, but I think you've already toasted to Gilbert Wells at least four times."

She's likely right, but the next toast isn't in celebration of Declan and Abby's son. This toast is all about her.

I grab my glass and raise it in the air. "To you, Greer."

CHARM

"To me?" She holds off on clinking her glass against the side of mine. "For what?"

"For existing." I go the extra step and lightly tap my glass against hers.

I down the entire contents in one gulp. There's just something about champagne that makes it go down so fucking easy.

Her glass is still in the air. I can't help but notice her hand is now trembling.

"What's wrong?" I ask softly.

"We can't go back to where we were in East Hampton, Holden."

She made it clear before we said our goodbyes after our weekend together that I was a part of her past. Now, I'm not.

"We can't," I agree. "Is there a chance we can move forward as something more than what we are now?"

"What are we now?" The question rushes out of her.

Before I can formulate a response, she's sliding off the chair she's been sitting on next to my dining table.

I stand, too.

Her gaze drops to the jeans and T-shirt I'm wearing. I bought the shirt last year from a vendor who was selling her wares at a market in Brooklyn. Kirby desperately wanted a pink one in her size because it was adorned with a picture of a rainbow. She chose a matching one for me that is blue. I don't wear it often, but it's comfortable.

"We're two people who like each other." I test the waters. "We're two people who liked fucking each other."

Her eyes widen. "Holden!"

"I'm not lying." I chuckle. "We had fun, Greer. Let's have more fun."

She shakes her head. "While you're trying to steal my business away from me? No, thank you."

I step closer to where she's standing. I'm close enough that I could circle her waist with my hands, but I don't. Instead, I cross my arms over my chest. "I'm trying to buy your business at a very fair price. Our offer is incredibly generous."

She doesn't argue that point.

"I can't stop thinking about you," I confess.

She drags her top teeth over her bottom lip. "You're not making this easy for me."

"I'm not making what easy for you?" I push because I want her to explain what she's feeling. I need to know if she wants me as much as I want her.

She pushes her hair over her shoulder. "You know exactly what I'm talking about. Do you want me to admit that I'm wildly attracted to you? Because I think you're already well aware of that fact."

"Wildly attracted?" I repeat the key phrase in what she just said.

She stomps away from me, leaving a faint hint of her perfume in her wake. It's floral and will forever remind me of our time at the beach.

I follow behind her because I have no choice in the matter. My feet may be doing the work, but my desire for her is the fuel behind every step I'm taking in my effort to catch her before she storms out of my home.

"Greer," I say her name loud enough that it stops her in her tracks. "We need to talk about this. Ignoring what we both want won't make it disappear."

She turns abruptly to face me. There's a fire in her eyes that I haven't seen in weeks. "What do we both want?"

I'd ask her what she thinks we want, but she needs to hear it from me first, so I'll happily oblige. "To kiss, to touch. You want me to fuck you again."

She shakes her head, but her stuttered breaths tell a different story, as do her rushed words. "You don't know that."

I narrow the distance left between us with measured steps. As soon as I'm close enough, I reach out to touch her chin. "Tell me I'm wrong. Look me in the eye and tell me you don't want me. Tell me you don't think about what it felt like to be with me."

"I can't," she whispers. "I can't tell you I don't want you."

That's all I need to hear. Leaning forward, I drag the pad of my thumb over her bottom lip, waiting for her to signal this is not what she wants.

She leans forward too, tilts her head, and slowly closes her eyes.

I take what she's offering to me and claim her pillow-soft lips in a deep, slow kiss.

CHAPTER THIRTY-NINE

GREER

I FALL INTO HIM, resting my hands against his chest.

The kiss is everything, and then some.

He cups his hand around the back of my neck, owning the kiss and me. I give in to it all because it feels so good. It's almost too good.

A phone ringing in the distance makes me pause. He does, too, but quickly dismisses it when he kisses me again.

The incessant ringing quiets as Holden starts to guide me toward the wall. He doesn't say a word. He doesn't need to. I know that I'm about to feel things I haven't felt in weeks. This man takes me to places I've never been before.

The phone starts ringing again. Each shrill bite of the sound in the air haunts me.

"I think it's mine," I whisper against his lips. "I have to check it."

He trails kisses over my neck, heading toward one of the

shoulder straps of my dress. "Voicemail will pick up or they'll call Krista."

I whimper as he slides the strap aside before he kisses the spot under it. "Holden."

"I need you naked, Greer," he growls. "Jesus, do I want to fuck you. I'm hard as stone here."

My hand falls to the front of his jeans.

The man is not lying. I can feel the outline of his rigid cock straining against the denim. With just my right hand, I fumble with the button before I free it. When I move to tug on the zipper, his hand joins mine. Our fingers tangle before we lower the zipper together.

"On your knees," he orders. "I need your mouth on my dick."

The plea in his voice is so needy that it catches my breath in my throat. I grab hold of his hands for leverage. I'm partway down to my knees when my phone starts ringing again.

Mild concern is now full-blown panic within me. My heart feels like it's thundering through my chest wall.

I dart back up to standing. "I have to get it, Holden. Olive. What if it's about Olive?"

I instantly realize what I've done. I've revealed a secret that I intended to hold onto tightly for as long as I could.

His gaze searches my face. "I'll get the phone."

He darts to where I left it by the front door when we came in. He scoops it up as it rings, but his gaze never leaves me.

Just as he hands it to me, the ringing subsides.

I scan the screen. Three missed calls from Martha.

I don't care what happens next. All I care about is that my daughter is safe, so I press the button to call Martha back.

She doesn't answer. My sweet angel does.

"Mommy?" Olive breathes hard into the phone. "Are you okay? I tried calling a thousand times."

Holden's gaze catches mine just as he takes a step back to give me more air to breathe and room to think.

"I'm okay, sweetheart," I whisper into my phone. "Are you?"

"Grandma gave me her phone to call you." She sniffles loudly. "We went to see a play in the park. There's a lady with a box of kittens. Grandma said I can't have one, but she said you had the last word."

"Grandma's right," I say, keeping my eyes on Holden.

A soft smile spreads over his lips as he listens.

"Why can't the last word be yes?" she whispers.

"We can't get a kitten right now, Olive," I tell her.

"Are you sure?" she questions. "I'll take care of it all by myself."

For a few days, until the responsibilities of pet ownership would fall mainly on the shoulders of her grandparents, since I work so much.

"I'm sure." I bow my head because this unexpected collision of my real life and the man I spent the best weekend of my life with is hitting me like a freight train. My emotions are all over the place. "I'll talk to you more about it when I get home."

"Will that be soon?"

"Yes," I say, sealing the fate on what I know would have been an unbelievably fun afternoon in Holden's bed. "I'll be home in just a little while."

"I love you, Mommy!" she screams into the phone.

"I love you, Olive," I say without any hesitation. "I'll see you soon."

I end the call and take a deep breath before I cradle my phone close to my chest and look Holden dead in the eyes.

"You're a mom," he says with a grin. "Aren't you?"

"Olive is my daughter. She's everything to me."

"She's a very lucky girl." He walks toward me. "I bet you're a kick ass mom."

I can't hold in a laugh. "I have my moments."

His hand jumps up to cradle my chin. "You need to go to her now. From what I gathered, there's some sort of kitten emergency."

"Olive believes there is." I sigh. "Today it's a kitten she wants. Last week it was a hamster. Such is life with a seven-year-old."

"Seven?" Holden tilts my chin up. "That seems like a fun age."

"Tell that to my heart." I pat the center of my chest. "She's growing up too fast for my liking."

Studying me carefully, he leans forward to kiss my cheek. "You're even more remarkable than I thought you were, Greer."

"Because I'm a mom?"

"Because you're you."

He kisses me again, but it's on my lips this time. It's tender and soft, and if it's meant to make my toes curl in my shoes, it hit the mark.

"Do you want me to order you a rideshare?" He motions to where his phone is sitting on the same table mine was. "Do you live far from here?"

We're currently in Tribeca, so I nod. "I live on the Upper East Side, but at this time of day, the subway will get me there easiest and quickly."

Nodding, he opens his mouth as though he's about to say something but then slams it shut.

I grin. "What is it, Holden?"

"I may be far off base here, but I can't help but wonder if

your refusal to sell Sweet Indulgence isn't all about how much you hate me."

My head falls back in laughter as I playfully punch his bicep. "I don't hate you."

"You hate the fact I'm trying to buy you out." He kisses my cheek again. "You love the sex."

"I really like the sex." I make that subtle correction because the actual L word has no business in any discussion involving the two of us.

"In that case, it's a hard like. "

I drop my gaze to the front of his open jeans. "About that… you should zip up."

He does, chuckling the entire time. "We'll pick this up soon?"

"Will we?" I question.

"We will," he answers. "We both want it."

I should point out that want and need are two very different things, and although I want desperately to be fucked by him again, I'm not sure I need it because it comes with a host of complications that have far-reaching impacts on my business.

"I need to go," I say, taking the easy way out.

"I know." He grips my arms in both hands. "Give me your number, Greer."

Seconds pass as I contemplate the ramifications of that.

"You're overthinking it." He laughs. "I promise I won't send you a thousand texts a day or call you telling you how much I miss you."

"In that case, I'll text you by the end of the day today so you have my number."

He eyes me skeptically. "You'll need my number to do that."

"I have it." I try to gently pull away from him. "Krista

gave it to me a few days ago. She gave me your brother's number, too."

His grip on me tightens as a wicked smile settles on his lips. "And you had the willpower to not call or text me?"

"I can resist you," I whisper, finally tugging free of his grasp.

"Maybe." His tone deepens. "The question is for how long?"

I want to say forever, but that very well could be a lie. Hell, it would be a lie. He's completely irresistible and he knows it.

I don't bother saying a thing. Instead, I scoop up my purse on my way out, and without a glance back, I exit his apartment and head home to the life I've worked so hard to build.

CHAPTER FORTY

Holden

A MAN'S fist is not a replacement for the body of a beautiful red head with lips that could take him to his knees, but I worked with what I had after Greer left.

I was going to change and go to the gym, but since I was nearing the point of utter exhaustion, I fell onto my bed.

Thoughts of her crowded my mind, but it was the look on her face when she was about to drop to her knees to take my dick in her mouth that pushed me to palm my own cock.

I came, and after another shower, I thought I'd fall into a deep sleep. I gave up on that after five minutes. I got dressed, had a tall glass of water, and took off out of my apartment, headed to nowhere in particular.

Part of me is considering taking a stroll along a few streets on the Upper East Side, but that will land me right in stalker territory if I run into her.

If I do venture to her part of the city, I want it to be after she extends an invitation to me.

My stomach reminds me with a growl that I'm hungry. The mini-meal I shared with Greer wasn't enough to fill me up.

I have no issue eating alone, but if I can convince a family member or friend to join me, that makes for good food with a side of great company.

I slow my pace while glancing at the contact list in my phone.

The choices are widespread from business contacts to people I've lost touch with.

I'm about to send a text to Rook to see what he's up to when my phone's screen lights up with an incoming call.

Laughing, I answer immediately. "Rook."

"This shit is getting old, Holden." He chuckles.

I immediately jump back in my mind to our conversation at the hospital last night before we went our separate ways. We hugged, said goodbye, and agreed to meet up later this week for a drink or dinner.

"What shit?" I ask because I'm lost.

"Look to your left." He's still laughing. "This is unreal."

My gaze darts to the left, and I join in on the laughter as I end the call.

Standing just a few feet away from me, holding a pizza box, Rook shoves his phone in the back pocket of his jeans.

By the time he's right in front of me on the sidewalk, my laughter has subsided, but I'm still sporting a wide grin on my face. He is, too.

"How the fuck does this keep happening?" He shakes his head. "What made you choose that shirt to wear today?"

I glance down at the black T-shirt I'm wearing. It bears the logo of the boarding school we attended when we were teenagers. I balked when my grandparents told me I was heading upstate to go to the Buchanan School. I wanted no part of it, but the experience was one of the best of my life.

Not only did I meet Rook and Declan, but I also learned a lot about myself during my time there.

We all became Buck Boys, as the students and alums are called. I've been an ardent supporter of the school since I graduated. I go back yearly to speak to the graduating class about business and life. I donate monthly to their various programs.

"The real question is what made you choose to wear it, Rook?" I point at his shirt, which so happens to be an exact match to mine.

The fact that we both have on faded jeans only adds to our twinning look.

"I need to go shopping for new clothes." He gives me a side hug before shoving the pizza box at me. "That, my well-dressed friend, is a pepperoni pie from Franzini's."

I'm not surprised. Rook knows the eatery in Brooklyn makes my favorite slice. It doesn't hurt that one of the paralegals who works for Rook's law firm is the sister of the guy who owns Franzini's. I know Rook gets a deal whenever he places an order, but he's a stellar tipper, so it all balances out in the end.

I glance past him. "Where's Kirbs?"

"Still with Chesca," he says. "I get her tomorrow."

"So I'll see you again tomorrow?"

"Of course you will. Come over for dinner." He gestures toward the double glass doors of my building and the doorman standing at the ready to open them. "Do we need to make a beer run, or do you have some?"

"I have a few bottles in the fridge."

"It's time to eat." He takes off toward the door. "Did you find some chocolate cigars we can surprise Declan with?"

Since I'm the one who brought up the idea of getting Declan cigars at the hospital during the wee hours of this morning, I need to get on that. Rook thinks it'll be hilarious to present Declan with a box of chocolate ones. I think our old friend would prefer a real cigar to celebrate the birth of his son, but I'll defer to Rook on this.

"I'll get some," I say.

"I know you will," he calls back over his shoulder as he enters the lobby of my building after passing the doorman a few bills. "You're the guy with all of the candy connections in this city."

"WHAT'S HER NAME?" Rook asks as I walk into my main living area with another bottle of beer for him in my hand.

We finished the pizza within minutes after we sat down to eat. After that, we talked about Declan, Abby, and their newborn son. The look on Rook's face during that conversation told me he's as excited for our mutual best friend as I am.

I pass it off to him. "Who?"

"The woman who has you smiling like that." He tilts the bottle in his hand toward me. "You haven't smiled like that in years, Holden."

I drink from the water bottle I opened for myself during dinner. "The smile is all about baby Gilbert."

"Bullshit."

I bark out a laugh. "Can't a guy be happy for his best friend?"

"I'm your best friend," he decides. "That's how I know you're not on cloud nine over the new baby. You're crazy about someone, so who is it?"

"If there was a woman…and I'm not saying there is…I wouldn't say I'm crazy about her."

"So you are crazy about a woman."

"Fuck you, Rook."

"I'm a goddamn lawyer, Holden." He tilts the bottle in his hand slightly. "I'm an expert at reading between the lines, and the lines here spell out great sex with a beautiful woman."

"She is beautiful," I say because I can't argue that point with him. "I'm not talking about fucking her with you."

"That means it's the best sex you've ever had."

"Leave," I demand with a grin. "Just go if you're going to keep pulling that."

"What's her name?"

"Greer," I tell him. "We met in East Hampton."

His eyes widen. "During your last trip there a couple of months ago?"

I nod in acknowledgment. "We spent the weekend together. Our paths crossed here again recently."

"In the city?" he questions. "Did you two pick up where you left off?"

I down another mouthful of water. "No."

"Why not?"

"I'm trying to buy her company at the moment." Closing my eyes briefly, I shake my head. "Her business partner wants out. Greer wants to hold onto it."

"Sounds messy." He chuckles. "I take it you're the enemy in her eyes now?"

I half shrug, since I'm unsure how to answer that. I would have agreed without question before today, but she was seconds away from taking my cock between her perfect lips just hours ago.

"It's complicated, Rook." I set my bottle on the table. "I want her."

"And her company," he finishes my thought. "It would be a lot less complicated if you chose which you want more. Greer or her business."

That answer is easy.

I want Greer.

There will always be another company to buy, but from where I'm standing, there's only one Greer Irwin.

CHAPTER FORTY-ONE

Greer

"DID WE INTERRUPT YOU EARLIER?" Martha asks as she stacks three books on the coffee table. Olive borrowed them from the library last week. "I handed my phone to Olive so she could call you about the kitten. Bruce was watching her outside the market while I ran in to get some fresh veggies. I had no idea she tried to call you as many times as she did."

I reassure her with a comforting pat on the middle of her back. "You could never interrupt me, Martha. Olive couldn't either, or Bruce. You're all way more important than anything else."

The soft smile she gives me in return melts my heart. One of the best things that came out of my failed marriage is my relationship with Martha and Bruce. I don't know what I'd do without the two of them. The fact that they love taking care of Olive and me feels like a gift.

I'll never be able to repay them.

"You're very important to us, too." She kisses my cheek. "I know things with Aaron were a mess, but we see you as our daughter."

That hits the center of my heart in the best way. I swallow hard to chase away a rush of emotions that I know have the potential to make me cry.

"Olive is up in the craft room making paper kittens with Bruce." Her gaze catches mine. "She chose our menu for dinner tonight."

"Let me guess." I tap the center of my chin. "Hot dogs and mac and cheese?"

Her head shakes. "Our sweetheart wants grilled chicken, mashed potatoes, and a garden salad with cherry tomatoes on the side. Blueberry pie is on the dessert menu."

Surprised by that, I furrow my brow. "That sounds more like Bruce's favorite meal than Olive's."

"I think she wants it because he does love it so much." She sighs. "He was talking about dinner on our way home from the play. Olive decided that she'd request that menu to make him happy."

"It makes me happy, too," I say, although I'm still full from the food I ate at Holden's.

"Were you at work when Olive called?"

I swear, sometimes it seems as though she can read my mind.

"I was meeting with the man I told you about," I admit.

Her face lights up with a brilliant smile. It reaches all the way to her eyes. "Meeting or *meeting*?"

The subtle difference in how she says meeting the second time makes me laugh out loud. "Martha!"

"There's no law that says a young, beautiful, single mom can't have some fun, Greer." She glances at the stairs leading up to the second and third floors. "You deserve to have as much fun as you can as often as you can."

"I'm not sure about that."

"Why not?" she spits both words out quickly. "You've devoted your entire life to Olive since the day she was born, and the business takes up so much of your time, too. I know you want to fulfill Celia's dreams, Greer, but…"

"Who had a dream?" Olive comes racing around the corner.

It looks like my little sneak took the back staircase to get to this floor. That's her usual trick when she is on the hunt for a candy before dinner since that staircase leads straight to the kitchen.

"Is that a cinnamon chew in your mouth?" I ask to change the subject.

Her tongue darts out to show me what's left of the small candy. "They are so good, Mom. They're the best."

"I agree." Martha's hand dives into the pocket of her dress to scoop out three of the brightly wrapped candies. "I always keep a few right here in case I need a little hit of spice."

"Mommy is the best candy maker in the world." Olive runs toward me with her arms outstretched.

I take her in for a hug, holding tightly to her.

"One day, I'll be the best candy maker in the world, too," she whispers. "I'll go to our store every morning. I'll tell people how great our candies are, and everyone will keep coming back for more."

Martha smiles softly at me as I cling to my daughter. "Sweet Indulgence is a very special place."

It is, and it's part of my family's legacy now.

I'm not sure I have the strength to let it go.

I RAP QUIETLY on the door to Krista's apartment. She lives in a two bedroom on the third floor of a walk-up in Brooklyn. Her apartment is a testament to the best this city has to offer. Her neighbors are phenomenal, and the view is as New York as one can get, with the skyline of Manhattan in the distance.

I'm not sure how she's going to leave this all behind, but she will. I realized earlier as I heard my daughter talk about a possible future at the helm of Sweet Indulgence that I can't let the company go.

What I can do is let my surviving best friend go.

I can encourage her to chase her dreams.

Krista swings open the door with a wide grin on her face and what looks like a spot of pink cloud on her nose.

I fall into laughter immediately. "You have cotton candy on your nose."

"Oh, fuck." She swipes her hand across her nose. "I was craving it so badly. I sent Howie out to get me some earlier."

I lift a hand in greeting to her fiancé. "Hey, Howie."

"Hey, you!" he calls from where he's sitting in an armchair reading a book. "There's plenty more cotton candy on the table."

I take a step in and glance at their small dining table. It's covered by an array of see-through containers. Each holds a different shade of spun sugar.

"I'll pass."

"Smart move." He slides to his feet. "I'm going to take my book to the pub across the street. I indulged my fiancée's cotton candy craving, so it's time to satisfy mine for a cold beer."

He scoots past us, stopping to kiss Krista on the cheek before he hugs me. "You love each other. Never forget that."

"We won't," we whisper in unison as he walks out of the apartment.

As soon as the door is closed behind him, Krista looks into my eyes. "You said you needed to talk tonight, Greer. I take it that means it's important."

"It is," I say, waiting for an invitation to sit since my knees are quaking.

"I'll get us some water and we can talk." She hugs me tightly. "Whatever it is, I'll always love you."

"I'll always love you, too," I whisper. "Always."

CHAPTER FORTY-TWO

GREER

"I BROUGHT YOU SOMETHING." I dig in the pocket of my jeans and tug out a small dark blue velvet bag. "I thought you should have it."

Krista leans back slightly on the comfy red couch we're sitting on. She purchased the piece while we were in college. Celia and I both told her she'd regret it, but she hasn't.

When she moved into this apartment, she told Howie that his pristine white couch had to go. I was there when that conversation happened, and he didn't hesitate for a second before telling her that he'd do everything he could to make her happy.

They sold the white couch days before Krista and this red couch moved in. Since then, the room's décor has transformed to complement it, including two gorgeous black wingback chairs that face the couch and a distressed wood table with just a hint of red stain on it.

Their home is welcoming and exudes warmth. I always feel like family when I come over.

"What is it?" she asks, eyeing the bag as though whatever is inside it might bite her.

I drop it in her lap. The dress she's wearing is one she took from Celia's closet on the day we packed up her things. It was months after she died, but we both cried for hours as we tucked her life into a few cardboard boxes.

Krista's gaze catches mine briefly, so I nod. "You'll like it. I know you will."

She nods in understanding. "I know I will, too. You've always been the most thoughtful person when it comes to gifts."

I try.

I've always viewed gifts as an expression of what I feel for the receiver. I've been known to spend days, if not weeks, choosing birthday gifts for Martha and Bruce. The time I invested paid off. Every gift I've ever given either of them has brought tears to their eyes.

Her fingers make quick work of the lazy knot I tied the bag's two woven strings in. She digs her hand in all while keeping her eyes on me.

I see the instant she touches what's inside because a tear streams down her cheek. "Oh, Greer."

I'm overcome with emotion, too, but I hold in my tears and smile. "It belongs to you now."

She yanks the small silver cube from the bag. It was designed to resemble a child's toy block, so each of the six sides contains a letter. It was a random purchase that Celia made weeks before Olive was born. The three of us promised then that whenever one of us had a baby, we'd pass it along.

It was sitting on a shelf in Olive's room since the day she was born. When I told her this morning that Krista and Howie are having a baby, she's the one who ran to get the block. She placed it in my palm and told me it was time to pass it on, since I've told her the story about where it came from many times.

"What about our Olive?" She smiles through a veil of tears.

"She wants you to have it."

She nods softly. "She's such a good girl, Greer. You're an incredible mom."

That's the greatest compliment she could ever give me. "You'll be a great mom, too."

"I hope so." She takes a deep breath. "I really hope so. I'm going to need you to share all your wisdom with me. I'll need pointers every day about how to be the best mom I can be."

I reach for her hands and cradle them in mine. "My tip for today is slather on the sunscreen. Not just on the baby but you and Howie, too. From what I hear, the California sun is brutal."

Her gaze jumps over my face. "Greer?"

"You need to go chase your dreams," I whisper. "I want that for you."

She lunges at me, tugging me into a big hug. She cries with her face against my shoulder. I hold onto her tightly, sure I can feel the tension leaving her body.

"I'll call Jameson," she whispers. "I'll call him and tell him the deal is a go."

"No," I say evenly. "Don't."

She moves back from our embrace to look at me. Her hand swipes her cheeks, chasing away the last of her tears. "I'm fine with you making the call, Greer."

I rehearsed what I wanted to say to her on my way here, but all those carefully chosen words have gotten lost now.

"I'm not selling," I start, stopping to blow out a breath. "I'd like to dissolve the agreement we had about selling the company together. I want to hold onto my half, Krista."

Her brow furrows. "Carden will be on board for that, Greer. Jameson already mentioned the possibility of buying me out so they can partner with you."

She's making this harder than it needs to be.

"That can't happen," I tell her. "I don't…"

"Sure, it can happen," she interrupts me. "Once we dissolve that clause in our contract, I'll hammer out a deal with them and then all that's left is for you to approve it."

I rub my hands over my thighs, smoothing out the denim of my jeans. "I won't approve it."

Her eyes instantly well with tears again. "What? Why not?"

I knew before I got here that I had to tell her the truth. I can't fumble my way through a bunch of lame excuses for not agreeing to partner with one of the most successful candy conglomerates in the world.

"Are you scared they'll force you out?" she asks, jumping to an obvious conclusion. "That's it, isn't it? You think they'll make your life hell so you'll eventually throw your hands up in the air and give in and sell to them."

They might, but I'll never have to worry about finding out if it happens.

"I'm not scared of that." I thread my fingers together, anxiety driving every one of my movements. "It's something else."

"What is it, Greer? Please tell me."

I glance at her face to see understanding in her expression. I hope it's still there after I confess what I need to. "I slept with Holden Sheppard."

Her mouth falls open. "No, you didn't."

I hold in a laugh. "I did."

She jumps to her feet, still holding tightly to the silver cube. "It was sometime before the meeting, wasn't it? That's why you couldn't wait to get out of there."

Rubbing the back of my neck, I nod. "We met in East Hampton when I was there. We both used fake names, so I had no clue I spent that weekend with Holden."

"You spent the entire weekend with him?" Her hand leaps to her mouth. "So when you walked into the meeting, was that the first time you'd seen him since you two slept together?"

"Yes." I stand, too. "I almost fell over."

"I saw it firsthand." She laughs. "This explains everything, Greer. It explains so much."

"Does it explain why I can't agree to you selling your half of the business to him?"

She purses her lips. "Maybe, but what if it's a good thing for you if I sell to him?"

"It's not."

She wraps her arm around my shoulders. "He might be the guy for you, Greer. You know what they say about how thin the line between love and hate is."

A bubble of laughter falls from my lips. "I'll never love him. I don't hate him, but that doesn't mean I'll ever go into business with the man. That will always be a hard no."

CHAPTER FORTY-THREE

Holden

JAMESON SPRINTS toward me as I exit the elevator on the floor that houses our executive offices. It's a typical move for him when he wants something from me.

I'm just about to turn around and step back into the open elevator to earn a laugh from my brother, but the woman who snuck around me to get inside has already pressed a button, sending the doors sliding shut.

"Have a nice day, Mr. Sheppard," she says as she disappears from view.

I toss her a smile at the very last second. "You too."

Jameson reaches me just as the elevator takes off to one of the floors below us. "I needed to talk to her."

"Her?" I jerk a thumb over my shoulder toward the elevator. "Who is she?"

He lets out a hearty laugh. "Jesus, Holden. Try and keep up. She's our new accounting manager. I introduced you to her a couple of months ago on the day she started."

"Nope." I cross my arms over my chest.

"Yep," he says, mimicking my stance. "It was right after you came back from East Hampton. The day after, I think. I remember because she told me I had a great tan, and didn't say a word about you."

My brother always seems to have a great tan.

"I should have known you'd forget that meeting." He slaps the center of my back. "You had just spent the weekend with Greer. Your mind was not on business."

He's right about that, so I shrug off the comment. "You can take the stairs and meet her in the lobby."

"Her name is Carol," he says with a smirk. "I can also just call her and say what I need to say."

"Which is?" I gesture toward the corridor that leads to our offices.

"To tell her what a great job she's doing."

Leave it to my brother to compliment every employee whenever he gets the chance. That's who James is.

"Did you hear the good news?" He elbows my side.

I glance at him before I dart a finger into his bicep. "What good news?"

"The Sweet Indulgence news."

"What?" I ask, my voice catching in my throat.

Any news that remotely involves Greer is news I want to hear right fucking now.

"You really like her," James accuses, but there isn't a teasing note in his tone. "I don't know her, but she's built a solid business with Krista. That tells me a lot about her."

It tells me that she has strength and fortitude. It tells me the woman has grit and a will to succeed that not many people possess in this industry.

I loosen my tie slightly. "What's the news?"

"She really didn't tell you?" He motions for me to step to the left to allow room for Sasha to pass.

She's on a call, so all we get is a weak wave from her.

Jameson waves back. I nod because I know Sasha isn't focused on us at the moment. She takes her job seriously, and that has always meant she blocks out everything but the task at hand.

"Greer didn't tell me a thing," I say before I go on. "I haven't spent a lot of time with her. The last I heard, she wasn't interested in selling to us."

We reach the open door to Jameson's office, and he's the first one to step inside. My office may be bigger, but my brother's is a better reflection of who he is as a person. There are framed pictures of his wife and son on his desk. He even took one of us with his phone at the beach house a few months ago. It's in a dark wood frame in the center of his desk. I keep meaning to ask for a copy of it, but the request always gets lost when a business matter pops up.

Before taking his seat behind his desk, he motions for me to sit in one of the two guest chairs that face him.

I settle into the left one because the right one has a lump on the seat that always jabs my thigh. I've complained to my brother about it more than once, but he tells me the chair once belonged to our grandfather, so it stays as is.

"Krista and Greer had a clause in their partnership agreement that didn't permit either to sell the business without the other selling as well."

"That's complicated." I lean back in my chair.

"That's putting it mildly." James touches the corner of one of the framed pictures of his wife. "My guess is they didn't see an end in sight to their partnership when they signed that document. They do now."

Crossing my legs, I loosen the knot on my tie more. "Do they?"

"Krista called an hour ago to tell me Greer has proposed they cut the clause from their contract."

"Which means Krista can sell her half to us," I finish his thought before I point out something my brother is well aware of. "We don't partner with companies. We buy them."

"That's not a hard and fast rule, Holden."

He's right. We've never put it in writing, but the intent of our purchasing fledgling candy companies and taking them under our wing has always been clear. We're broadening our customer base and expanding our reach.

Jameson calls our end goal "*global candy domination.*" I call it good business.

"What would we gain by partnering with Greer?" The question is almost laughable coming from me.

All I want to do is partner with her, but I want a bed to be involved and plenty of orgasms for her...*and me*, but her pleasure is all I think about.

"I'm the one who did the initial research into them," he states bluntly.

"I know," I stress the point. "You view the company as a worthwhile acquisition. My question is, do you still view it through that same lens now that we won't have complete control?"

"You don't get it, do you?" he says, exasperation evident in his expression.

"I don't get what?" I ask calmly because that's what he needs from me.

Jameson needs me to listen to him. For too long, I didn't, and silencing his voice is something I will never do to him again.

"I tasted every single product they're selling." He stares

at me. "They're all great, but some have the potential to make us millions, Holden."

"Millions?" I question for clarity.

"Tens of millions," he amends his first declaration. "If we buy Krista's stake in the business and can convince Greer to mass produce what she's already producing on a small scale, we do a test run and distribute to a handful of our global locations."

We've taken this approach plenty of times in the past and have enjoyed good results in most cases, but I've never seen this look in my brother's eyes before. I can tell he's viewing this through a new lens. He's considering how Sweet Indulgence offerings will complement what we're already selling under our brand.

"Long term, I see us phasing out Sweet Indulgence entirely. We'll offer Greer a boatload of money to sell her half to us, and she'll accept," he says as though it's a foregone conclusion.

I laugh so hard my head falls back.

He chuckles, too. "What's so fucking funny?"

I regain my composure and smile at my younger brother. "You're underestimating her will to succeed, Jameson. She's committed to Sweet Indulgence."

His gaze drops to the picture of his wife. "She sounds a lot like my wife. Sinclair's been working hard for years to make a name for herself in the literary world."

My sister-in-law's ghostwriting career has launched her into a solo and very public endeavor. She's penning a fact-based book on our grandparents. Interest in the project is already off the charts.

"They are alike," I agree with a brisk nod. "Sinclair has never given up on her dreams. Don't expect Greer to give up on hers. If we do happen to partner with her, we're in it for the long haul."

Jameson shoots me a sly smile. "Something tells me you would be good with that."

I don't argue the point because he's right.

I'd be more than happy to partner with Greer in any capacity for as long as she wants.

CHAPTER FORTY-FOUR

Greer

"THAT SETTLES IT." Martha claps her hands together as her face beams bright with a smile. "Bruce and I will cash in all of our investments and become your silent partners. This is perfect, Greer. It's just perfect."

It's a disaster waiting to happen.

"I…well…no, Martha." I shake my head. Hard. "I can't let you do that."

Her head cocks to the left. "Why not?"

I could list a million reasons why it would be a bad idea, but I go with the first one that pops into my head. "I already have some leads on people who want to invest."

I don't bother mentioning that both of those people are my parents. When I bemoaned to them that I was on the hunt for a new business partner, they both got way too excited at the prospect of moving back to New York to work "hands-on" with me every single day.

I love my folks, but their lives are running smoothly, without the complications of spreadsheets, lost orders, and unhappy customers.

Besides, I need to find someone who has some business acumen so I'm not chasing after them about every decision they make.

"Is one of those people your lover?"

I'd cringe, but laughter is my first reaction. "Martha!"

"There's nothing to be ashamed of, Greer." She drinks from the martini glass in her hand. "I've had lovers."

Okay.

This conversation stops now.

Since we're out in the small yard behind the house and Olive is already in bed, I can't hold out hope that she'll come racing in with a problem that needs to be solved in an instant. Bruce is out for a stroll, so he's not going to rush to my rescue either.

"I can't partner with him." I sip from my glass.

If Martha were ever looking for a way to spend her evenings, she'd make bank as a bartender. This apple martini she made me is the best I've ever had. I decide to use that to steer the current conversation we're having straight off the rails.

"This martini is divine, Martha."

Her left eyebrow perks. "You told me that twice already, Greer. I know what an attempted diversion looks and sounds like."

She tilts her chin toward me.

I pat her hand as if I'm chasing away a silly notion. "I was simply complimenting you on the great drink."

"You were simply trying to get me to drop the subject of your lover."

"Holden," I spit out his name so she'll stop referring to him that way. "His name is Holden."

"He must be a good man. My money is on him being a strong man. He's handsome, too, I bet?"

"You got all of that from his first name?" I finish what's left in my glass, hoping that she'll offer to make me another.

That doesn't happen. She just smiles as I place the empty glass on the small white table set between our chairs. We're in the corner of the yard near one of the two white lilac bushes Bruce planted the week after we moved in.

"He's okay to look at." I shrug.

A giggle falls from her lips. "I'm going to take that to mean he's beautiful."

That's not a word I'd use to describe a man, but it somehow fits Holden Sheppard. He is beautiful, handsome, gorgeous, great in bed…

"You're daydreaming about him," she says bluntly. "Naughty daydreams."

"If by naughty you mean me telling him to keep his big hands off my business, then yes, it's a naughty daydream."

"Big hands, you say?" She sips from her glass.

I try as hard as I can to keep a straight face, but it's all in vain. "I can't want someone who is trying to steal my business."

"You can want anyone you damn well please, Greer." She balances the base of her glass on her thigh. "I hate disagreeing with you, but steal may not be the appropriate word here. From what you've told me, it sounds like he's being upfront with his desire to partner with you. Partner is the important word in that sentence, dear."

I know she's right, but I tilt my head back and close my eyes. "Why are you so rational?"

"It comes with age," she uses the same line she always does when I question how she's so wise. "Maybe a partnership with this Holden fellow is just what you need."

I glance at my empty glass.

"I'll make you another if you promise to hear him out," she pleads Holden's case for him even though they've never met. "Listen to what the man is offering, take a few days to think it over, and then decide what's right for you."

"And for Olive," I whisper.

"Our girl has her entire life ahead of her." She moves her glass from her thigh to the table. "She may decide to take over the business, or she might go to medical school. Maybe she'll teach grade school."

"The world is her oyster," I agree with a nod.

"Olive and Celia would want you to do what's best for you." She reaches for my hand to squeeze it. "It's time to think about that. Put Greer first."

"That's hard for me," I say, my voice cracking as I think about Celia and every dream she never got to fulfill.

"Do you remember how long you debated going to The Hamptons?" She winks. "If you don't, I'll remind you. It was weeks, Greer. Weeks."

She's right. I did have a war brewing within me about that. Part of me didn't want to leave Olive for that long, but the other part of me knew it was what I needed. After seven years, I needed a few days to catch my breath.

"You and Bruce are the reasons I did it," I tell her.

"We'll always be here for you." She squeezes my hand again, tighter this time. "We want what's best for you. You're the one who needs to decide what that is without taking everyone else into consideration. Think about what you want your future to look like."

For the first time in what feels like forever, I'm not sure about that.

I think I may want Holden Sheppard to be part of my future. The real question is, do I see him as a business partner or more?

Is there a chance he could be both?

CHAPTER FORTY-FIVE

Holden

> Unknown: We should talk.

I STARE at my phone's screen, hoping like hell I'm looking at a text message from Greer.

Just as I'm about to type out a response, asking the sender to confirm their identity, they shoot another message my way.

> Unknown: It's me. Summer Time.

I may be standing in the middle of the library, but I almost let out a loud "fuck, yeah!" I refrain not only because the librarian would give me hell, but I'm with Kirby, and the little angel always calls me out when I curse.

"You look happy, Uncle Holden." She stares at me from where she's been standing next to a shelf that houses her current reading obsession.

Lately, she's been obsessed with a series of girl detective

novels that her dad and mom are teaching her to read. Since I had a few hours free in my schedule today, and Rook had a last minute order to appear in court, I offered to bring Kirby here to return the books they had read together and to pick out a few new ones for the coming week.

"I'm always happy when I'm with you."

Doubt taints her expression. "Are you texting a girl right now?"

I should be, but I don't want Kirby to think I'm neglecting the very important process of picking out just the right books. I'm here for her.

"Not right now, no." I smile. "I'll text the nice lady back in a little bit."

She closes the short distance between us with hurried steps. "Do you want to kiss the nice lady?"

Everywhere for hours, but I keep that to myself.

"I need to talk to the nice lady about business," I tell her.

"What's her name?"

"Greer," I say without hesitating.

I may not share everything with Kirby, but I try not to put her in a position where she feels I'm keeping a secret from her.

We have a special bond that rivals the one she has with Rook's brother, Milo. We both view the almost six-year-old as smart and intuitive. She trusts us to give her the straight facts whenever we can.

"I like that name." Her blue eyes shift from my face to something behind me. "A boy from my day camp is here."

"A good boy or a bully?" I ask, although I can tell by the way she's smiling that the boy in question will land on Santa's nice list this year.

Kirby likes him. That's all I need to know.

"We should say hi to him, Kirbs."

"What?" Her hand jumps up to cover her mouth. "No way."

I steal a glance over my shoulder at a little boy with blond hair and a man with him who is sporting the same color hair. I'm not an expert at pinpointing family dynamics from afar, but something tells me that I'm looking at a dad and his son.

"What's the problem?" I ask, keeping my tone even as I fight to keep a smile from creeping over my lips. "It's good manners to say hi to someone you know when you see them."

"Who says?"

"Me." I perk a brow. "I'm a good manners expert."

"I heard you tell my dad to get lost on the phone last week." Her hands drop to her hips. "That's bad manners."

I've been telling Rook for years to keep our calls off speakerphone, but he doesn't listen. "I was teasing him."

She glances past me. "It doesn't matter. Bode is leaving now."

I reach for her hand. "We can catch up to them. There's an ice cream stand two blocks from here. You can buy Bode a cone."

"I don't have any money." She fidgets on her feet. "What if he says no?"

"I'll spot you a ten." I smile. "Sometimes people do say no, Kirbs, but you never know if they will until you ask the question."

She tugs on my hand. "Can we come back and get some books after?"

"You bet."

"Let's go." She sets off in a run, dragging me with her.

We're out of the library and heading down the sidewalk hot on the heels of Bode, when I spot a beautiful woman with red hair across the street.

"Hurry!" Kirby urges. "He's going to get away."

Faced with the choice of chasing her friend or pursuing the woman I can't stop thinking about, I do what needs to be done.

As we weave our way through the pedestrian traffic to catch up to Bode and who I think is his dad, I call out, hoping my voice carries over the noise of this city. "Greer!"

She stops, turns toward me, and smiles brightly. Her hand darts in the air just as a bus speeds past on the street, blocking both our views.

When it's gone, she's still there with the same smile on her face. "Holden!"

"I'll call you!" I yell. "Give me an hour. I've got an ice cream date now."

"It's not a date!" Kirby screams loud enough that it grabs everyone's attention, including Bode and the man he's with.

I can't hear it, but I see Greer laughing.

Jesus, she's so fucking beautiful, and I'm the luckiest guy in this city that I get to talk to her as soon as I make this ice cream non-date happen.

Greer sends me a final wave before she disappears into the foot traffic.

I straighten the lapel of my suit jacket and extend my free hand to the blond guy holding tightly to little Bode's hand. "I'm Holden Sheppard. My niece, Kirby, would love to buy you and Bode an ice cream if you have the time."

Kirby squeezes my hand lightly. I steal a glance at her face to see her beaming.

This day is shaping up to be a good one, and it'll get even better later when I talk to Greer.

CHAPTER FORTY-SIX

Greer

MY HEART FLUTTERED in my chest when I saw Holden holding tightly to the hand of a little girl who can't be that much younger than Olive.

Seeing him like that broke open something inside of me. For the first time since we said goodbye in East Hampton, I viewed him through a lens that wasn't clouded by business.

I saw him before he spotted me, but I looked away because I was overcome with emotions. I don't know if he'll ever become a part of my daughter's life, but seeing him looking down at the girl at his side convinced me that he's not the big, bad business stealing brute I've been making him out to be.

When he called my name, and I looked at him for a second time, I saw a flash of the man I met at the beach house more than two months ago. He may have been wearing a tailored suit and expensive tie today, but he was relaxed and at ease.

I loved seeing him like that.

Glancing up, I realize I've arrived at my destination. Smiling, I step through the open doorway and breeze inside, stopping briefly to say hi to the doorman.

"Greer!" A woman screams my name from across the lobby. "Your crew set everything up this morning. It's perfect."

The crew she's referring to consisted of Krista's brother, Burt, and a friend of his. The duo almost always volunteers to set up when someone orders a candy buffet.

Krista's younger sister is our usual hostess, but she's out of town with friends, so that duty has fallen on my shoulders.

I'm not complaining. I'm in the lobby of a gorgeous building on Park Avenue headed toward a sprawling penthouse.

I glance down at the calendar on my phone to jog my memory. I had the job on the forefront of my mind until I saw Holden. Everything I was thinking about was erased in that second.

"Hi, Minka," I say the name I noted in my calendar for this event. "How are you?"

"So excited." She backs that up with a slight twirl to show off the lacy pink dress she's wearing.

I'm decked out in the outfit I typically wear when I take on the role of candy buffet hostess. One of my dark green Sweet Indulgence T-shirts is beneath a black blazer. I opted for black jeans and heels today to give off a semi-professional look.

"It's going to be a fun afternoon." I smile because it will be fun and profitable for my company.

The candy buffets started as a side hustle, but they currently make up a good percentage of our yearly revenue.

"Let's get upstairs." Minka dashes toward a bank of

elevators. "The bride-to-be has no idea that all of her favorite candies will be waiting for her."

I take pride in knowing that.

As we board one of the available elevator cars, Minka turns toward me. "I gave your number to two friends already today. One needs you for a fifth birthday party next month. The other is a corporate job. It's some sort of retirement party in a few weeks."

"Thanks, Minka," I say, grateful for the business she's sending my way.

"There will be a lot more." She winks. "We're expecting more than fifty guests, Greer. Get ready to have a very full calendar for the next few months."

That's all the extra assurance I need to know I'm making the right choice by holding onto my half of Sweet Indulgence. All I have to do now is find the right partner.

THREE HOURS LATER, I exit the elevator with a smile on my face and a nice cash tip in my wallet.

I told Minka that it wasn't necessary to tip me more than she had when she paid the invoice for her event. We've always had a policy of payment upfront, since we realized pretty early on that people change their minds, and when that did happen, we were stuck with an overabundance of candy that we had to sell at a discount rate.

My smile widens even more when I see who is waiting for me on one of the leather benches set up against the wall to the left.

"Greer!" Holden calls out my name as he gets to his feet. "It's good to see you."

I feel exactly the same way about him.

"I'm sorry I'm late," I apologize as he walks toward me.

"You're not late."

He's wrong. I'm definitely late for our planned meeting in this lobby.

When he texted me shortly after I arrived, I told him I'd be free two hours later. When I realized that wasn't going to happen, I texted him again and added an extra thirty minutes on.

I gave him the address of the building, so we could meet out front before going for a drink. The drink was my idea, and he was on board without question.

"I'm guessing you were here for an event?" he asks, taking in my outfit as he rakes me from head to toe.

Surprised that he jumped to that conclusion based on my clothes, I tug on the lapels of my jacket to straighten them. "You can tell that based on what I'm wearing?"

His chin lifts. "By what you're wearing on your head."

My hand leaps up to find one of the fake metal tiaras that Minka was putting on everyone's head as they arrived. She snuck one on mine when I was busy explaining the ingredients in one of our most popular hard candies to a party guest. I must have forgotten about the tiara that is adorned with three pink stones.

I snag it off my head with a swipe. As soon as it's in my hands, I carefully try to bend it. It gives without any resistance, which means it'll be the perfect surprise for Olive.

"You're going to give that to your daughter, aren't you?"

My gaze pops up to meet Holden's. "How do you know that?"

"You're already adjusting it to fit her head." He reaches for it. "May I?"

I hand it off to him. He delicately moves the ends in, being mindful of the sharp metal on the edges. Once he thinks it's the perfect size for my little girl, he bends the edges over so they're dull to the touch.

He holds it up to look at his handiwork. "How's that?"

"It looks perfect to me." Something colorful on his wrist catches my eye. I laugh a little as I point at it. "What's that?"

He hands me the tiara before pushing the sleeve of his suit jacket up far enough to reveal a colorful beaded friendship bracelet.

"It's a gift from Kirby," he says proudly, flipping his wrist over to reveal six beads spelling out Uncle H.

I skim a fingertip across them. "It's beautiful. That's the little girl you were with earlier?"

"Yeah." He gazes at the bracelet. "I've been there for her since day one. I'm lucky I get to spend as much time with her as I do."

There is so much more to this man than meets the eye.

"Are you ready for that drink?" he asks, buttoning his suit jacket. "Are you hungry? I could go for a little food alongside our wine."

"I'd like that." I fish my phone out of my purse. "I need to make a call first."

He nods, as if he understands completely that I have to check in at home. "Take all the time you need, Greer. I'm not going anywhere."

CHAPTER FORTY-SEVEN

Holden

WE BOTH CLEARED our plates at Atlas 22. The seafood restaurant is quickly becoming a favorite of mine. It's located in the West Village, and the owner is a great guy who appreciates all of the candies I deposit in his hand as an added tip whenever I'm in.

I didn't have any to offer today, but he didn't mind. He was too busy chatting with Greer about the trio of lollipops she pulled out of her purse to give to him when he mentioned his kids.

She made a point of inviting all of them to Sweet Indulgence's store next week for a private testing of a new candy that's about to hit the market.

Her heart, head, and soul are in that business. Jameson is a fool if he thinks she'll ever sell her half to us.

"When you texted me earlier, you said we should talk," I remind Greer. "Do you want to do that here or at my place?"

Her answer is swift and concise, "I want that to happen at your apartment."

My hand immediately darts in the air to motion for the waiter to come over. "I'll settle up."

She scans her phone's screen as I do that, even though it takes longer than I'd like, since the kid who served us is determined to talk baseball with me. I'm surprised he remembered that we had a brief conversation about his favorite team the last time I was in here.

As soon as he takes off, I glance at Greer. "Are you ready?"

She drops her phone into her purse and smiles. "I'm as ready as I'll ever be."

So am I. I have no idea what the topic of discussion will be, but I'm all in regardless. I could sit for hours and just stare at this woman. The fact that I get to do that in the comfort of my home is a bonus.

I stand and place a hand on the back of her chair as she slides it back a few inches.

She gazes up at me. "You're kind of charming."

"Kind of?" I laugh.

"That's what I said." She stands, too. "I kind of like that about you."

I'll take the compliment. I wish to fuck I could snap a picture of the way she's looking at me, but if I drag my phone out of my jacket pocket now, the moment will be lost.

I stare at her to cement this moment in time to memory.

A soft smile coasts over her lips. "What are you thinking about?"

"I kind of like you too," I say. "I kind of like everything about you."

AS SOON AS we're in my apartment, Greer slips her shoes off. She lets out an audible sigh of relief as she does. "Finally."

I toe out of mine, too, but there's no relief to be had since my shoes are custom-made. It's money well spent. Jameson has told me more than once that it's wasteful, but he has yet to discover the comfort that comes with shoes that are designed to fit your feet like a glove.

"If you have a seat, I'll rub the pain away." I wiggle the fingers on my right hand. "I promise it'll be relaxing."

"Can you promise it won't lead to you massaging other parts of me?"

"I can't promise that." I shake my head. "A guy can dream, can't he?"

Rubbing the back of her neck, she smiles. "I'll take a rain check on the foot rub."

"Cash it in whenever you want."

She watches intently as I slide my suit jacket off and place it over a decorative chair in the foyer. The designer I hired to help me decorate this place thought it added a 'touch of whimsy' to the room. It might, but it's become more of a spot for me to deposit my jackets, keys, and whatever else I lug in here.

My cuff links end up on the chair's cushion, followed by my tie.

"You're not getting naked, are you?" Greer asks through a stuttered giggle. "I mean, I wouldn't complain about it, but we do need to talk."

I wade my way through all of that to come to the conclusion that she's not against seeing me nude at some point tonight.

"I'm getting comfortable." I point at her. "You can lose the jacket if you want."

She doesn't need to hear anything else to be convinced to shrug off her jacket. When she does, she lets out another sigh. This time it's louder.

"Maybe you're the one who needs to get naked, Greer."

Her eyes light up. "I need to talk to you about that."

"What's there to talk about?" I stalk toward her. "I have no issues with you stripping right here."

Her hands leap to the center of my chest. The fingers on her right hand skim the buttons on my vest. "I have an issue with doing that and being your business partner."

This conversation is going just as I wanted it to. I anticipated that she'd want to steer clear of partnering with Carden if she was interested in me on a personal level.

It may break Jameson's heart not to get his hands on Krista's half of Sweet Indulgence, but he'll get over it. He'll have to.

I reach down to cup her hand in mine. "Tell me what you want, Greer."

Silently, she scans my face. Her gaze locks on mine. "I know you said that you're not interested in more than what happened at the beach."

"That was then. This is now." I kiss her palm lightly. "You said the same to me."

"This is now. That was then," she says, smiling brightly.

"I want to see where this could go," I admit. "I want to take you to dinner, lunch, drinks. I want to talk to you, laugh with you, and *fuck*... I want to fuck you again."

"To be clear," she starts before she plants a soft kiss on my chin. "I'm not partnering with Carden. I won't approve a deal between you and Krista."

"Understood." I smile broadly.

She bites the corner of her bottom lip. "You don't have to look so happy about it."

I fake a frown. "Is that better?"

"Your brother will be upset, won't he?" she asks, genuine concern in her tone.

"For a split second." I kiss her cheek. "He'll get over it."

"Krista will, too," she says, but I hear the uncertainty in the words. "She'll have to."

"Do you have another partner in mind?"

Shrugging both shoulders, she gives her head a shake. "Not yet, but I'll contact a few people who may be interested."

"No one who swims naked in pools, right?" I tease.

She kisses my jaw softly. "Definitely no one like you."

CHAPTER FORTY-EIGHT

Greer

I UNDRESSED him before I let him get his hands on me. Peeling back each layer of his clothing to reveal his glorious body left me in awe.

Holden Sheppard is magnificent.

I look up from where I'm kneeling. I've been here, pleasuring him with my lips, mouth, and teeth since I tugged his boxer briefs down.

His cock was hard and aching for attention, so I couldn't resist.

He drags a hand through my hair, pushing it back from my face. "If you keep doing what you're doing, I'll come down your throat."

I circle the crown with my tongue, smiling as I do. "That's not a bad thing, is it?"

"It is if I want to fuck you in the next two minutes."

He tugs on my hair, encouraging me to stand. I enjoy one

last lingering lick along the length of him before I oblige and push up to my feet.

"I was having fun," I say, pretending to be upset.

He sees right through me. "Lose your clothes and you'll have even more fun."

"You want me to strip?" I tease with a fingertip poised on my bottom lip. "Right here. Right now."

He glances around his bedroom. It's as stunning as the rest of his apartment. The king size bed is the anchor of the far wall. A white tiled fireplace faces it on the opposing wall. Beautiful art and a stylish silver lamp are the only accessories the space needs. It's minimalistic but still impressive.

"Now, Greer." He leaves me where I am to stalk toward a dresser near the bed. After sliding the top drawer open, he pulls out a condom package.

When he turns to face me again, he's still as hard as stone. His face is etched with raw need. It's exactly what I feel inside.

He rakes me from head to toe. "Get naked."

"Help me?" I ask because I want to see his expression as he exposes every part of me.

He steps toward me. As he gets closer, he places the corner of the condom package between his teeth.

His hands get busy tugging my T-shirt over my head before he unclasps the front of my bra.

"I need a minute," he growls, the condom package falling to the floor. "To suck on this."

His lips circle my right nipple. The sensation is so overwhelming that it makes my knees weak. I stumble forward a step.

That stops what he's doing. He pops back up to kiss me hard. "I'm aching for you, Greer. Nothing feels as good as fucking you."

It's the same for me. Sex with this man is my bliss.

I tug on the button on my jeans to free it, before I grab hold of the zipper pull. His hand swats mine away. As he takes over sliding my pants down, he drops to a knee to trail kisses over the skin of my thigh.

My hands fall to his hair. I rake my fingers through it, feeling a sense of calmness that I haven't felt since I left him in East Hampton.

When he looks up, there's a soft smile on his lips. He doesn't need to tell me what this means to him. I feel it, too.

Gazing into his eyes, I see something I never thought I would. I see a future with Holden.

HE TENDERLY WASHED me in the shower after we made love. The sex was different. It was as mind-blowing as every other time we've shared ourselves with each other, but today, there was more emotion wrapped around it.

As he entered me, he whispered how divine it felt to be that close to me.

When I came, he told me I was the most beautiful thing he's ever seen, and when he climaxed, he called out my name in a growl.

It was guttural and raw and followed by a kiss so lush and deep I felt my toes curl as he slowly slid his body from mine.

I wait for him to finish drying off. I'm dry courtesy of his thoughtful touch. He wrapped me in one of his robes after, even taking the time to fold up the sleeves until my hands were visible.

He wraps the towel around his waist, tucking in the end so it stays put. A quick rake of his hands through his hair, and he's smiling at me. "I should take my contact lenses out."

"Yes, please." I nod vigorously. "Holden Sheppard in glasses is one of my kinks."

That earns me a hearty laugh. "I want to know the other ones."

"In time."

"We have all the time in the world, Greer." He reaches for a bottle of contact lens solution and a container to hold his lenses that are on a shelf. "I don't mean tonight, but…"

"I know what you mean." I glance out the bathroom door toward his bedroom. "I should go look at my phone, just in case."

"Go," he directs me with a wave of his hand and a smile. "Check on your girl and I'll get all hot for mine."

I can't help but laugh. "You have to know how good you look in those glasses you wear."

"All I care about is that they make you want me."

I want him for so many reasons. The glasses have fallen to a spot near the bottom of the list. His compassion, warmth, and the respect he's shown me regarding my role as a mom and a businesswoman top the list now.

"I do want you," I whisper.

"You have me," he says evenly. "I'm yours for as long as you want."

Forever dances on my tongue, but I keep that word to myself. I'm part of a package deal, and the thought of introducing him to my daughter both thrills and terrifies me.

"I'll go check on my little girl." I take a few steps forward to kiss his bare shoulder. "Then I'll meet you in the kitchen."

"I'll be there." He spins around quickly to kiss me on the lips. "No rush, though. Take as much time as you need. You're always worth the wait."

CHAPTER FORTY-NINE

Holden

I SPRINT to get to where Rook is waiting for me. It's been just over an hour since Greer left my apartment. She wanted to get home to kiss Olive goodnight, so I suggested we meet up for dinner later this week. She was on board for that.

Something important shifted between us today. It's not going to be easy telling my brother that any chance of a deal with Sweet Indulgence is now dead, but he'll get it. I know he will once I explain that something substantial is brewing between Greer and me.

"You look happy," Rook says as soon as I'm near him. "Are you in love?"

I have no fucking idea. I thought I was in love when I married Finella Livesay. I popped the question and went through with the ceremony because I thought it was the right move for me. At the time, it was. Not only did it quiet Finny's questions about whether I'd ever take things to the next level, but it won me a race. My grandmother awarded me the role of CEO of Carden because I got married before my brother.

Dollar signs and control were what pushed me to marry Finella. Her infidelity tore us apart. I mourned the relationship briefly before I put the entire fiasco behind me.

"I'm in a hard like," I tell him.

His brow furrows. "Frame it however you want. I'm more concerned with how you came to choose that shirt and those pants."

I glance down at my charcoal gray pants and the black button-down shirt I'm wearing. I plan on going to the office after we visit Declan and his family.

My gaze slides to what Rook's wearing. It's black pants with a charcoal gray sweater.

I huff out a laugh. "At least it's not an exact match today."

"Close enough." He chuckles. "Did you get the goods?"

That brings more laughter out of me. "The goods? It's a box of chocolate cigars, Rook."

I hand it off to him, so he can inspect it, although he knows exactly what they taste like since he's a big fan of Wolf Candy's chocolate bars.

"Why don't you make these?" He taps the corner of the box on his palm. "You could corner the market. Your reach is widespread."

"Nothing we come up with will compare to what Nikita Wolf is making," I admit. "Her chocolate sales beat ours every day of the week in this city."

Nodding, he glances at the building Declan and his family live in. "It's time to fight over who gets to hold our new nephew."

Neither of us is related to Gilbert Wells by blood, but he's our family. He will always be our family.

"You can hold him first," I offer as we enter the lobby. We both nod in appreciation at the doorman as he holds open one of the heavy glass doors. "When he cries, and he will, I'll take him from you."

Rook pats my shoulder as we walk side-by-side toward the elevators. "You do have a way with kids, Holden. You're going to be a good dad one day."

I press my finger into the call button before I glance at him. "As good as you, Rook."

"Don't get carried away." He grins. "You'll do all right. My daughter loves you. Gilbert will, too."

I can only hope he's right. My friends' kids and Jameson's son are a big part of my world. I'm not counting on smooth sailing when it comes to meeting Greer's daughter, but maybe someday, that little girl will see me as a friend.

I EXIT the elevator on the floor that houses the executive offices of Carden Confectionaries. It's well into the evening now, but there are still people milling about. Everyone who works for us understands our vision and knows that if they do a great job, they'll be awarded appropriately.

Yearly bonuses are a given here, so I'm not surprised to pass one of our sales staff in the corridor on the way to my office.

I also breeze past the woman I practically ignored the other day. "Hi, Carol."

She stops mid-step to look right at me. "Good evening, Mr. Sheppard."

"Holden," I correct her, even though only a handful of our employees have been given the go-ahead to call me that.

"Holden," she repeats my name in an almost whisper.

"Are you on your way in, sir? Do you need me to help you with anything?"

My gaze drops to the wide gold band wrapped around her ring finger. The birthstone pendant hanging off her necklace is another clue that Carol has a family to get home to. There are at least six colorful stones on the pendant.

I was tempted to buy one just like it for my grandmother years ago, but I hesitated because my relationship with Jameson was fractured at the time, and I thought the pendant would only serve as a reminder of that whenever my grandmother looked at it.

"I'm good," I assure her. "You should get home."

"I'm on my way out for the night," she says, and I swear there's a sigh of relief wrapped around the words. "Two subway rides and I'll be home sweet home."

I don't know if the good mood I'm in is all related to Greer, or if holding baby Gilbert has something to do with it, but I whip my phone out of the pocket of my pants and initiate a call to the private car service we use when needed.

Jameson tends to use it more than I do, but I can't fault him for that. He has a family to rush home to every night.

I order a car for Carol and end the call quickly.

Her gaze trails over my face. "What did you just do, sir?"

"I made sure that you'll get home in time to enjoy some of your evening." I point toward the elevator. "The car will be in front of the building in less than five minutes. Your driver is named Atticus. Point him in the right direction and he'll get you there in good time."

She steps toward me as though she's about to hug me, but she stops short. "Thank you, sir."

"Holden," I remind her. "It's Holden."

"Right." She grins. "If you're looking for Jameson, he's left for the day."

I'm not surprised.

I'll break the news of the lost Sweet Indulgence deal to him tomorrow. For tonight, I'll clear my desk of old business. It's the best way I know to get my mind off of Greer for at least an hour or two since all I want to do is reach out to her, so I can hear her voice one last time tonight.

CHAPTER FIFTY

Greer

I TIE a pink ribbon around the base of Olive's ponytail. "All done."

"Is it nice?" she asks, tugging on the end of it. "I hope it's nice, Mommy."

"The ponytail is perfect," Bruce says as he stands in the doorway of Olive's room. "The dress is, too."

"Do I look fancy enough, Grandpa?" She spins in a circle, showing off her light blue dress. "I know the museum is a fancy place."

I hide a smile behind my hand because my daughter loves a day trip to any of the museums in the city. It's not just that she's fascinated by the art. Olive loves to people watch.

"You look like a young lady who is going to show her grandpa the sights and sounds of the museum today," he tells her. "I'm very proud to be going there with such a smart and well-dressed girl."

That brings a big smile to her lips. "You look good too, Grandpa."

Bruce skims a hand over the front of his short-sleeved checkered shirt. "Thank you."

"Can we get something for lunch after?" she asks with a sly smile. "Maybe something round with some little pepperonis on it?"

"We have to get pizza," he insists. "It's our tradition now, isn't it?"

She rushes over to hug him. "I love our traditions, Grandpa. I love you."

I watch their tender embrace, grateful that my ex-husband's parents stepped into a situation that their son ran from.

The day Olive was born, Bruce and Martha lost a son because he wasn't ready to be a father. They tried to talk to Aaron about the joys of being a parent, but he wanted nothing to do with it.

He stormed out of their lives just as they stepped into mine to help me in any way they could. They've reconnected with Aaron since, but they've never wavered in their devotion to Olive.

"Can you meet us for pizza, Mom?" Olive glances at me. "Or we can bring some to the store for you."

I was planning on spending the majority of my day in New Jersey at our production facilities, but if I stay in Manhattan for the morning, I can make a few calls. It's time for me to reach out to people who I think may be interested in buying Krista's share of the business.

It's a short list given that I need to be comfortable working with them, but there's potential there.

Considering that the museum they're headed to doesn't

open until ten-thirty, I know my daughter will be more than ready for pizza by noon. "At noon?"

Bruce nods in agreement. "We'll bring some sodas, and apple juice for Olive."

She scrunches her nose. "Good because the bubbles in soda tickle my nose."

I gather up her hairbrush and the rest of the package of hair elastics from the foot of her bed. "I hope you have a fun morning, you two."

Olive races back across her room to wrap her arms around my waist. "Oh, we will, Mommy. I know you have fun at work, but I hope it's extra fun today."

I love that she views my work as fun. In many ways, I do, too, but right now I feel like the weight of the world is on my shoulders.

Krista is doing her best to find a new co-owner, but so far nothing has worked out on her end.

"You know we will do anything for you, Greer." Bruce catches my eye. "I talked to Martha again last night about things, and our position on that business matter hasn't changed."

The fact that they're still trying to convince me to partner with them warms my heart. "You've already done so much for me."

He looks at his granddaughter. "We can never repay you for what you've done for us. You gave us a little girl to love."

"It's me." Olive laughs. "You're talking about me, Grandpa."

"Of course I am." He leans a shoulder against the doorjamb. "Should we double check with Grandma to see if she wants to go to the museum with us?"

"No." Olive shakes her head. "Grandma is going to have

tea with some friends today. She wants to talk to them about cro…something."

"Crochet." Bruce nods. "We'll leave her to that."

"Can we go now?" Olive runs back to Bruce, grabbing his hand in hers. "We can walk through the park."

This city has so much to offer all of us, but a mid-morning stroll through Central Park is one of the best.

"You can walk with us for a bit, Mom, right?" she asks hopefully. "I can show you where Grandpa sometimes feeds the pigeons."

I can't say no to that, so I don't. I nod. "Give me a minute to grab my things and I'll meet you downstairs."

"I'll race you!" Olive yells as she takes off ahead of Bruce.

He hangs back for a few seconds. "I meant what I said, Greer. We can never repay you for letting us into Olive's life. Whatever you need is yours."

"You don't owe me a thing." I rush toward him to wrap my arms around him. "Thank you for loving her as much as I do."

"Always." He kisses the top of my head. "We will love that little girl forever. We love you, too."

"I love you," I whisper.

"Grandpa!" Olive yells from the bottom of the stairs. "I beat you."

Bruce gives me one last kiss on the top of my head. "I'll go down and keep her busy until you're ready to go."

I watch as he walks away, wondering how I got so lucky in life. I have a beautiful family and a man I can't stop thinking about.

I haven't been this happy in a very long time. It feels good. It feels so damn good.

CHAPTER FIFTY-ONE

GREER

"I TALKED to Nikita Wolf about buying my half of this beautiful business," Krista announces as she walks into Sweet Indulgence with a bottle of water in one hand and what smells like a cup of coffee in the other.

I'm about to ask if the coffee is for me because I could sure use it. I didn't grab a cup at home because I wanted to stroll through Central Park with Olive and Bruce. On my way here, Burt texted me to say he had a family emergency and needed to leave. He was vague with the details. That made sense since I texted Krista right after that to ask what the emergency was.

Burt was called in for a last minute audition for an off-Broadway musical.

It seems the family emergency was all about him hoping his family could watch him on the stage one day.

Krista slides the coffee cup across the checkout counter toward me. "I got it just the way you like it, Greer."

CHARM

I'm hoping that's because she views it as a celebratory gift. Partnering with Wolf Candy would be ideal. Nikita Wolf has built her very successful business from the ground up. Combining her premier chocolate with our candy seems like a win-win to me.

"Thank you," I whisper. "You said you spoke to Nikita?"

"I did." A smile blooms on her lips. "She mentioned that Holden Sheppard was in her store yesterday."

I suddenly wonder if he's out canvassing for a potential partner for me. If that were the case, he would have told me when I saw him.

"He was buying something for a friend." She sighs. "He seems like a great guy, Greer. Are you sure there isn't a chance for more between you two?"

I want nothing more than to tell her there's not only a chance, but we're going to pursue things to see where it all leads. Right now, though, I want to hear about what happened when she asked Nikita about buying her out.

I decide to go the direct route, so Krista doesn't wander off course again. "What did Nikita say about buying your half of Sweet Indulgence?"

She unscrews the cap of her water bottle and takes a long drink. If she's trying to forcefully push me into agony, she's doing a great job.

"It's a no," she says. "She loves our products but is looking to expand her business, so she's focused on that right now."

A small jolt of disappointment courses through me, but partnering with Wolf Candy was a long shot.

"I take it you haven't had any luck finding someone to buy me out?"

"I'm working on it," I say, honestly.

"We'll find someone." She lifts her bottle in the air, motioning for me to do the same with my coffee cup.

I do, smiling the entire time. "What are we toasting to?"

"To the future." She grins. "To my life in California, and the beautiful life you've built here."

We both turn in unison when the store's door swings open and Olive comes racing in.

Bruce is on her heel with a pizza box and a paper bag with twine handles.

"Pizza delivery!" Olive yells. "Krista, you're here!"

My little girl runs toward Krista at breakneck speed, darting around several displays until she's got her arms wrapped around my dearest friend.

"I've missed you," Krista whispers as she strokes Olive's hair. "You're getting so big."

Olive glances up at her face. "One day I might be taller than you."

Krista's eyes fill with unshed tears. "You're so beautiful, Olive."

"You're not crying, are you?" Olive hugs her tighter. "What's wrong?"

"I'm so happy to see you," Krista explains as she shoots me a look.

I know it well. She needs me to save her from the overwhelming emotions she's feeling. This doesn't happen every time the two of them are together, but as Olive's gotten older, it's become more frequent.

Olive steps back before she comes to me. When her arms wrap around my waist, I feel the same sense of gratitude I do every time I get to hug her.

"There's enough pizza for all of us," she tells me. "We can have a fun lunch break."

"I'd love to share that pizza." Krista's voice wavers. "I always like hanging out with all of you."

Bruce sets the pizza box on the counter along with the paper bag. "I'll run to the back to get napkins."

"I know where they are!" Olive screams, setting off in a sprint to grab a handful of the napkins I keep on the desk in the back room. "I'll race you again, Grandpa."

A low chuckle falls from between Bruce's lips. "Something tells me winning a race against that little one isn't in the cards for me."

He leaves the room, walking at his usual, unhurried pace.

"He's so good with her," Krista whispers once Bruce is out of earshot. "They love her so much, Greer."

"They do."

She twirls her engagement ring around on her finger. "I know raising her hasn't always been easy."

"I've loved every second of it," I say, my voice breaking. "I love her so much."

"Me too."

I reach for her hand to quiet her anxiety. I can always tell when Krista needs reassurance that everything is okay. "She's growing up so fast."

"She really is." She smiles through a sob. "I can't believe how much she looks like…"

"Mom!" Olive interrupts Krista at the precise moment I know I would have broken into tears. "You had some pink napkins back there."

I turn my attention to my little girl, tucking a strand of her hair behind her ear. "I got those just for you."

"I knew it." Her entire face beams with pride. "I'm starving. Can I dig in?"

The bell above the door signals a new arrival, so I steal a glance in that direction.

Two women walk in. One of them is holding tightly to the hand of a toddler. All three of them look to the left, before their gazes shift to the right as they take stock of everything in the store.

"I'll handle them," Krista offers with a hand on my forearm. "You enjoy the pizza."

I pick up the box and the bag with the beverages, and point toward the corridor that Olive and Bruce just came from. "Let's go eat in the office."

Olive looks at Krista. "I'll save you two pieces."

Krista bends down slightly, scooping the four-leaf clover pendant hanging around Olive's neck into her hand for just a moment before she kisses my daughter's forehead. "I can't wait."

I hear the emotion that's still swimming in her voice, but she stands up straight, clears her throat, and gets to work helping our customers.

CHAPTER FIFTY-TWO

Holden

I WALK into my office to find my brother behind my desk. He's sipping on a coffee while he stares at my laptop screen.

"Snooping doesn't look good on you, James," I say. "Did you at least get me a coffee?"

"Why would I?" he barks back with a grin. "You broke my heart. I may never recover."

That tells me all I need to know about why he's hanging out here. I had a meeting this morning that kept me out of the office. I stopped for a quick bite for lunch. I used the time to plot out exactly how I'd tell my brother about the lost Sweet Indulgence deal. It seems he's already heard about it.

"You'll recover." I round my desk to smack his shoulder. "Get out of my chair."

He moves to stand. "Mine is more comfortable."

"That's debatable." I drop my phone on my desk.

Another sip of his coffee is followed by a heavy sigh. "Unless you tell me that the reason we're not partnering with

Greer is because you don't want to mix business and pleasure, I'm about to yell at you."

"You're not going to yell at me."

His brows perk. "So there is something going on between the two of you?"

"There is," I admit. "We're navigating through it, but spending time with her is the best, James."

His gaze jumps over my face. "You're falling for her. You're falling in love with her, aren't you?"

I'm not ready to admit that to myself yet, so I sure as hell won't admit it to my younger brother. "We like being together."

It's not exactly what he wanted confirmation of, but he takes it with a grin. "Good. I want you to be happy, Holden."

"I'm happier than I've been in years," I say with confidence.

"That makes losing the deal worth it."

"Thanks, James." I pat his shoulder. "We'll find you another company to obsess over."

"I already found three." He holds three fingers in the air. "All are great fits for us. I'll forward you the specs later today."

Just like that, he's moving on.

"Sounds good." I tilt my chin up. "How are Morgan and Sinclair today?"

"Perfect as always." He smiles. "You can stop by for dinner tonight if you're free."

"I'll be there unless I get a better offer."

"Understood." He laughs. "You like Greer more than you like me."

All he gets from me in response is a hearty chuckle.

"After all the shit you went through with Finella, you

deserve to be happy." He lowers his tone. "I'm sorry I wasn't around when your marriage fell apart."

Since we weren't talking at the time, James didn't know anything about my divorce until it was final. He helped me pick up the pieces afterward. To me, that counts for a lot.

"That's my past," I remind him. "I'm focused on my future."

"With Greer?" he asks with his left eyebrow cocked. "This could be your forever, Holden. Can you see yourself having kids with her?"

I'm nowhere near thinking about that yet, but I fill him in on the most important person in Greer's life. "She has a daughter. Olive. She's seven."

Jameson's eyes light up as he smiles. "That's fantastic. Have you met her yet?"

"No." I shake my head. "I'm hoping we'll get there in time."

He pokes a finger into the center of my chest. "You will. When you do, Olive will think you're great. Just like Morgan does."

I can only hope that's the case.

The closer I get to Greer, the more I want things to work out between us. What started as a weekend of fun has the potential to morph into a lifetime of memories. I'm not going to get ahead of myself, but I can see it in the distant future, and I like the way it looks.

I'M ABOUT to indulge in a late afternoon treat that has the potential to turn my day around.

After I got to the office earlier and had the brief discussion with my brother about Greer, all hell broke loose.

One of our deliveries was lost somewhere between North Dakota and New York State. A store with our name on the awning in Seattle caught on fire. It was contained to a corner of the storeroom, and no one was hurt, but it did shake up the two employees who were present.

I called them both personally and assured them that we're here for them. Marc is scheduled to fly out there tonight to address the situation in person. He's an expert at handling a crisis, so I know the employees will be taken care of. Marc will deal with all the insurance issues, too.

I swing open the door to a café that I've become familiar with over the past few years since it's around the corner from my office tower.

I spot Greer immediately as soon as I'm inside. Her hand jumps in the air to greet me, but the smile on her face is what I can't take my eyes off of.

I was surprised when she texted me asking if I could spare a few minutes for a coffee. I was out of my office and in the elevator before I texted her back that I was all in.

I go in for a hug when I'm close enough to make it look natural.

There's absolutely no resistance from her. In fact, she doubles down by kissing me lightly on the cheek. I pull back far enough to look into her eyes.

"If there weren't so many people here, I'd kiss you," I whisper.

"Do it," she challenges.

Without any hesitation, I cup a hand behind her neck, tilt her head ever so slightly, and claim her mouth in a kiss that leaves no question about how desperately I want her.

CHAPTER FIFTY-THREE

Greer

THAT KISS WAS JUST what I needed.

I left a meeting that didn't go as planned right before I walked into this coffee shop around the corner from Holden's office. I saw it as an opportunity to steal a few minutes alone with him. Fortunately, he viewed it through the same lens when I texted to ask him to meet me.

I breathe in a mouthful of air as he watches me intently. "What's going on, Greer?"

"You're the best kisser I've ever known."

A smile parts his lips. "I'll own that title with pride. I'm working toward being the best of everything in your life."

He already is. He's proven he respects me in a way my ex-husband never did. Holden gracefully bowed out when I told him I wouldn't approve a sale between Krista and Carden. He honored my decision.

I chew on the corner of my bottom lip. "You are already the best at a lot of things."

"That involve my mouth?" he whispers. "If there weren't so many people here, I'd go down on you."

Laughing, I slap the center of his chest playfully. "That only works with kissing, not with oral."

"Stop by my apartment later and I'll satisfy both of our cravings."

Considering it, I sigh. "It would need to be after Olive goes to bed. Bruce and Martha love reading her bedtime stories, but I prefer to do it."

He nods. "Of course. Are Bruce and Martha your nannies?"

I shake my head. "They're my ex's parents."

I'm not surprised when he steps back an inch or two. "Oh."

It's the reaction I was anticipating. I want to explain more, but dumping my sordid past on him while we stand in line waiting to order coffee isn't how I saw this unfolding.

"I want to share more about all of that," I tell him while gazing into his eyes.

He adjusts his glasses slightly. "I really want to know more about that."

I tug on his tie to straighten it. "Tonight? We can talk about it a bit when I come to your apartment. I don't have to rush home, so if you want to take your time kissing me goodnight after we talk, I'm all for that."

It's a roundabout way of expressing my hope that after I tell him about my ex and what happened between us, he won't want to end things.

"I'm all for that, too." He lightly brushes his lips over my jaw for a kiss. "Come by whenever you're ready, Greer. I'll be waiting for you."

"Hey, Holden!" A man's voice calls over the noise in the coffee shop. "There you are!"

We both turn in unison to see Jameson approaching us. As soon as he spots me, he taps his palm against his forehead. "Shit. I'm sorry, Greer. I didn't see you there."

"It's fine," I say as I notice him silently mouthing the words "*I'm sorry*" to his brother. "How are you?"

"I'm great, thanks. You?"

I turn my attention back to Holden. "I'm the best I've ever been."

A soft smile coasts over his lips as he stares into my eyes. "Me too."

Jameson clears his throat, luring his brother's attention toward him. He shoots him a frustrated look, but he doesn't say a thing.

"We need your signature on some documents, Holden," he explains. "I wouldn't have tracked you down if this wasn't urgent. It's regarding the fire."

"What fire?" I blurt out, my gaze volleying between Holden and Jameson.

Holden reaches for my elbow, grazing a finger over it. "One of our locations in Washington State caught fire. Everyone on site is fine."

"I'm glad everyone is okay," I say. "I'm sorry about the fire."

"Me too," Jameson adds his voice to the mix. "I'm also sorry I have to drag my brother away."

"Duty calls." I smile at Jameson. "I'll grab my coffee to go."

"Put it on Carden's tab." Jameson gestures to the barista counter. "Feel free to do that anytime you're in the neighborhood."

"That's very generous of you. Thank you."

He nods at me. "It's the least I can do. You've put a smile on that guy's face lately. That means something to me."

I look at Holden to find him grinning at his brother as he playfully admonishes him, "James, enough."

"He means something to me," I admit. "I hope the fire recovery goes smoothly."

"Thanks," Jameson tugs on the sleeve of Holden's suit jacket. "Let's go."

Holden gifts me with one last kiss. This one is in the center of my forehead. "I'll see you tonight, Greer."

"Tonight," I whisper. "I can't wait."

MARTHA STANDS in the open doorway of my bedroom with her arms crossed over her chest. The jean jumpsuit she's wearing has a multitude of pockets. From where I'm standing, I can see the head of one of Olive's favorite small stuffed animals poking out from one. Another is barely hanging onto the corner of a dishtowel.

Martha is beautiful in a simply elegant way. She has exquisite bone structure and long hair that was once light brown but has now become soft waves of gray. She's always garnering second glances from the people we pass on the sidewalk.

Her heart is just as beautiful as her face. I love my mom, but Martha has filled a spot in my life I didn't know was empty.

"You're thinking about something," I say with a teasing glance. "Tell me what's on your mind."

"Slip some clean undies and a fresh T-shirt in that tote you're taking." She points at the weathered brown leather tote I've been carting around all day.

I chose it this morning because I wanted to take my laptop

with me so I'd have Sweet Indulgence's sales data at the ready if a potential buyer asked to see it.

The meeting I had right before I met up with Holden at the café didn't get past the initial handshake stage. As soon as I mentioned how small of an operation Sweet Indulgence is, I was shown the door.

I'm not deterred, though. There are still plenty of fish in the financial sea of Manhattan. With Krista and I both on the hunt for someone to take over her shares in the company, we can't fail.

"Excuse me?" I laugh. "Are you saying what I think you're saying?"

Martha steps closer to me, lowering her voice even though Olive is fast asleep in her bedroom at the far end of the hallway. "A sleepover isn't the worst idea, Greer."

Shaking my head, I scoop up the handles of the tote to place it over my shoulder. "I'm not sleeping over at Holden's apartment."

"Bruce and I are here for our girl," she reminds me. "You can get home before she wakes up if that's your concern."

I sigh. "I'm not sure what my concern is."

"Then maybe there isn't one." She moves to within a few inches of me, so she can tuck a strand of my hair behind my ear. "I've never known anyone more worthy of happiness than you. You sacrificed everything, Greer. It's time for you to start thinking about you again."

I place a hand on her shoulder and squeeze. "None of it was a sacrifice. I'm so lucky."

"Then go get lucky." She winks. "Have fun tonight. If you happen to fall asleep, I'll call at six-thirty to wake you up. Will that give you enough time to get back here before she wakes up?"

I nod. "Okay. If I do happen to drift off, I'd appreciate that call."

"Or if you happen to not fall asleep at all?" she asks with amusement in her tone.

I move in for a hug. "You're the best, Martha."

Her hand lightly strokes the back of my head. "So are you, my darling dear."

CHAPTER FIFTY-FOUR

Greer

I PLACE my tote on the seat of one of the chairs next to Holden's dining table. After Martha left my bedroom to head down to the kitchen to make her nightly cup of tea, I took her advice. I slipped a fresh pair of lace panties in my bag along with a blouse.

I'm currently wearing a light blue T-shirt and white jeans. I have no idea how the night will go, but if I do stay over, I'll be able to walk out of here in something slightly different than what I arrived in.

It's not that I'm worried about an early morning walk of shame. There will be absolutely no shame attached if I spend the night in Holden's bed. It's what I want. I can't speak to what he'll want, but I'm hoping it's the same thing.

"Can I get you anything?" he asks from where he's standing near the door.

He greeted me with a hug and a soft kiss in the lobby of the building. I was grateful to see him waiting for me when I got out of the rideshare. As we rode the elevator up, he reached for my hand, weaving his fingers in between mine.

It was contact I wasn't aware I needed, but it gave me strength and courage.

Very few people in my life know my story.

I've kept it that way for many reasons, including the need to protect Olive. She knows most of what happened before and after she was born, but I've shielded her from the majority of the details surrounding my divorce from Aaron.

"I'd love a glass of wine," I say without hesitation.

I won't indulge in more than one, but I know the alcohol will calm my nerves a bit. I could use that right about now.

"I'll pour one for each of us."

He breezes past me. His cologne lingers as he does. I inhale deeply. There's just something so comforting about the small details. His glasses, his cologne, and the sound of his laughter have all become a part of who he is to me.

I smile when I spot the friendship bracelet on his wrist. I'm wearing mine tonight, too.

As soon as he's back in front of me, he hands me a glass half-filled with deep red liquid. I smell it with my eyes closed because it's just that good. I can't help but smile when I have my first taste because it's a notch above anything I would ever buy for myself.

He sips, too. "It's good, isn't it?"

"Very."

Nodding, he takes another drink before placing his glass on the dining room table. "You're nervous, Greer."

He's right, so I don't argue the point. "I am."

"Talking about the past isn't easy." He tilts his chin down. "I know that from experience."

"Because of your divorce?" I whisper.

"Yeah." He moves a step closer to me, stopping to rest his

hand on the back of one of the chairs. "Finella and I were on and off for years before I asked her to marry me."

I shouldn't feel even a bite of jealousy since we didn't know each other then, but I do. It's irrational, but the thought of him loving someone else enough to ask her to marry him stings.

"How long were you married?" I ask, placing my hand next to his on the back of the chair.

His hand inches forward until his fingers brush against mine. "Until I caught her in bed with a friend of mine. It wasn't that long after we got married."

Shocked that any woman would cheat on him, I shake my head. "I'm so sorry that happened to you."

"It was rough," he says curtly. "In other ways, it wasn't. To be honest, we probably shouldn't have gotten married in the first place, but there was some family pressure."

I didn't have to deal with that. I married Aaron because I loved him, or I did until the day it all fell apart.

"I'm sorry you went through that, Holden."

His gaze finds mine. "I appreciate that, but it was for the best. Finella wasn't right for me."

I want him to say I am, but we're not there yet. He doesn't even know the details of my divorce.

I take a deep breath. "I was married to a man I met in high school. On the day we got married, I thought Aaron and I would go the distance."

"Aaron," he repeats my ex-husband's name. "What happened with him, Greer? What went wrong with you and Aaron?"

I take another sip of my wine. "Maybe we should sit down before I tell you about that. It's going to take a while."

He finishes the last of his wine in one swallow. "I'll meet you on the couch after I grab a refill. Do you want more?"

I want to get this conversation over with, but I'm determined to do that without too much alcohol. "I'm good."

He starts to walk away, but stops to curl his hand around the back of my neck. Looking into my eyes, he kisses me softly. "You have no idea how glad I am that you found me naked in that pool."

I can't help but smile. "I feel the same way."

"We were both right where we needed to be that night," he says matter-of-factly. "We're right where we need to be tonight, too."

I believe that with every fiber of my being.

"I'll be right back." He kisses me again. "Go sit down and get comfortable."

CHAPTER FIFTY-FIVE

Holden

GREER IS A BUNDLE OF NERVES, and I wish to fuck I could make that all go away for her. I don't know what happened in her marriage, but something is tearing her apart.

I walked back into the main living area with a full glass of wine and a clear view of her profile. Her gaze was cast down to her lap. Her shoulders were bouncing slightly as though she were filled with nervous energy.

I'm sitting next to her now, waiting for her to say something. At least two minutes have passed since I sat down, so I bite the bullet and start the conversation. "How long were you and Aaron married?"

"Too long." She half-laughs. "We got married after college. He filed for divorce seven years ago."

Seven years ago.

They had a baby seven years ago, too.

I can't help but wonder if they're connected.

Since she doesn't say another word, I ask a related question. "You mentioned your ex's parents read Olive bedtime stories sometimes. I take it they live in the city?"

I want to know more about Aaron, so asking about his parents seems like a solid path to get me there.

"They live with us," she says. "Martha and Bruce live with Olive and me."

Surprised by that, I just nod.

"I have a townhouse on the Upper East Side. They have their own space on the top floor. It's not a full apartment since there isn't a kitchen, but they have a bedroom, a bathroom, of course, Martha's craft room is up there, and there's a nice little sitting area for them."

I never had a close relationship with Finella's folks. In fact, I haven't heard a word from them since we divorced, but I like it that way. We had nothing in common other than their daughter, and I always wondered if her father could tell I wasn't committed to the relationship as Finny was.

"They've helped me with Olive since she was born," she says with emotion lacing her voice. "I lived in an apartment back then, and they stayed at a hotel close by until they found a rental in the same building."

I lived in an apartment back then, not we.

I replay that in my mind once and then again.

"Where was Aaron?" I blurt out. "Did you separate before Olive was born?"

Her bottom lip trembles slightly as her gaze scans my face.

I instinctively reach for her hands to hold them in mine. "If you're not ready to talk about this, Greer, I completely understand. We can stop for now. I don't want to push…"

"Aaron left me the day Olive was born." She lets out a sob. "He wasn't ready for kids. He wanted no part of it, so he just walked out of the hospital and never looked back."

WHAT KIND of piece of shit did she marry? Who the fuck waits until his wife gives birth to tell her he doesn't want to be a father?

Jesus.

I gently run a hand over Greer's hair as I hold her against me. She's been crying for the past few minutes. I'll hold her forever if that's what she needs from me.

"I have to tell you something," she whispers.

"You can tell me anything."

She pulls back to look at my face. There's a deep sense of sorrow in her eyes that I'd do anything to chase away. I don't want her to feel pain. If I could carry that burden for her, I would.

She glides a hand over her mouth before swiping it across her cheeks. "I love Olive with my whole heart. She's everything to me."

"I know." I catch the last tear streaming down her face with my thumb. "I can hear it in your voice when you talk about her. I can feel it, Greer."

She nods silently, perching her hands together near her lips as if she's in prayer. "I lost my best friend in the world seven years ago."

Fuck. That year put this woman through the wringer.

"Christ." I exhale audibly. "You've been through a lot, Greer. I wish I had known you then."

A soft smile coasts over her lips before it disappears. "My friend's name was Celia."

"What was Celia like?" I ask because I've never felt anything but gratitude when someone asks me that question about my grandparents.

Talking about them helped me navigate my grief. It's

been years since her friend died, but mourning doesn't follow a set timetable. It hangs over a person like a storm cloud, letting chaos loose when you least expect it.

"Beautiful," she begins before taking a sharp breath. "Brilliant, kind, caring, and funny as fuck."

I laugh. "She was special."

She nods. "So special. Her aunt raised her. We met in grade school, but then she had to transfer to a school in Queens. My mom made sure we still got to see each other, though. She always made sure that we were a part of each other's lives."

"Your mom sounds amazing, Greer."

"Oh, she is." She grins. "She lives in Denver with my dad and my grandma, but they were ready to move back and help me raise Olive. They came for Cel's memorial service, of course, and to meet Olive."

"But, Aaron's parents stepped up to help with their granddaughter?" I ask.

Her top teeth scrape her bottom lip slowly. "She truly is their granddaughter. They've never viewed Olive as anything but family, even though…"

"Even though what, Greer?"

I think I know the answer to that question, but I suspect she wants me to hear it direct from her.

She shakes her head slightly. "Olive isn't Aaron's daughter."

Warring emotions crash over me like a tidal wave. I'm falling in love with her. I know it. I feel it. There's no denying it, but she's telling me that she was married to a man when she gave birth to another man's baby.

That doesn't automatically equal an affair. She could have gone the IVF route with donor sperm.

She squeezes my hand slightly, luring my attention back to her face.

Her eyes lock on mine. "Olive isn't my daughter either. I mean, she is. Of course, she is, but I didn't give birth to her. I adopted her."

I'm confused, but don't say a word because I hope she'll fill in the blanks for me.

"Olive is Celia's daughter," she whispers. "Cels died the day Olive was born. It was before she had a chance to hold her for the first time."

CHAPTER FIFTY-SIX

Greer

HOLDEN STARES AT ME. He's speechless. I don't blame him. I just dumped a lot in his lap.

"She passed away from an amniotic fluid embolism." I take a deep breath in an effort to calm my emotions. "Not enough oxygen was flowing to Celia's brain. There was nothing that could be done."

"Fuck, Greer." He rakes a hand through his hair. "I'm so sorry. I'm sorry for you and for Olive."

I nod in appreciation for his kind words. "Olive knows about Celia. I've always talked about her. She has some of Celia's favorite trinkets on a shelf in her room. There's a framed picture there of Celia when she was pregnant. Olive wears Celia's favorite pendant on a gold chain around her neck sometimes."

Holden watches intently as I tap my fingers on my chest. "Her heart is as pure as Celia's was."

He rubs a hand over his jaw. "Tell me about her."

"Celia had a soft spot for animals." My laughter envelops the words. "She convinced me to volunteer at an animal rescue with her when we were teenagers. I ended up loving it."

Holden smiles. "Olive wanted a kitten. You two must have passed that on to her."

Holding back tears, I smile, too. "She's so much like Celia."

He squeezes my hands. "It's truly remarkable that you stepped in to take care of her."

"I can't imagine not doing that," I admit. "When Celia was pregnant, she worried about a lot of what-ifs since she didn't have any family. Her aunt was her only relative, and she died when we were nineteen."

"What about Olive's dad?" he asks the question I knew was coming.

I scratch the back of my neck. "It was a one-night stand. They didn't even exchange fake names."

He laughs at the reminder of our three-day stand in East Hampton. "Understood."

"She was determined to raise Olive on her own. Celia had chosen the baby's name as soon as she knew she was having a girl." My voice breaks. "Celia was scared about the possibility of something happening to her in the future, so she had a lawyer friend of hers draw up a will. She named me her baby girl's guardian."

"You took it a step further and adopted Olive?"

"I had to," I tell him. "It felt right."

He lifts my hand to his lips to kiss my palm. "I'm sorry you went through all of that, Greer."

"Thank you." I rest my head on his shoulder. "When Aaron walked out, his parents stepped up. We have a beautiful little family now. It may seem unconventional from the outside looking in, but we're happy. They truly are Olive's grandparents in every way that matters."

"That's what families are," he says, kissing my temple. "They're people who love each other through thick and thin. Martha and Bruce sound like good people."

"They're the best." I smile even though he can't see it. "Their son was the worst."

"Their son is an asshole."

I sigh. "Aaron didn't want to be a dad at that time. I had to be a mom. I wanted to be Olive's mom, so I didn't fight him on the divorce."

"Does he visit his parents often?"

I fight the urge to ask him if we can talk about Aaron later, but he's curious, and my answer won't change whether I address this now or a month from now.

"He moved out of state shortly after our divorce was finalized." I take a breath to gather my thoughts. "He showed up on my doorstep about a year ago asking to see his parents."

"Did that surprise you?" He runs his hand over my shoulder, soothing me.

"A little," I answer honestly. "He wanted to talk about us. I told him there would never be an '*us*' again. He has moved away again since, but did come back a few times to take his parents out for dinner. They always met him at a restaurant. Aaron knows that I want nothing to do with him. I never will again."

He kisses my head again before motioning for me to shift slightly so I can see his expression. "You're an unbelievably strong woman, Greer. I'm in awe of you."

That touches me deeply. I've always strived to be a source of strength for those around me, especially my daughter.

"I know it's soon, but I'd love for you to meet Olive," I

say without giving it a lot of thought. "Only if you'd like to meet her."

"Are you kidding?" He laughs. "I'd love to meet her."

"You can come over for dinner one night," I suggest. "Martha and Bruce do date nights twice a month, so we can plan for one of those nights. That way you won't be thrust into meeting everyone at once."

"You name the night and I'll be there," he says as he stares into my eyes. "Meeting your daughter will be an honor."

I tilt my chin up in a silent offering. He obliges, lowering his mouth to mine.

AN HOUR LATER, I roll onto my back, laughter falling from between my lips. "That was something else, Joe."

Holden chuckles as he swipes a hand over his brow. "Why am I sweating so much? You're the one who rode me."

"You did plenty of the work." I look over his nude body, noting that he's semi-hard even though he just came. "It looks like you could go again."

"Give me a minute to catch my breath." He pats his rock hard stomach. "I need to get rid of the condom and grab something to drink. You wore me out."

"You wore me out," I whisper. "You always do."

His head snaps toward me so our eyes lock. "I love fucking you, Greer."

"I love fucking you, too."

His gaze lingers on mine, and his lips part as if he needs or wants to say something else, but nothing escapes him but a heavy exhale. "I want to eat you. That was my intention when I dragged you in here."

"You didn't drag me in here," I correct him with a slap on his chest. "You took my hand and brought me in here."

"True," he agrees with a brisk nod. "Then I tore your clothes off, dropped mine on the floor, and told you to get on top of me."

That pretty much sums it up, other than the fact that he took a slight detour to slip on a condom.

"Fair warning that my mouth is going to be on your pussy exactly five minutes from now." He glides his tongue over his bottom lip. "I'll need at least an hour to savor that."

"An hour?" I purse my lips together.

"Two it is."

Shaking my head, laughter bubbles out of me. "I'll come in the first two minutes, Holden. I won't need an hour or two. You're an expert at oral."

He kisses me softly. "I love the taste of you. Only you, Greer. You'll grant me an hour to enjoy myself. Promise me you will."

I'm not going to argue that point with him. Why would I?

"When I'm done eating you, I'll order something in for us to eat." He slides away from me to swing his long legs over the side of the bed. "You can stay for a while, can't you?"

I watch him stand, marveling at how cut and defined his body is. "I need to be home before Olive wakes up in the morning."

"I'll make sure you are." As he turns back around, I notice the tissue in his hand. The condom is gone, so it makes sense.

"Thank you."

"For what?" he asks, squinting slightly. "For wanting to have as much time with you as I can? You have to know by now that I'll take whatever you can give me. I'm falling for you, Greer."

It feels like my heart is ricocheting inside my chest. I'm scared to admit how I'm feeling, but he's worth the leap of faith, so I nod. "I'm falling for you, too."

He holds my gaze for a few seconds before he smiles. "I'll be right back. Promise me you won't go anywhere."

"I won't," I tell him. "I'm yours for the entire night."

CHAPTER FIFTY-SEVEN

Holden

I STAND NEAR one of the windows in my office and look out over the city that has been such an integral part of my life.

I love New York, but there have been moments when I've hated it.

After my marriage crumbled, I thought about leaving it all behind.

My brother wasn't talking to me at the time. I'd disappointed my grandmother by not giving her the heir to the family business that she desperately wanted.

I never felt like a failure, but I was pretty damn hard on myself.

Everything has turned around now, though. I'm the CEO of the company my grandparents worked tirelessly to build. I work side-by-side with my brother, and I'm an integral part of his life now.

Then there's Greer.

Fuck, I'm so lucky I met her. I feel grateful that she views me as a man worthy of her time and attention.

And tonight...tonight I get to meet her daughter.

"What are you looking at, old man?"

Chuckling, I glance over my shoulder to see Jameson decked out in a sharp looking two-piece suit. He's even wearing a tie. It's a solid look for him.

"I'm looking at my brother looking like the COO that he is."

He tugs on the lapels of his suit jacket. "It's nice, right? I had it made just for me. Trying to follow in my big brother's footsteps."

That hits me right in the center of my chest because recently I've been feeling like I've been the one chasing his footsteps.

He may be seven years younger, but his life is exactly where I want mine to be.

I don't need a newborn baby to fulfill me at the moment, but I would like to have a family someday in the future. Admitting that to myself has been hard. Allowing myself to imagine that family including Greer and her daughter is fucking scary, but the thought has crept into my mind since she confided in me about Olive's birth last week.

We've seen each other a few times since. We've talked more and fucked more. Every second I spend with her helps me to realize what a gift she is.

"I like it," I tell him. "I'm proud of you, James. I don't know if I tell you that enough."

"You don't." He shoots me a smile. "I'm proud of you, too, Holden. I'm proud of how far you've come since the Finella bullshit happened."

That feels like a lifetime ago.

"Why the new suit?" I effortlessly change the subject

because my ex-wife doesn't warrant another second of my time.

"I'm taking my wife out for dinner tonight." He brushes a hand over the sleeve of the jacket. "Before you ask, Berk and Astrid are watching Morgan. I argued the case for you, but Berk and Astrid are a package deal with Stevie, so they won out."

Sinclair's oldest brother and his wife have a nine-year-old daughter who is in love with her baby cousin. Denying Stevie time with Morgan isn't something I'd ever willingly do. Besides, I have plans that are too important to cancel, even if those plans involve my nephew.

"I'm meeting Greer's daughter tonight."

I wait for my brother's reaction, and it's exactly what I anticipated. He rushes over to where I am to grab me for a bear hug. "This is big, Holden. It's huge."

He's right. It's a monumental step, but it feels natural. I want a future with Greer, and Olive is an integral part of that.

"Take Olive some candy," he says.

Since I sat him down a few days ago and explained that Greer is a mom, he's now aware of Olive's name. I didn't dive into the details of her birth or the resulting collapse of Greer's marriage.

That's Greer's story, and I won't tell it without her permission.

I grin. "Have you forgotten her mom owns Sweet Indulgence? She's already eating some of the best candy in this city."

"In this country," he corrects me, fake frowning while he does. "It still hurts that we didn't score that deal."

"You're already over it, James."

"True." He winks at me. "Don't tell any lame jokes tonight."

My arms cross my chest. "I don't tell lame jokes."

"Says the guy who only tells lame jokes." He rolls his eyes. "What was that one you told Sinclair the other night about a bike?"

I laugh because it's a joke Stevie texted me earlier that day.

"Something about a bike falling down?" he tries to remember the setup.

"The bike fell over because it was two tired," I say, chuckling while waving two fingers in the air.

Despite his protest about the jokes I tell not being funny, he laughs out loud.

"You know how happy I am for you, don't you?" he says as his laughter fades. "No one deserves this more than you, Holden."

The fact that I can hear the sincerity in his voice and see it in his eyes hits me hard.

"Denia would be proud of us." I choke up a bit when I mention our grandmother's name.

"You're right. She'd be damn proud of us." He shoves his hands into the pockets of his pants. "We grew up."

"You grew up," I point out. "I've always been the more mature one."

His right hand escapes his pocket just before he darts his middle finger in the air.

I huff out a laugh. "My point exactly, James. That's mature."

He steps forward to wrap his arms around me. "I love you."

We don't say it often enough, but I'm working on changing that. "I love you, too, James."

CHAPTER FIFTY-EIGHT

Greer

IT'S surreal to see Holden Sheppard standing in the foyer of my townhouse. He's holding two flower bouquets. They're both dotted with multi-colored roses. One is larger than the other, but that's the only difference between the two.

"I hope you like roses," he whispers before he leans closer to kiss me softly on the cheek.

His gaze scans the main living area off to the right and the staircase to the left. I know exactly who he's looking for.

"Olive is upstairs making something for you." I smile. "It's a surprise."

It's a friendship bracelet to add to his collection. This one will spell out his first name. She asked what his favorite color was, and since I don't have a clue, I told her to surprise him. She said the beads would look like a rainbow when she's done.

"A surprise?" he questions with a perked brow. "Give me a hint."

Shaking my head, I wave a finger in front of him. "Not a chance."

He pushes his glasses up the bridge of his nose. "I had to try."

"You'll see the surprise soon enough." I motion toward the hallway that leads to the kitchen. "Do you want something to drink? I've got water, soda, wine, beer…"

"A glass of water would be great." He shoves the larger bouquet toward me. "These are for you, Greer."

I take them and inhale the soft scent of the roses. "They're beautiful, Holden."

His gaze rakes me from head to toe. "You're beautiful."

I know he'd tell me that regardless of what I'm wearing. My look tonight is courtesy of my daughter. She chose our outfits. Mine is a pink sundress with a scoop neckline. Olive's dress is frilly with pink polka dots. She insisted that I help her fasten the gold chain with the four-leaf clover charm around her neck. She kissed it before she tucked it inside the neckline of the dress. She said she didn't want it getting in the way of the polka dots.

She doesn't fuss much about her clothing, but when I told her that a friend of mine was coming for dinner, she insisted on wearing something special.

"Follow me," I say with a smile. "I want to put these in water."

Holden's response is a brisk nod.

The sound of his shoes on the hardwood taps out a steady beat as we cross the narrow hallway until we enter the expansive kitchen. This room is one of the reasons why I purchased this home. It's a welcoming space with more than enough room for at least a dozen people to gather.

When I first looked at it with my real estate broker, I made a comment about picturing Olive and a group of her friends hanging out here together after school. A few do come by regularly for playdates, so it's always fun to see them sit at the table, sipping lemonade and drawing pictures.

"Your home is wonderful," Holden says from behind me.

I love this house. I've worked tirelessly to make it into a home that I feel comfortable and safe in. I want Olive to feel that, too. I hope she always does.

"Thanks." I turn to face him. "Have a seat while I put these in water."

He nods again, but this time follows it up with a heavy exhale. "Okay."

"You're nervous, Holden. Aren't you?"

His right hand drags a slow path over the front of the light blue sweater he's wearing. He's paired it with dark gray pants. It's a casual look but still put together enough to impress anyone. "You can tell?"

I lean forward to kiss him softly. "She'll like you. I told her all about you."

His eyes widen. "What did you say?"

"That you're becoming a good friend to me," I start with that before leading into the more mundane stuff. "That you also run a candy business, and you have a brother."

"Good. I sound boring."

I toss my head back in laughter. "You are anything but boring."

"Greatest compliment ever." He smiles.

Part of me wishes we were spending the night together, but that won't be happening. I plan on saying goodnight to him on my stoop before sending him on his way.

I've never introduced a man I've been seeing to Olive before. It makes sense since I've only dated a couple of men since she was born. Neither of those relationships lasted beyond a few weeks.

CHARM

Thundering steps interrupt the moment as Olive scoots down the back staircase.

I've memorized the sound of every creak of the floorboards and each rattle of the railing as she holds tight to it.

She'll come into view in mere seconds.

I glance in the direction of the staircase just as her feet appear. I shift my gaze to Holden's face as he stares intently at the staircase until Olive is at the bottom of it.

She marches over on bare feet and presents her right hand to Holden. "Hello, sir. My name is Olive Irwin. It's very nice to meet you."

Her small hand disappears as he closes his hand around it. He shakes it gently. It's barely even a movement, but his gaze stays locked on her face. "Hi, Olive. Please call me Holden."

She looks up at him. "I really like those glasses. Are they real?"

I laugh hard enough that I can't step into the conversation to tell her that it's an impolite question. One of her teachers at school last year always matched her eyeglasses to her outfit. On the last day of school, she accidentally dropped them on the floor. One of the students stepped on them in his haste to help, and that's when the secret was revealed.

She told him not to worry about the damage because they weren't helping her see at all.

"They are." Holden slides them off his face and hands them to her. "Take a look for yourself."

Instead of holding them a few inches in front of her, she perches them on her nose, being careful to keep a finger pressed against the center of them. "Wow. Everything looks silly to me."

Holden chuckles. "Everything looks perfect to me when I look through them."

She snaps her head to the right to look at me. "Mommy, you look funny."

I tap her shoulder. "I hope you mean I only look that way when you have those glasses on."

She slides them off, handing them back to Holden as she does. Once he has them firmly in his grasp, she turns her attention back to me. "You're beautiful, Mom. Isn't she beautiful, Holden?"

With the eyeglasses back in place, he looks right at me. "She's the most beautiful woman I've ever met."

Olive's gaze drifts from me to Holden. "I think so, too."

CHAPTER FIFTY-NINE

GREER

I WISH I had my phone nearby so I could capture the look on Olive's face as Holden hands the smaller rose bouquet to her. I've seen my daughter smile broadly at many things, but this may top the list.

Her eyes are wide, her lips parted, and she's bouncing up and down. "For me? These are for me?"

"Just for you," he repeats what he said when he first offered the bouquet to her.

"Wowie," she whispers. "Sometimes Mom gets me flowers or my grandma or grandpa does, but they don't look like this."

Holden takes pride in that. I can tell by the way a grin has firmly planted itself on his lips. "I'm glad you like them."

"Like them?" she asks with a slight shake of her head. "I love them. Thank you, Holden. Thank you to the moon and back."

"That's a pretty big thank you," he says. "I'm happy they make you happy, Olive."

"Wait." She stands perfectly still for a second or two. "I have something for you, too. It's in my pocket."

She's about to shove the bouquet back at him, but I take it instead. "Thanks, Mom."

Her left hand dives into one of the pockets on her dress. When she scoops it back out, a few beads are visibly peeking out from her closed fist.

"I made this myself." She half-shrugs. "I know we're not real friends yet, but I think you'll still like it."

"We're friends," he says with a tender note in his voice. "Some people are instant friends."

"That's what we are." She nods vigorously. "You're my instant friend, so here."

Her fist opens to reveal the beaded bracelet. "I put your name on it for you."

Holden takes it from her. His gaze wanders over the entire thing. He takes a second to run his fingertip across the beads. As soon as he's done, he slips it on his wrist. "It's perfect, Olive. Thank you."

"It kind of matches your sweater," she comments, stepping closer to him. "I'm really glad you like it."

"I do." He looks down at her. "I'll treasure it forever."

"That's a long time," she says in barely more than a whisper. "If it ever breaks and you need me to fix it, just tell my mom."

Holden looks at me. "I will."

"I'm going to put your flowers in some water, Olive." I motion behind me to one of the lower cupboards. "Why don't you pick out a vase for them?"

"I'll do that," she says before she sprints in that direction.

Holden leans in to lower his voice so only I can hear it. "I think she likes me."

"She does," I agree. "Her mom does, too."

His right eyebrow perks. "This is already shaping up to be the best night I've had in a long time."

"DINNER WAS DELICIOUS." Holden swipes a linen napkin over his lips.

"I made the salad." Olive's hand pops in the air. "I think I did a pretty good job."

"You did," Holden says. "Did you help with the roast chicken and sweet potatoes, too?"

"I shouldn't say, but that was all grandma," Olive whisper shouts. "She got it all ready for Mom this afternoon and told her when to put it in the oven."

Laughing, I own it. "Martha loves to cook. I'm still learning, but she's the expert around here."

"Grandma is a very good cook." Olive nods. "She's good at sewing, too. She sewed a really pretty dress for me. Do you want to see?"

Since that question is clearly directed at Holden, he nods. "I'd love to see it."

"I'll get it," she announces before she takes off in a run toward the stairs.

As soon as she's out of view, Holden reaches for my hand. He cups it in his before he drags it up to his lips to kiss my palm. "You're a great mom."

The compliment is unexpected but welcome. "That's all I really want to be."

The sound of movement above us lures Holden's eyes to the ceiling. "It sounds like she's moving furniture up there."

"She might be."

"That would give us time to kiss." He cocks a brow. "A chaste one, of course."

I lean closer to press my lips to his for a soft kiss. "Like that?"

"How can a kiss like that make me want you so much?" he whispers. "Why can't I get enough of you?"

I want to tell him it's the same for me. I can't get enough of him. I don't know if I ever will.

The rumble of Olive's feet on the stairs pulls us apart. Holden gives my hand one last squeeze before he drops it.

Olive appears again, but this time, she's dressed in blue. It's the dress that Martha sewed for her just last month. They chose the material together, and Olive sat by her grandmother's side as she worked on her vintage sewing machine. I captured so many images and videos of that because I want to remember it forever.

"What do you think?" Olive spins in a tight circle to show off the dress. "It's so pretty."

Holden's gaze lingers on the pendant hanging from the gold chain around her neck that is now in view. She's tugging on it. I know that move. She does that when she's extra excited.

"You're looking at my necklace, aren't you?" she asks before Holden can say anything. "It's my good luck charm. A four-leaf clover."

He leans forward to get a better look. "With two small diamonds."

"Right." She nods. "My first Mommy gave it to my Mom. I get to wear it whenever I want."

Grateful that I explained Olive's birth to Holden, I glance at him, but his gaze has dropped to his lap. When he does look up, he's focused solely on Olive.

"The dress and the necklace are beautiful, Olive."

She takes a step closer to him. "I was wearing this necklace when I won the spelling bee at school."

He smiles gently. "You must be very good at spelling."

"Average." She laughs. "But whenever I wear this, good stuff happens."

She's now directly in front of him. Her fingers toy with the four-leaf clover charm. "Do you think they're real diamonds. Mommy said they might be, but maybe not."

He stares at the pendant, his gaze never leaving it. "Those are real diamonds, Olive."

I've always suspected they were, too. Celia told me she treated herself to the pendant when she saw it at a market while on a beach vacation with some friends from work. She was struck by the idea that the pendant might bring her good luck.

It did in many ways, and not in others.

It is something tangible that bonds her to Olive, so I hope my daughter treasures it forever.

"I'll take extra good care of it." The pendant disappears into her fist when she closes her hand around it. "Can we have dessert now, Mom?"

A phone's chime fills the air. Holden mutters an apology under his breath before he tugs the phone from his pocket. When he looks up, his gaze catches mine. "I need to take care of something."

"My home office is at the end of the hall." I motion in that direction. "It's the last door on your left."

"I'll be right back." He slides out of his chair, stopping to glance at Olive before he disappears out of view.

CHAPTER SIXTY

GREER

I GLANCE toward my closed office door. It's been fifteen minutes since Holden went in there. I know the weight of responsibility that comes with running my small business. I can't begin to imagine what he's faced with every day.

That makes me even more grateful that he's made my daughter feel so special tonight.

His attentiveness to her has been touching. During dinner, they talked about dinosaurs and astronauts. Olive told Holden about her dream to not only run Sweet Indulgence one day, but also to sail a boat around the world. He told her he has a sailboat, which was news to me.

I could tell that impressed my daughter because she talked about it non-stop until I finally cleared the plates. After dinner, when he showed interest in her necklace, her shoulders pushed back and her smile widened.

She likes him. Nothing could make me happier.

The door to my office swings open. That lures Olive to

her feet since she's been stealing glances at it since Holden went to make that call.

As soon as he's on the approach, I can tell that something is wrong. His steps are determined and heavy, and the expression on his face is unreadable. It's obvious that he was given very bad news just now.

"Are you okay?" I ask as soon as he's stepped into the kitchen.

"Yes," he answers succinctly. "I do need to go, though. I'm sorry."

"Oh no." Olive stomps a foot on the floor. "I wanted to show you the pictures from my birthday party. Mom made a scrapbook out of them with pieces of wrapping paper and all the cards from my friends."

With a slight smile on his face, he drops to one knee in front of her, making sure he's giving her his full attention. "When's your birthday, Olive?"

"I was born on March 4th," she says proudly. "Seven years ago on March 4th."

His gaze scans her face before dropping to her necklace again. "That's a very special day."

"That's what my grandpa says." She laughs. "He always tells me that March 4th is the best day of the year."

"I think he's right." Holden drops his chin as he sucks in a deep breath. "I'm sorry, I do need to go."

Her small hand lands on his shoulder. "That's okay, Holden. Will you come back for dinner again?"

He swallows hard. "I will. I promise I will be back."

"Good." Her fingers tap dance over his shoulder. "When you come back, I want to show you a picture of my first mom."

"You can show me now." His voice wavers slightly. "I can spare a few minutes to see that before I go."

"There's one by the front door." She sets off in that direction. "Mommy put it in a pretty gold frame. I'll go get it."

"I'll help," I call after her.

The frame is special. It belonged to Celia. She treasured it because her aunt had given it to her as a gift for high school graduation. After she passed, I had the last image I had taken of the two of us printed to fit the frame. When we moved in here, I placed it on the foyer table along with a few other important pictures, including some of Olive and me and a couple of Martha and Bruce.

As I brush past Holden, I reach for his hand. He takes mine in his, squeezing it slightly. We walk side-by-side toward the foyer, dropping hands as soon as we near Olive.

She pushes the frame at Holden. "Here it is. You can see that I look like her."

He carefully takes the frame. He studies the picture, not saying a word as he does. The image was taken just a few months before we lost Cels. She had just moved back to Manhattan from Buffalo, so I could help her when the baby arrived. We were having lunch at a restaurant in the West Village. The light from one of the windows was hitting her just the right way, so I shifted my chair to get closer to her and snapped the photo.

"Do you think I look like her, Holden?"

My daughter's voice lures his gaze to her. His bottom lip is trembling as he nods slowly. "You do look like her, Olive."

"I'm the luckiest girl ever because I had two mommies."

He hands the frame to me, keeping his gaze on Olive's face as he does. "I think so, too."

"Do you really have to go?" she asks in a whisper. "You can't stay for just a little while longer?"

He finally glances my way, and I see something I've never seen in his eyes before. Sadness.

It's not unexpected since I always catch a glimpse of that when I tell anyone about losing my best friend.

"He really needs to go," I answer for him. "We need to finish the dishes and get you ready for bed soon."

Olive lets out a deep sigh. "Okay, Mommy."

"Thank you both for dinner." Holden holds my gaze for a few seconds. "I'm really glad I came."

"We are too!" Olive taps the bracelet on his wrist. "Don't forget to call Mommy if this breaks. She'll fix it right up. She can fix anything."

"Your mom is a remarkable woman." He looks at her before he shifts his attention back to me. "Tonight was special."

"It was," I agree. "I'll talk to you soon."

He nods, turns to open the door, and walks out of my home without another word.

CHAPTER SIXTY-ONE

Holden

JAMESON BANGS his fist against my apartment door. "Open the door or I'll use my key. "

I glance in that direction but remain seated on my couch. I don't say a word because as soon as I start talking, I know I won't stop.

I've spent the past two days in here. Alone.

I called in '*sick*' the morning after I had dinner with Greer and Olive. I did that because I was hung over.

I went straight to a bar after I left Greer's house. I thought numbing everything I was feeling in half a bottle of whiskey was a good idea. It wasn't. I ended up having to call Rook to get me home.

He didn't ask questions. He told me he loved me, and whatever it was he'd help me through it.

He can't. No one can.

I've avoided everyone since then, including Greer and my brother. I should have known it would be Jameson who would show up at my door ready to barge in.

"When did I give you a key?" I mutter as he uses it to unlock the door.

"Holden?" he asks as he approaches where I am. "What's wrong? Tell me what's wrong."

I glance in his direction. He's wearing another new suit, and he's had a haircut in the last few days.

I, on the other hand, haven't shaved in days, my hair is a mess, and I'm wearing nothing but a pair of sweatpants.

I hang my head. "Jameson."

He sits next to me. His hand darts to my shoulder. "What happened? You've been out of touch for days. That's not like you."

I start to tell him, but the words get caught in my throat. All that comes out is a pained sound.

He leans closer. "Whatever it is, I'm here for you. I'm not going anywhere, Holden."

I pat his knee. "Thank you."

"When's the last time you ate anything?" He glances at the bottle of scotch on the coffee table. "I see you've been consuming enough fluids."

I laugh for the first time in days. "I've had water. Bottles and bottles of water. I haven't touched the scotch since early yesterday. "

I thought it would serve as a foolproof hangover cure. All it did was make me pass out.

"I'll order some food." His hand dives into one of the pockets of his suit jacket. "What do you feel like eating?"

"A sandwich?" I say without any real conviction attached to it. "A burger?"

He rubs a hand over his smooth jaw. "Get in the shower. We're going to Crispy Biscuit."

I know what he's doing. He's pulling me out of my pity and tossing me back into the real world.

I'd protest, but it's not a bad idea.

Getting out of here and breathing some fresh air will help.

I drag myself to my feet as he does the same. Before I can walk away, he's got his arms around me.

"I know you're going through something," he says. "Talking about it will help."

Maybe it will. Maybe it won't, but he's the guy I need to confide in.

I step back and nod. "I'll get ready to go."

"We'll video chat with Sinclair on the way there," he promises. "Morgan is awake. You'll get a few smiles out of him."

As I look at him, I have to swallow hard to hold back the barrage of emotions I feel. "You're a great father, James."

His gaze scans my face. "I'm a great brother, too. I'm going to prove that to you tonight."

WE WALK NEXT to each other as we approach Riverside Park. It's not quite dark yet, but dusk is settling over the city.

It was my idea to come here because I feel anchored here, and it's always provided me a refuge from the hustle and bustle of my daily life.

East Hampton is the place I tend to run to when I need time to breathe, but I can't leave town now. Truth be told, I'm not even sure I could fully process what I'm going through at the beach house since that's where my life changed so dramatically.

The bench I prefer is vacant, so I point at it. "Over there, James."

"I know," he says. "I followed you here once."

That brings a smile to my face. "When?"

He shrugs. "It was years ago. We argued. You stormed off. I gave chase, but I dropped it when I saw you sitting on the bench. You looked like you needed some '*me*' time."

I spent the last two days drowning in the silence of time alone. I shut off my phone, essentially cutting myself off from everyone, including Greer. When I powered it back up after my shower, I saw three text messages from her and one missed call. Her voicemail was simple and to the point. She wanted me to call her back when I had the chance.

I'll make that happen as soon as I know what to say to her.

We sit side-by-side on the bench, watching silently as people pass us by on the path a few feet away.

Jameson crosses his legs, but he doesn't initiate the conversation. He knows I want to do that. Experience has taught him that.

"I've always wanted to be a dad," I say in a low tone. "That's always been a dream of mine."

That can't be news to him, since I cooed and blew kisses at his phone when we video-chatted with Sinclair and Morgan on our way here.

"You'll get there, Holden," he assures me. "When you do, you'll be stiff competition for the world's greatest dad."

That hits me hard because being a good father is what I want. I want to be there for everything. I don't want to miss anything in my child's life, and yet…

"I am a dad," I say the words for the first time out loud. "I found out that I'm already a dad."

He turns to the side to look straight at me. "What the fuck? You have a kid? When did that happen?"

I take a deep breath to steady my racing heart, but it does fuck all.

"Seven years ago." I rake a hand through my hair. "I had a one-night stand when I was in East Hampton."

"Seven years ago? And you're just finding out now that you have a kid?"

Nodding, I glance at the beaded friendship bracelet on my wrist. "I found out two days ago."

His brow furrows as he tries to put the pieces together. "How did you find out? Did this woman just appear on your doorstep? Do you have a son or a daughter, Holden? Tell me everything."

"The woman passed away." I give more details, trying to build up to saying what needs to be said. "Her best friend raised my daughter. She adopted her."

His gaze jumps over my face. "Your little girl lost her mom?"

"She never knew her," I explain, glancing at the bracelet again. "She died on the day she was born."

He sits in silence with his hand covering his mouth.

"I wasn't there for her." I scrub a hand over the back of my neck. "I haven't been there for her. She grew up without me, James."

He throws an arm over my shoulder to comfort me. "You know now. Things can be different now, right? You can be part of this girl's life."

I clasp my hands together in my lap. "I already am. I met her the other night, James."

"What?" His expression shifts instantly. "What's she like? What's her name? Does she look like you?"

"She's smart." I smile. "Kind. She's full of love to give. I can see grandmother in her face. She has her nose. Her eyes are the same color as ours."

He nods. "What's her name, Holden?"

"Olive," I say my daughter's name for the first time to my brother. "Her name is Olive Irwin."

CHAPTER SIXTY-TWO

Holden

"OLIVE IRWIN?" Jameson repeats. "Greer's daughter?"

I nod. "She's my daughter, too."

He gives me a look that reads all kinds of skepticism. "I'm lost, Holden. You believe Greer's daughter is your daughter? Did she adopt Olive? How long has she known you're Olive's dad?"

It's a lot to have thrown at me, but I brought him here to listen to my story, so I need to tell it.

"Almost eight years ago, I met a woman at a bar near the beach house."

He doesn't look the least bit surprised. He also doesn't say anything.

"I had just finished picking up a birthday gift for grandmother." I shake my head. "She mentioned wanting a gold four-leaf clover charm and she hinted that she wanted diamonds on it. I got her one with two diamonds."

CHARM

"One for each of us," he says, jerking a thumb back and forth between the two of us.

"Yeah," I affirm with a nod. "I couldn't find anything like that, so I had a jeweler custom make it for me."

"You were always a goddamn show off with the gifts." He pats the center of my back. "You always made me look bad."

With a smile, I shrug that off. "Finny and I were on the outs at that time, and this woman was fun, James. She bought me a drink, but didn't indulge. When I had my fill, she suggested we go back to my place, but grandmother was there, so..."

"So you ended up at her place?"

"A hotel," I answer. "She said her hotel had paper thin walls so she suggested one of the nicer ones that border the beach."

"You couldn't say no," he rightfully assumes.

"She was pretty," I tell him. "Friendly and I needed the fun."

"What was her name?" he asks the question I've never once asked myself since that day.

That's been haunting me since I left Greer's home the other night. My daughter was conceived on a night when I didn't have the decency to ask the name of the woman I took to bed. I didn't offer mine either. Maybe if I had, things would have been different.

"Celia," I say, and then add to it, "I found that out the other night while I was at Greer's. When we slept together, we didn't exchange names."

"Lay out for me how this all came to light, Holden." He pats my back again. "I think I'm missing some pieces."

"When I was at Greer's for dinner, Olive showed me a dress that her grandma made her." I stop to consider what I'll say next. "She had the charm around her neck on a chain. It was the charm I had custom-made for grandmother. When I woke up the morning after Celia and I were together, the charm was gone. She took it out of the pocket of my jeans."

"It makes sense that I never saw grandmother wearing it."

I nod. "I couldn't take my eyes off the charm. Then Olive told me her birthday, and the timing lines up. I saw a picture of Celia with Greer, and I knew. I know. She's mine, James."

"Wow," he whispers. "That had to have knocked you on your ass."

"It threw me," I admit. "After I saw the charm around Olive's neck, I excused myself. Greer assumed I needed to make a call, so she directed me to her home office. I didn't call anyone. I tried to catch my breath."

"Understandable," he says.

"Then came the birthday reveal and the picture of Celia." I look up at the sky. "It hit me so hard, James. I slept with her nine months before Olive was born. I'm her dad."

"We need to look at this from a rational place, Holden. The first step, if you haven't already taken it, is talking to Greer."

Without glancing at him, I nod.

"I know you may not want to hear this, but a paternity test is important, Holden," he says evenly. "I hate to ask, but you used protection, right?"

"A condom." I rest my head in my hands. "I always use one. It could have broken, though. That happens."

"It does," he agrees. "The paternity test will put any questions to rest."

My heart is telling me Olive is mine, but I suspect James won't be the only person suggesting a paternity test. I'm sure Greer will want it, too. I don't even know how I'll tell her that I believe I'm the father of her daughter.

It's as fucked up as it is miraculous.

"If you need me to go with you to talk to Greer, say the word," he offers. "I'll back you up in whatever way you need."

I appreciate the offer, so I pat his knee. "I'll handle it, but thanks for this, James. I needed this."

"I won't breathe a word of this to anyone," he promises. "Until you're ready to share the news."

"You're going home to tell your wife, aren't you?" I ask, although I already know the answer. "You'll tell her as soon as you can."

"I'll call her as soon as you walk away." He chuckles. "You know, Sin, though, she'll keep the secret."

I don't intend on keeping my daughter a secret for very long. I want everyone I love to know I'm the father of a beautiful little girl named Olive.

I WALK by Sweet Indulgence even though it's shuttered for the night. Jameson and I parted ways at the edge of the park when he hopped into a taxi.

He offered to have the driver drop me at my apartment building first, but I needed fresh air and time to think.

The conversation I'll have with Greer will be the most important one of my life.

She has dedicated herself to making sure my daughter has had the best life possible. That only makes me love her more.

Love.

I was falling head over heels for Greer before tonight. Now, all I feel is wonder, awe, and gratitude.

I stop directly in front of her shop and press the button to initiate a call to her.

She answers on the second ring. "Hey, Holden. Hi."

"Hi," I say back, smiling like a kid in a candy store. I laugh lightly when I realize I am indeed in front of a candy store. "I'm sorry I've been out of touch."

"Was it a licorice emergency?" I can hear the grin in her voice. "Or was it a caramel catastrophe?"

"Let's hope I avoid both for the foreseeable future."

"You and me both," she says, her voice bright and breezy. "Speaking of which, I'm meeting with a potential new partner tomorrow. I think this may be the one."

I'm too overwrought with emotion to ask many questions, so I ask the only one that matters to me right now. "Can you meet with me tomorrow, too?"

"Meet as in a coffee or meet as in more than a coffee?"

I'd give anything to be in a bed with her right now, but I can't go forward with what's building between us until we talk about Olive. "Let's start with a coffee."

I'm just about to tell her that I want us to drink that coffee at my apartment, but I hear rustling on her end.

"Olive had a nightmare," she says in almost a whisper. "I need to go take care of her."

I close my eyes and take a breath deep enough to fill my lungs with air. "Text me tomorrow to let me know what time works."

"I will."

"Oh, and Greer," I begin, hoping I'm catching her before she ends the call. "Tell Olive I love the bracelet."

"That will make her happy." She sighs. "I'll talk to you tomorrow. Good night, Holden."

The call ends, and I stare at my phone. I'd trade my entire fortune for the opportunity to comfort Olive after she's had a nightmare.

All I can hope for at this point is that I get the chance to do just that soon.

CHAPTER SIXTY-THREE

Greer

I ADJUST the collar of my blouse before I step into Palla on Fifth. The café is one of the nicest in the city. I don't stop here often because it's out of my way and the price of a coffee is almost double what I pay near my store.

It's worth every last drop, though. I don't know how they prepare it or where they source their beans, but it's a true treat.

I spot the man I'm meeting as soon as I'm inside. His arm leaps into the air to wave me over.

Rocco Jones reached out to me yesterday after his wife stopped into Sweet Indulgence to pick up some candy for their son. Dexie Jones made an off-handed comment about how her husband should have invested in a candy store because she loves sweet treats so much. I took a shot and told her that I was actually looking for a new partner.

Twenty minutes later, Dexie left Sweet Indulgence with a bag of candy and a smile on her face. She called her husband while she was with me to tell him about my business. When she switched the call to speakerphone, I was greeted with the voice of what I could tell was a kind man.

It turns out, Rocco is an angel investor who has made it his personal business to pair with companies that are looking for someone with the financial means to take them to the next level.

He's a tall man with dark brown hair and blue eyes. He's dressed casually in jeans and a black button-down shirt. I admit I'm surprised given that he's worth billions.

"Greer?" He extends a hand to me as soon as I'm close enough.

I take his hand in mine and shake it firmly. "Greer Irwin. It's so nice to meet you, Mr. Jones."

"That's my dad's name." He lets out a deep chuckle as he pulls on the back of a vacant chair across the table from where he was seated. "Why don't we sit?"

My gaze drifts to the barista counter. I'm nervous, and one of the only ways I know to calm down is to fill myself with caffeine.

Just as I'm taking a seat, a woman with an apron tied around her waist comes over. "Hi, Rocco."

He goes in for a hug. "Palla, how's everyone?"

That launches them into a conversation about kids, spouses, and a family lunch that's set for this coming Sunday.

When that ends, Palla looks toward me. "Hi, I'm so sorry. Rocco and I haven't caught up in a bit. I'm Palla."

"It's good to meet you. I'm Greer."

"What can I get for you?"

I tell her I'll take a coffee with a shot of caramel syrup. She promises it'll be ready in no time flat before she makes her way back to the barista counter.

"Palla is married to my cousin," Rocco says. "We don't see each other nearly as often as I'd like."

I nod. "This is such a special place."

"When we launched, I knew it was a gem." He smiles. "I told Palla and my cousin, Arlo, we'd do great things here. We have."

"You're an investor?" I ask, surprised by that.

"I am." He nods briskly. "Palla and Arlo are good people. They had a vision that they shared with me, and I jumped in to help."

He's exactly what I'm looking for in my business.

"I sampled all of the candy my wife brought home with her." He shoves a hand through his hair. "It was all very good, Greer. I'm impressed with the products."

That's a big step in the right direction toward a partnership.

"If you're open to it, I'd like to take a look at your financials and set up a time to speak with you and your partner together."

"Of course." I nod since it is Krista's shares that he'll be buying, and that negotiation is between the two of them.

I know she'll be excited that I found someone genuinely interested in a potential deal.

"This could be good for both of us." He smiles. "I understand you have a daughter. I have a son."

I already know that, since Dexie showed me at least a dozen pictures of their son, Bryant, on her phone. I did share a few of Olive with her because it was impossible not to.

"Your daughter must love that you own a candy business." He smiles at the barista who drops off my coffee at the table.

"Thank you," I say to her before I direct my attention

back to him. "Olive loves it. She's seven, so her dream at the moment is to run the business one day."

"Maybe our kids will end up as partners on that." He laughs. "You never know where life will take you."

I know where it's taking me later today. I get to see the man I'm falling in love with. I can't wait to tell him that I may have finally found a business partner.

CHAPTER SIXTY-FOUR

Holden

A SOFT KNOCK at my apartment door tells me the doorman let Greer up without notifying me. I don't blame him. When he gets busy helping other residents with packages and deliveries, his attention is easily diverted.

I take a deep breath to try and slow my racing pulse, but it's useless. I'm sure at some point I won't feel this thundering sensation against my chest wall, but that's not going to happen tonight.

I swing open the door to find her wearing the same T-shirt and shorts she was on the day we met.

It's a trip back in time to a moment I'll never forget. I had no idea when I turned around in Mrs. Frye's pool that I was coming face-to-face with the mother of my child.

"Holden!" she says my name with so much exuberance that I can't help but smile. "I brought champagne."

This moment would be perfect if she had any idea about the bombshell I'm about to drop in her lap. She doesn't, though. The champagne is meant to celebrate something other than the fact we share a child. My guess is that she found a new business partner.

Her gaze trails over my suit. "You look professional."

I point to where my tie would normally be. "I lost the tie an hour or two ago."

"And no glasses?" She tilts her head. "I still like you."

I think I love you.

I keep that to myself because it's far too intense to precede what I need to say to her.

"Good." I kiss the center of her forehead. "I like you, too."

"Will you pop the cork on this?" She lightly shakes the bottle of champagne. "We can toast to the very real prospect of me having a new business partner."

"I will." I take it from her. "I'd like to talk first."

"His name is Rocco Jones," she says. "He's an angel investor. He would be the perfect partner, Holden. He'll offer advice and guidance, and he has a million connections that can open a lot of doors for me."

I listen to every word because this is important to her. That makes it important to me, too.

I know who Rocco Jones is. I met the guy once at his grandmother's restaurant. Calvettti's serves the best Italian food in the state. The Calvetti family has touched the lives of many people in this city. If Greer has the opportunity to partner with one of them, I see that as a solid move for her.

"I'll know more soon," she says, eyeing the champagne bottle. "Where do you keep your champagne glasses?"

I reach for one of her hands. "I need to talk to you about something."

Her gaze scans my face slowly. "It's something serious, isn't it?"

"Very," I admit. "Life changing."

"For me or you?" she questions.

"Both of us, Greer."

She glances at the champagne bottle again before her gaze drifts to the couch. "Let's sit and talk. We should sit and talk, right?"

I squeeze her hand. "We should sit and talk."

Her fingertip traces her bottom lip. "Okay."

I lead her toward the couch in silence. I'm about to change her life forever, and I have no idea if anything will ever be the same between us again.

THE BEST WAY TO address a difficult situation is by jumping all in. My grandparents taught me that. It's how they handled all of the bullshit that came up, be it in business or with their family.

I have no fucking idea if jumping all in is what is best here. I don't know how to handle this, so I ease in slowly.

"Years ago, I had a pendant custom-made for my grandmother for her birthday."

Greer smiles. "Of course you did. You were probably the perfect grandson."

"There's not a chance in hell that's true." I chuckle. "I did like buying my grandmother gifts, though. She appreciated them. They meant something to her."

"What did the pendant look like?" she asks, her fingers trailing a slow path over my thigh.

I don't brush away the contact because I need it. I look into her face so our eyes are locked because I want her to see how much she means to me. "It was a four-leaf clover charm."

Her smile widens. "Like the one Olive wears?"

I bypass the direct question with an answer I hope softens the truth that's about to come out of my mouth. "It had two diamonds on it. One for my brother and one for me."

"That's wild." She scratches her upper lip. "You said you had it custom-made?"

"A jeweler in East Hampton took care of it for me," I explain. "I had him engrave two letters on the back of it."

She slides her hand from my thigh to her lap. It's shaking. I want to reach out and grab it, but I don't.

"An H and a J?" she whispers. "Was it an H and a J?"

"For my brother and me to remind my grandmother how lucky we were to be her grandsons." I close my eyes briefly. "I knew when she saw it, she'd love it, but she never got the gift."

She's on her feet in an instant, moving to the left before stepping to the right. "Celia said H and J were the initials of the jewelry designer. She said she picked it up at a market in The Hamptons when she went there for a party weekend with some people she worked with."

Standing, I swallow past the lump in my throat. "She took it out of the pocket of my jeans after we spent the night together."

She lets out a loud bark of laughter while shaking her head. "You did not sleep with Celia. She wouldn't have taken that from you."

I stand stoically, aching to reach out to take her in my arms, but she's walking backwards now, creating physical distance between us.

"I slept with Celia," I say clearly. "We went to a hotel after meeting at a bar. We spent the night together without exchanging names. When I woke up, she was gone. The charm was gone, too. I had shown it to her at the bar. She said it was beautiful. I can't say why, but she took it and the box it was in with her when she left, Greer."

"That can't be right," she whispers. "Maybe you're wrong."

"I'm not."

She rubs a hand across her forehead as tears drop onto her cheeks. "She got pregnant around that time, Holden. It can't be. You're not…"

"I'm Olive's dad," I say as tenderly as I can. "I believe with everything I am that Olive is our daughter."

CHAPTER SIXTY-FIVE

Greer

I FALL BACK onto the couch because my legs don't have the strength to hold me up. My entire world is spinning around me. None of this makes sense.

None of it.

Celia wasn't a thief.

Looking up at Holden, I ask through a sob, "Do you want the pendant back?"

He sits next to me. "Fuck, no, Greer. No."

My heart feels like it's ricocheting around in my chest. I swear I can't feel the floor beneath my feet, and there's not enough air in the room to fill my lungs.

There's another much more important question to be asked, but I can't form the words. I can't ask him if he's going to take her away from me.

I glance down at my hands, willing logic to step into this so I can think clearly.

"I know you'll want me to take a paternity test, " he whispers. "We can arrange for that as soon as possible."

He's being logical. Why wouldn't he be? He's the one who knew that my Olive might be his biological daughter.

"When did you realize?" I ask quietly. "How long have you known that she could be yours?"

He tilts his chin up, and I can't help but wonder if he's going to correct me and say he is Olive's father, not that he *could* be.

"When I saw the pendant around her neck the other night." He taps his shoe on the floor. "The picture she showed me of you and Celia confirmed it."

"It was a one-night stand," I point out. "That doesn't mean…"

"Olive has my eyes," he says calmly. "She resembles my grandmother."

"You're imagining that."

He nods ever so slightly. "I know this is a shock, Greer. I get that it's incredibly overwhelming for you."

That's an understatement.

The man I thought I was falling in love with is suddenly claiming to be the guy who knocked up my friend during a one-night stand forever ago.

I push to my feet again because I will never find clarity here with him.

I want to talk to Bruce and Martha. I need to speak to a lawyer. I have to hug my daughter.

"I have to go."

He's on his feet, too. He reaches for me but stops short of touching me. "Greer, please. We should talk more."

"I need to talk to other… there are other people I need to talk to right now."

Nodding, he steps back. "I understand."

I walk to the table to grab my tote bag. My gaze lingers on the bottle of champagne I brought with me.

I foolishly thought he wanted me here to tell me he was falling in love with me. I would have confessed the same to him before we toasted with champagne and made love.

The excitement I felt about finding a potential new business partner paled in comparison to what I'm feeling for Holden.

Or what I thought I was feeling.

"Can I call you tomorrow?" he asks from behind me. "Would that be okay?"

I glance over my shoulder as I reach the door to his apartment. "Maybe not. I need time."

"I'll give you some time," he says in a gentle tone.

It's only a promise of a brief reprieve, but I'll take it.

***

MARTHA HANDS me a mug of tea. I didn't ask for it, but she made it because she can tell that I'm spiraling.

I was in tears when I got home.

She appeared in the hallway as soon as she heard my first sob. I fell into her arms. I didn't say a word, but she offered many. All of them were comforting and focused on how she'd do anything to help me. She said we're a family and she'll help me through whatever it is.

Whatever it is.

It's the knowledge that my daughter's father may have just wandered into our lives.

Bruce walks into my den, closing the door softly behind him. It's unnecessary since Olive is fast asleep, but Bruce is a man who values privacy and will do anything necessary to protect his granddaughter.

I stare at them both as they sit side by side on the small pink loveseat that is opposite my desk. The loveseat was an impulse buy right after I moved in. When I first saw it, I pictured rainy afternoons with Olive curled up on it, having a nap.

I don't think she's fallen asleep on it once, but she's tucked her dolls in to sleep on it.

The purchase was worth every dime I spent on it.

"We want to help you, Greer." Bruce smiles gently. "You know you can tell us anything. There's no judgment here. We will always love you no matter what."

I know that and believe it deep within my bones.

These people are my family. They are Olive's family. They need to know what's happening.

"The man I've been seeing, he…"

"Holden?" Martha interrupts. "Olive says he's the nicest man she's ever met and his smile makes her smile."

That sends an ache through my heart. I brush away a falling tear.

"Did he break up with you?" Bruce asks in his best protective dad tone. "Give me his address and I'll have a talk with that young man."

I manage a small smile. "It's not that."

Bruce leans forward slightly. "Tell us what it is, dear."

"There's a chance that he might be Olive's dad." I take a breath as both of their mouths drop open. "He slept with Celia around the time she got pregnant. She stole that four-leaf clover charm from him."

"Oh, my," Martha whispers.

Bruce glances at her before he locks his gaze on my face again. "Did he know about Olive before you met him on your trip?"

"No," I answer quickly. "He had no idea I was a mom."

He considers that for a second or two. "Let's do the right thing. You deserve to know the truth. He does, and Olive sure as hell does."

I close my eyes and drop my chin. "A paternity test."

"Yes." His voice fills the room. "Let's find out if he's her dad. Would he be the kind of father she deserves, Greer?"

I look at Martha before I level my gaze back on Bruce. He's always been like a dad to me. He's given me advice whenever I've asked. He's held me when I've cried. He stepped up to take care of a little girl when his own son walked away.

"I think he has the potential to be as good a dad to our Olive as you've been to me," I tell him.

A single tear streams down his cheek. "You love this man, don't you? I think there's a chance you've fallen in love with him."

"I have," I admit for the first time out loud.

"Then it's settled." Bruce pushes to his feet, motioning for me to do the same. "Give me a hug, my girl. Tomorrow we'll make a few calls to find out what the next steps need to be to get that paternity test done."

I rush into his arms. Martha stands and joins in the embrace.

I cling tightly to my family. I have no idea what the future holds for Olive and me, but I know we'll get through it.

CHAPTER SIXTY-SIX

Holden

IT'S BEEN three days since I tore Greer's world apart, and I still haven't heard a word from her. Jameson has reminded me twice since then that I need to ask her to consent to a paternity test for our daughter.

I did speak to Rook about this after handing him a dollar. I told him it was to retain him and to buy his silence. He assured me that he would never repeat anything I told him in confidence even to Declan.

From an attorney's point of view, Rook suggested I seek out an expert in family law to help navigate what comes next. He threw out a couple of names of law school buddies.

I have yet to call either.

I want to talk to Greer before I take another step.

Grabbing my suit jacket off the back of my chair, I start toward my office door. A walk in Riverside Park will help me think more clearly.

Just as I'm about to swing it open, a soft knock comes from the other side.

It's well past quitting time, so everyone, including my brother, has left the office. The cleaning crew is milling about. That's why I shut my door. It's not that I don't like making small talk with them. I enjoy it. They're an incredible group of people who work hard for us.

Tonight, I didn't have the heart to dive into any conversations. Solace has been my best friend since Greer walked out of my apartment.

I swing the door open and instantly feel a sense of relief wash over me. "Greer."

"Hey," she says softly. "I went by your apartment. You weren't there, so I thought I'd try Riverside Park."

I love that she knows where I go when I need to think.

"Obviously, you weren't there either, so I thought I'd try here." She glances into my office. "Are you working late?"

I haven't done much work over the past three days, so I shake my head. "No. I was just on my way out."

"Can we go somewhere?" she asks. "Unless you'd prefer to talk here."

"We can go wherever you want." I look into her eyes. "You lead because I'll follow you anywhere."

"Your apartment?" she asks tentatively. "I'd like to talk there."

"I'll order a rideshare." I tug my phone out of the pocket of my suit jacket. "Have you eaten dinner, Greer? I can order some food to be delivered for when we get to my place."

"I'm not hungry."

I'm not either, even though I've barely eaten anything since I last saw her. "Okay."

"We should go down to the lobby to wait for the car," she says before starting toward my office door.

I watch her walk away from me, noticing the slight tremor in her hands as she does.

She's as torn up as I am, but we're going to talk. We'll figure out what comes next, and more importantly, we'll decide together what's best for our daughter.

I TOSS my keys and phone on the coffee table as I slide off my suit jacket. I fold it neatly before placing it over the back of a chair. My tie lands on top of it.

Greer stands silently watching it all.

"Do you want something to drink?" I ask. "Water, wine, soda…I could make you a coffee, but I'm not promising it'll be any good."

She smiles slightly. "I'm fine right now. Thank you."

I motion toward the couch. "Do you want to sit?"

Her gaze volleys between the couch and me. "I don't think so."

That's a sign that she wants to be ready to bolt for the door if need be. Unless she's going to tell me that she'll fight me on the paternity test, I won't give her a reason to leave.

She's been Olive's sole parent for her entire life. I can't blame her for trying to protect her little girl.

I glance at the watch on my wrist. The time isn't relevant. Unless I check, I have no idea if it's night or day. It's been that way since I realized Olive is my daughter.

When I look up, I find Greer staring at me. "I think you're her dad, too. She has your eyes, Holden. I didn't see it before, but I do now."

I blow out a quick breath, relieved that this conversation is not beginning as I thought it would. "I felt a connection to her immediately. My heart knew right away when I met her."

313

"I need to say something." Her bottom lip trembles. "I don't think I need to say it, but I think I should."

"You can say anything to me, Greer."

She nods briskly. "Okay. Here goes..."

I step closer to her, watching as she tucks her hands in the front pockets of her jeans before she tugs them back out quickly.

She's a ball of nervous energy. All I want to do is wrap my arms around her and hold her close. I need her to know everything will be all right.

"Do you want me to say something first?" I ask, almost kidding.

I'm trying to break the tension of the moment by giving her an out, but it may not be what she needs.

"Yes." Her eyes widen. "Say something, Holden."

I don't even consider what the next words out of my mouth should be. I just go with what has been sitting inside me for weeks now. The unspoken words that I wanted to express as soon as I saw her walk into the conference room for the first time. It was the day I found out her real name. It was also the day I realized I could have a chance with her.

"I'm falling in love with you, Greer."

Her mouth falls open. "What?"

"I know my timing is shit." I chuckle. "I wanted to tell you weeks ago, but I was scared. My track record with love hasn't been great, but I know what I feel."

She takes a tentative step toward me. "You were going to tell me before you found out about Olive?"

"Way before."

She closes her eyes briefly. "I feel things for you, too, but it's a lot right now. I don't know if I can say exactly..."

"You don't need to," I interrupt to save her from having to tell me she can't repeat the words I just said to her. "Your focus right now is Olive. I know that. I respect that. I love that about you."

The sound of a phone ringing breaks the moment. I know it's not mine because I silenced the ringer on the drive here.

"You should get it," I say. "It could be about Olive."

She drops her tote bag on the floor before bending over to search through it. As soon as she has the phone in her hand, she answers it. "I'm here. What's happening?"

The person on the other end of the call says something that makes Greer look right at me.

"We're coming," she whispers.

More silence from her as she listens intently.

"I'm bringing Holden with me." Her voice is strong. It's determined. "We'll be there as soon as we can."

My suit jacket is in my hand before the call is over.

"Olive hit her chin on the counter when she was brushing her teeth," she says in a rush. "She's fine, but she's asking for me."

"I can come with you?" I ask so there's no misunderstanding.

"I want you to." She holds out a hand. "I know she'd love to see you."

I kiss her hand softly. "I'd love to see her, too."

She motions to the friendship bracelet on my wrist. "Have you taken that off since Olive gave it to you?"

I hold up my hand, kissing one of the beads. "I never will."

CHAPTER SIXTY-SEVEN

Greer

"WHAT WERE you going to say back at my place?" Holden asks as we descend the stairs to the main level of my home.

I glance over my shoulder at him. His suit jacket is in the kitchen along with his cufflinks. The sleeves of his white button-down shirt are rolled up to his elbows. He looks comfortable and content.

I know a lot of that has to do with the fact that he read Olive her second bedtime story of the night. She hung on every word, and when it was time for her to go to sleep, he kissed her softly on the forehead.

The tears that were streaming down his face as he walked out of her room and brushed past Bruce and Martha were all the proof I needed that he's Olive's dad.

As soon as we reach the kitchen, I turn to face him. "I was going to ask you not to take her away from me."

He pulls me close, cradling the back of my head in his hand as I rest it against his chest. When I was about to ask the question earlier, I was on the cusp of tears. I don't feel that now because I know how he feels about me.

"I'd never do anything like that," he whispers as he holds me. "You're her mom."

I push back so I can look at his face. "You're her dad."

He nods. "We'll get the paternity test taken care of this week."

We discussed it in the rideshare here. Even though my heart is telling me they are father and daughter, I know the prudent thing to do is get the test done.

Celia and I never discussed who she was or wasn't sleeping with. She took that pendant from Holden nine months before Olive was born. My daughter's eyes are the same shade as Holden's, and even Bruce noticed that they share the same hair color, although he made a whispered remark to Holden that Olive was missing the gray streaks.

"Once it's confirmed, where do we go from there?" I ask quietly.

"I'll spend time with our little girl," he says. "We'll spend time altogether. I get to spend some quality time alone with you."

I let out a laugh. "I miss our quality time alone."

"You and me both," he quips.

"Soon," I promise. "We'll be together again soon."

He kisses my forehead. "I can't wait."

We stare into each other's eyes for what feels like endless moments.

"I'll book the paternity test this week," I whisper. "Is there a day that works best for you?"

"You name the time and place and I'll be there."

"We'll talk to her together when the test results come back." I smile. "I want us to tell Olive together that you're her dad."

"We will." He cups my face in his hands.

"I can't wait for our life together," I whisper, knowing it will help him understand how deeply I care for him.

He gazes into my eyes. "It's already started. This is just the beginning."

TODAY IS THE DAY.

I have an envelope in my hand. Holden does too as he approaches where I'm standing outside Palla on Fifth.

We agreed to meet here because I just had a coffee with Krista and Rocco. The deal for him to buy her shares is almost complete. I know he'll make an amazing partner for me, and with his business acumen and connections, Sweet Indulgence will reach new heights of success.

Holden and I briefly discussed the idea of him personally buying out Krista to keep the business in the family, but this is a wise move for me. I also don't want to complicate everything that's happening between us by dragging business into it.

Our relationship already has so many layers.

"You didn't open the envelope?" he asks before he kisses me softly.

"Neither did you."

He laughs, pinching my chin as he does. "I don't need to, Greer. Olive is ours."

I feel that, too.

Since the paternity test was done, we've spent time altogether as we waited for the results. Holden came over for dinner three nights ago and then took Olive and me out for ice cream. We visited him at his office yesterday. Olive had the chance to shake her uncle Jameson's hand even though we didn't introduce him that way.

Right now, he's just James to her, and he couldn't be happier.

"You'll marry me one day," he blurts out. "I'm putting that out there before the truth is revealed."

He taps the corner of his envelope on his palm.

"Would you still want to marry me one day if you're not Olive's father?" I have to ask, although I already know the answer.

"I love you, Greer," he whispers the words I will never hear enough. "Nothing will ever change that."

"I love you, too," I say for the first time. "Nothing will ever change that."

"You love me?" he asks as if he doesn't already know.

It was evident when we made love in his bed last night. It was tender and slow. I clung to him as I came, whispering his name into his ear.

I told him I loved him then, but it was just silent words that fell from my lips as he found his release.

"So much." I nod. "I love you, Holden."

"Fuck, I'm lucky."

I laugh. "Let's open the envelopes together."

"Good plan." He smiles. "Three, two, one, and then we go, okay?"

"Okay." I take a breath. "Three, two, one, go."

We rip the corners of each of our envelopes together. His paper is out before mine, but I keep focused on opening my envelope.

The sob that escapes him hits me in the heart just as I read the results.

"Congratulations, dad," I whisper as I kiss him. "It's a girl."

CHAPTER SIXTY-EIGHT

Holden

DINNER IS OVER. Martha and Bruce have gone for a walk, and the moment is here. I'm about to tell Olive I'm her dad.

I'm doing it with Bruce's blessing. When I arrived an hour ago, he took me into Greer's office, gave me the biggest bear hug of my life, and told me he knew I was up for the honor of being the father of his granddaughter.

He's a good man who loves deeply.

I'm grateful to be part of this family.

"Mom said you need to talk to me, Holden." Olive looks up at me. "It sounds important."

I drop the dishtowel in my hands on the counter. I was on cleanup duty. I'm the one who assigned that task to me.

I needed time to gather my thoughts. It's been a few hours since Greer and I opened the envelopes confirming I'm Olive's birth father. We agreed we'd tell her as soon as possible, so I came over with three flower bouquets in hand, and a bottle of good scotch for Bruce.

I thought the time it took to eat dinner would be long enough for me to prepare a speech, but I've got nothing, so I'm going to have to wing this.

I glance down at the T-shirt I'm wearing.

Olive's gaze follows mine. "Don't worry about it. I get all wet when I help with the dishes, too. Mommy said it's okay to make a mess when you're little."

"What about when you're big?" I ask.

She grins from ear to ear. "It's not so okay then, but I can wet my T-shirt too if it makes you feel better."

I look at the dark green Sweet Indulgence shirt she's wearing. "Maybe your mom can get me one of those shirts?"

"Ask nicely and she'll do it." She steps closer to lower her voice. "If you make your eyes look like this, that helps, too."

She bats her long eyelashes.

I can't help but laugh.

Greer walks into the kitchen from the hallway. "What's so funny?"

"His shirt," my daughter says, jerking her little thumb in my direction. "He's messier than me, Mom."

Greer's gaze volleys between the two of us. I can tell she's getting choked up, so I motion toward the main living area. "I think we should go sit down and talk."

"Okay." Olive reaches for my hand. "I'm sitting beside Holden."

I mouth the words *I love you* to Greer before I follow Olive into the other room.

ONCE WE'RE ALL SEATED, with Olive between us, Greer

takes the lead. "Do you know how you've sometimes asked me about your dad?"

"Oh, sure." Olive shrugs. "I think about him sometimes."

"What do you mean?" Greer asks.

"I think about if he's tall." Olive laughs. "If he has freckles. If he has a bald head. I sometimes wonder if he is good at basketball."

"He is," I say, without realizing I'm stepping in before I should.

Olive's head snaps in my direction. "Really?"

"He's really good," I tell her, stealing a glance at Greer as I do.

She's smiling. A soft nod of her head encourages me to keep going.

"He's pretty tall." I tap Olive's knee. "He's smart. His brother thinks he's smarter, but he's wrong."

'Wait!" Olive's hand darts into the air. "My dad has a brother?"

"He does."

Her gaze scans my face slowly. "Do you know my dad, Holden?"

This is it. This is the moment that my daughter finds out she has a father who loves her endlessly.

"I am your dad," I whisper.

Both of her hands leap to her mouth before she lets out a scream. "No way! You're pranking me."

I laugh. "I'm not. I just found out I'm your dad. "

Tears stream down her face so naturally the same thing happens to me.

"I'm happy," she whispers. "I have a dad and he's cool."

"I'm cool," I say to Greer. "Our daughter thinks I'm cool."

Olive jumps into my lap. "Can I call you dad?"

I swear I'm about to lose it. I don't know how I'm not sobbing right now. "I want you to."

"Okay, Dad," she tests it with a broad smile. "You're my dad."

Greer glides a hand over Olive's head. "Are you happy?"

"The happiest I've ever been." She looks into my face. "Are you and Mom getting married? Some people with kids get married."

I hand this question over to Greer by tossing her a look.

"We have lots of time to talk about things like that," she explains.

Olive looks up and into my face. "Do you love Mom?"

I stare into my little girl's eyes. "I love your mom very much."

"I do, too." She runs her hand over my jaw. "Are you happy that you're my dad?"

"It's the best thing that ever happened to me."

"To me, too," she whispers. "Do you like kittens?"

Greer laughs before tapping Olive's shoulder. "He's not going to say yes to adopting a kitten, Olive."

She glances back at her mom. "He might."

"No kittens for right now," I tell her.

"If we vote on it, I think we can get one." She rests her head on my shoulder. "You'd vote yes with me, Dad."

I hold her against me, feeling the rhythm of her small heart as it beats. I close my eyes to soak in this moment in time because it will live within me for the rest of my life.

I'm a dad. I'm the father of the most wonderful little girl.

"Right, Dad?" Olive presses me to answer. "You'd vote for a kitten with me. They're so cute."

"My friend, Declan, and his wife, Abby, have a kitten named Cindy," I say. "We can visit them whenever you want so you can play with her."

She bolts back up to a straight position to look directly at my face. "Seriously?"

"Seriously."

"I can't wait to meet Cindy." She smiles. "This is the best day ever."

"It is." I reach over to grab Greer's hand. "It really is."

CHAPTER SIXTY-NINE

Holden

IT'S BEEN two days since Greer and I told our daughter that I'm her father. I've spent as much time as I could with Olive and her mom since. Olive wanted to see where I live so I brought them here earlier for lunch.

Olive insisted on having a grand tour. It only took a couple of minutes because my apartment isn't large. At the end of the visit, she looked up at her mom and suggested I live with them.

Greer shot me a smile. I gave her one back, but there wasn't a discussion to be had at that moment.

This is all moving at warp speed, but I want my daughter to have the time she needs to adjust to all of this. Right now, it's a whirlwind of new discoveries, but we have a lot of lost time to make up for.

I don't want to rush anything. We have all the time in the world to be a family.

A loud rap at my apartment door tells me Rook and

Declan are here. I've already had a one-on-one conversation with my brother about the paternity test results and how things have been going since then. It's time to clue Rook into that and reveal to Declan that I'm a dad.

I swing the door open to find my closest friends with smiles on their faces.

It's almost seven p.m., so I'm not surprised to see a Franzini's pizza box in Rook's hands and a six-pack of my favorite beer in Declan's.

Rook may have an idea of why I called them both here, but Declan is clueless.

I motion for them to come in.

Rook bursts out laughing as he crosses the threshold. "Jesus, Holden. Enough with the twinning. Did you smuggle a phone into my apartment and hand it to my daughter so she can give you a heads-up about what I'm wearing every day?"

Declan and I join in the laughter since I'm wearing jeans and a blue T-shirt that's just a shade lighter than the one Rook has on.

"I may need to get in on this trend," Declan says.

He's still wearing the suit he's likely had on all day. Since Gilbert was born, he's gone back to working a few days a week, but he's making extra time to spend with his newborn.

They cross the apartment to drop the pizza and beers on the dining table.

As soon as they both turn around to face me, I look straight at Rook. "You're fired. You are no longer my attorney."

"Screw you!" he yells with a grin on his face. "I've never been fired before."

"You hired him for what reason?" Declan asks. "What kind of trouble did you get into?"

I approach where he's standing so I can be directly in

front of him because I know Declan, and a hug is in my very near future.

"I hired him to give me advice about a personal matter." I draw out the big reveal. "His advice was solid."

"You fired him, so can one of you tell me what the fuck is going on?" Declan looks at Rook before he levels his gaze back on my face.

"I'm a dad," I say proudly. "I have an amazing seven-year-old daughter."

"What the hell?" Declan stares at me. "Are you serious?"

"Her name is Olive," I tell him. "She's perfect, Declan. She's so fucking perfect."

That's it.

That's all it takes for him to pull me into him for a bear hug.

"How?" He chuckles. "Not how did it happen, but how did you find out?"

We break apart. "I fell in love with her mom. I met her daughter and realized she was my daughter."

He shakes his head. "Wait. You're saying you slept with this woman years ago, reconnected now, and she told you that she'd had your kid during your first go round?"

"It's way more complicated than that." Rook laughs, slapping Declan on the shoulder. "I'll grab some beers because this is going to take some time for Holden to explain it all to you."

IT'S BEEN four weeks since Olive found out she's my daughter. Tonight, I'm watching her spin around the dance floor in the ballroom at the Bishop Hotel Tribeca.

Martha made the pale green dress she's wearing. Olive said she felt like a princess in it.

I reach across the table to tap Greer's wrist to pull her attention to me. She reluctantly does. I can't blame her. She's been watching Olive dance, too. It's a sight to behold. As soon as I told my daughter that I knew how to tap dance, she wanted tap shoes.

For the past two weeks, we've been practicing in one of the spare rooms on the second level of Greer's house. Bruce has joined in with bare feet. It's become a family tradition after dinner.

"This wedding has got me thinking," I say as soon as Greer looks at me.

A soft smile spreads over her ruby red lips. "About what?"

She knows the answer to that question. As we were getting ready to come to Krista and Howie's wedding today, I dropped to one knee to tie my shoe. I heard her breath catch as I did, so I know we're edging closer to the day when I can finally ask this beauty to be my wife.

"When I get married, I have three solid choices for a best man," I tease.

Her eyes light up. "I have one choice for a matron of honor."

Since Olive is the flower girl today, she has already made it clear that when we get married, she's reliving that role for us.

"Martha?" I ask with a soft smile.

"You know it." She glances at Olive again. "It's been a month since she found out you're her dad. She's been asking me a question, Holden. She's going to ask you tonight."

"About?"

I expect her to say marriage or our living arrangements

since I've been spending a few nights a week at Greer's home. She's come to my apartment, too, but she's always in a rush to get back to her house before Olive wakes up.

"Her name." Her eyes lock with mine. "Olive Irwin-Sheppard is what she'd like to be called."

There's an instant lump of emotion in my throat. I knew this was coming when my mom met Olive last week. My daughter made a point of mentioning that she loved our surname. My mom pulled me aside to tell me that she thought Olive would make the request for a name change soon. Her grandmother's intuition was spot on.

"How do you feel about that?" I ask Greer.

"It has a nice ring to it." She smiles softly. "Olive Irwin-Sheppard. Greer Irwin-Sheppard. It all sounds good to me."

"Does that mean…"

I'm about to drop to one knee to ask her if it means she's ready for a proposal. I've been carrying an emerald and diamond engagement ring around with me for a week.

"It means one day after you move in with us, you'll get on one knee and it will have nothing to do with tying your shoe."

"I can move in tomorrow," I offer.

"We'll talk about when you should move in tomorrow," she counters. "We'll make it soon, Holden. We're a family. I feel it."

"Me too." I tilt my chin toward the dance floor. "Let's join our daughter out there."

She moves to stand, so I follow suit. I take her in my arms to kiss her deeply before we dive into the dancing crowd.

"I love you," I whisper. "I love you so fucking much."

"I love you, too," she says. "Until the end of time."

EPILOGUE

Holden

Three Months Later

I GLANCE at Greer as we drive up to the beach house in East Hampton. It's our first time here since we met.

"Is this it, Dad?" Olive asks from the back seat of my car. "This big house is our house?"

I reach for Greer's hand to kiss her palm before I answer. "It's our house. I think you're going to like it here."

"Like?" She laughs as she unbuckles her seat belt. "I already love it here. Is the water close?"

"Very close," I tell her. "We have a pool, too."

"No way!" She taps the back of Greer's seat. "Maybe Kirby can come with us next time, Mom. Can you ask Uncle Rook if she can come next time?"

Witnessing Greer become an integral part of my friend group has been a gift to me. She effortlessly fell into step with all of them. Rook and Carrie's daughter, Kirby, has become fast friends with Olive. They're about a year and a half apart in age, but that hasn't stopped them from making plans to make friendship bracelets together, go to the park for playtime, and even arrange sleepovers.

Greer has been coordinating all of that with Rook and Carrie.

It took Greer some time to adjust to Krista's move to Los Angeles, but they talk on the phone every day. Greer cried when Krista told her that her daughter would be named Ceci when she's born. It's a fitting tribute to the friend they both loved and lost.

Greer has been working closely with Rocco on mapping out a path forward for Sweet Indulgence. Before she officially signed on the dotted line to approve the sale of Krista's share to Rocco, we briefly discussed the idea of partnering on the business.

At the end of the day, and after hours of discussion, we decided our personal partnership would always be our priority. Adding the extra layer of a shared business interest to that is not something either of us views as a priority right now.

I'll always be available to offer her advice if she asks for it, but her business is going places and I couldn't be prouder.

"I'll talk to Rook." Greer shoots me a smile.

"Let's get inside." I swing open my car door. "There are bouquets of roses inside for my two favorite people."

"That's Mom and me!" Olive yells as she slides out after I open her door.

She races toward the house, looking up at how expansive it is.

As we follow her up the paved walkway, Greer glances in the direction of Mrs. Frye's house. Even though it's not visible from here because of all of the trees and shrubbery, it still brings back memories of the day we met.

"After Olive goes to bed tonight, I'll go over there and take a dip in the pool," I whisper in her ear. "I'll leave an umbrella close by so you can threaten me."

She lets out a laugh. "You're not funny."

"You laughed," I point out. "So, I am funny."

"Dad is funny." Olive nods as we get closer to where she's standing by the door. "He told me a joke last night about a pony that's sick."

"It had a sore throat," I set up the punch line.

"That's called a little hoarse," Greer says with a laugh. "That's it, right?"

Shaking my head, I playfully poke her in the side. "You'll pay for ruining my joke later."

"I sure hope so," she whispers.

It'll happen. I'll take her to bed late tonight and remind her of what we did in this house the first time we were here together.

"YOU ALWAYS MAKE me feel so good," Greer purrs as she snuggles up against me.

"Same." I chuckle softly. "How the hell did I come twice in thirty minutes?"

She slides the tip of her tongue over her bottom lip. "I had no idea after I blew you that you'd fuck me senseless minutes later."

My gaze trails over her naked body. "I want to go again."

She kisses the center of my chest. "Let's catch our breath first."

"I'll get a washcloth to clean you up," I whisper as I kiss her forehead.

We stopped using condoms the day I moved into the townhouse. That was almost two months ago now.

Greer is on birth control. We want another child, but we're going to take some time to enjoy our daughter together first. Rook directed us to a friend of his who practices family law. She's been helping us with the paperwork that's required to ensure I'm Olive's legal father on record. She's also handled our daughter's surname change.

"Okay," she murmurs.

I get up to head toward the bathroom attached to our bedroom. I stop in place when I notice the moonlight filtering in through the break between the sheer curtains that cover the large window overlooking the beach.

I tug them open more, allowing the light to stream in. It's dim, but it hits the bed in just the right way, casting a beautiful glow on the woman I love.

She's on her side. I can tell she's deep in thought. I hope to fuck she's thinking about the same thing I am.

"Let's go out to the pool for a glass of wine," she suggests. "The moon is beautiful tonight. Let's not waste that view."

"Last one to get dressed is getting pushed in the pool." I laugh. "Go."

She's out of bed with her sundress over her head in no time flat. I don't even have a chance to get my jeans in my hand before she calls it a win for herself.

"I'll get the wine," she says. "You get ready to get wet."

She slides on a pair of panties from one of the dresser drawers before she swings open our bedroom door and walks out, closing it with a soft click behind her.

I get dressed, taking time to pick a clean and pressed

button-down shirt. I clean my eyeglasses, brush my teeth and my hair, and look in the mirror.

If anyone had told me a year ago this would be my life, I would have laughed in their face, but I'm about to make it even better.

I head out into the hallway, stopping briefly to open the door to the bedroom Olive declared was hers now. She's fast asleep, dreaming of only good things, I hope.

I shut the door quietly, sprint down the stairs, and make my way straight out to the pool.

The tiny white lights that are strung from all the trees around the property are lit up. With the moonlight adding its own special magic to the moment, it looks like a fantasy come to life.

Greer is standing on the pool deck, looking at the still water. A light breeze is gently moving the skirt of her dress. Her long hair is cascading over her shoulders.

"The breeze is carrying the scent of the lilacs this way," she says. "Can you smell it, Holden?"

The fact that she knew I was behind her brings me joy. I can always feel it when she walks into a room. It's the same for her.

She's shared the significance of white lilacs with me. Knowing they were Celia's favorite flowers helps me appreciate them more when I sit in the garden of our home in Manhattan with our daughter.

It seems appropriate that they're adding a subtle touch to this moment.

I drop to a knee. "Turn around, Greer."

As soon as she does, her hands are clasped together on her chest. "This is it."

I smile because she's right. This is the moment I've been waiting a lifetime for. I know she has been, too.

"The day I met you, I had no idea what that would mean to me," I say, trying to swallow back my emotions. "I see forever when I look in your eyes. I love you endlessly. I will cherish you until my days on earth are over."

She steps closer. Tears are streaming down her cheeks.

"Please marry me, Greer. Please say you'll be my wife."

"I will!" she screams. "A thousand times over, my answer is yes, yes, yes."

I slip the ring on her finger and jump to my feet to kiss my fiancée. It's tender and soft, and mixed with both of our tears.

"You're a gift to me," I whisper to her. "You and Olive are my everything."

They are. They will always be, and I can't wait to find out what life has in store for all of us.

THANK YOU

Thank you for purchasing and downloading my book. I can't even begin to put to words what it means to me. If you enjoyed it, please remember to write a review for it. Let me know your thoughts! I want to keep my readers happy.
For more information on new series and standalones, please visit my website, deborahbladon.com. There are book trailers and other goodies to check out.
Feel free to reach out to me! I love connecting with all of my readers because without you, none of this would be possible.

Thank you, for everything.

THE BILLIONAIRE BUCK BOYS

They've got money, power and each other's backs but when it comes to love, these billionaires are about to lose control.

The *Billionaire Buck Boys* series follows a tight-knit crew of ultra-elite men who met at boarding school as young men and now dominate New York City. Boardrooms, penthouses, private jets – these guys play hard, win big and fall even harder.

Each book delivers a swoony, scorching romance with a powerful alpha who finally meets his match. When a Buck Boy, falls, they fall *all in.*

Read all of their stories, now.

WANT MORE? START HERE.
THE CALVETTI'S OF NEW YORK

He watches her every night. She lets him.

It started as a sinful little game, slow undressing behind thin curtains, locked eyes through open windows. But when she walks into a pitch meeting and finds her late-night voyeur on the investor panel, the stakes skyrocket. ***THIRST*** is a scorching, slow-burn romance dripping with tension, obsession, and the kind of heat that can ruin deals... or make you beg for more.

CHAPTER ONE OF THIRST

Dexie

"I don't understand why you haven't invested in window coverings for this place."

I turn to see my friend, Sophia Wolf, standing next to one of the large windows in my new apartment.

"I like the light," I answer quickly. "Besides, in my rental agreement it says that the building's superintendent will supply blinds and install them. The man is busy. I don't want to bother him about it."

"You pay rent which means it's his job to keep you happy."

Spoken from the lips of a woman who lives in a luxurious apartment with her novelist husband and daughter.

"Don't worry about it, Sophia." I put a cardboard box on the kitchen counter. "I really like this place. It's cheaper than my last apartment and there's a lot more room."

"I can't argue with that." She takes in the sprawling space. "Are you thinking of setting up your workstation over there?"

I haven't given it any serious thought yet because my time is limited. I work full-time in the marketing department for a cosmetics company and part-time helping Sophia with her clothing line.

My purse design business has yet to take off, but I'm determined to change that. I've put out some feelers to try and find a private investor for my company.

Supplies aren't cheap and even though I have a steady stream of customers willing to pay for my one-of-a-kind handmade purses, there's not enough cash coming in to take my business to the next level.

"I'm going to get all my stuff unpacked and then I'll figure that out."

She taps her heel on the hardwood floor. "That makes sense."

I point at a lamp on a table near where she's standing. "Can you turn that on? It's getting dark."

She hits the switch on the lamp and it instantly fills the room with soft light. "I have one more concern and then I swear I'll shut up."

I don't look at her as I open a box filled with dishes. "What?"

"Your bed is right in front of that window. Aren't you worried that your neighbors will watch you while you sleep?"

I picked this apartment because it has a loft feel to it. My bed is visible from my kitchen and the main living space. The only area that is separated by walls and a door is the bathroom.

I'm not shy. I've slept here for the past four nights and I haven't bothered to look out any of the windows to see if the people in the building next to mine are looking in.

"This is Manhattan." I stop what I'm doing and scan the

CHAPTER ONE OF THIRST

exterior wall and the arched windows that face the building next door. "People are too busy to stare in here."

"What if you bring a guy home, Dex?"

"A guy?" I pause as I tuck a lock of my pink-streaked blonde hair behind my ear. "You're worried that my neighbors are going to watch me having sex? Is that what you're asking?"

She laughs. "It's a possibility, no?"

"Not right now." I give an exaggerated shrug. "I don't have time to meet men. You can rest easy tonight knowing that my neighbors won't be getting a free show."

Her dark brown hair sways as she crosses the room to pick up her purse from where she tossed it onto the corner of my bed when she got here. It's one of my latest designs. Sophia is my walking talking billboard and so far, I've had a few customers seek me out because of her.

"I have to get home." She shoulders the navy blue bag. It's a perfect complement to the red blouse and white pants she's wearing. "I need to make dinner. Do you want to come by for a bite?"

I look around the apartment. I have too much to do tonight. There's no way I can spare the time it would take to get to her place, eat, visit and then trudge back here. "Thanks, but I'll pass."

"I'll talk to you later in the week." She hugs me tightly. "Call me if you spot any peeping Toms."

"Will do." My reply is swift. "I'm not sure what you'll do about it, but I'll shoot you a text if I catch one."

I arch my back in a stretch as I finally put away the last of my dishes. I don't own a lot, but my mismatched collection of

CHAPTER ONE OF THIRST

plates, bowls and glasses is enough for me. I've never thrown an elaborate dinner party. I only cook the basics. All of my spare time is devoted to my passion. If I'm not working on one of my handbags, I'm thinking about elements for the next design.

I ate a bowl of cereal for dinner after Sophia left, taking a spoonful in between unpacking boxes.

I've accomplished more tonight than I thought I would. I glance at my phone sitting on the worn laminate countertop and realize that it's nearing midnight.

Since I need to be at my office at Matiz Cosmetics nine hours from now, sleep has to be next on my schedule.

I hurry toward the bed. It's not the most comfortable I've ever slept in, but it's large and right now it's calling my name.

Just as I'm about to tug my pink T-shirt over my head and unbutton my jeans, I turn to the windows.

The building next door is close. It's also home to many apartments with dozens of windows.

Several of the windows are shuttered with curtains and blinds. Subtle hints of light peek around the edges. A few apartments don't have any window coverings and they're backlit enough that I can make out what's happening in the homes of my neighbors.

Television sets flicker, a woman dances past a window, and then my gaze settles on the apartment directly across from mine.

I know that the low light coming from the lamp in the corner makes me visible to the person standing with their back to me.

There's a light on in their apartment too. It's not too bright, more of a gentle glow that casts just enough warmth that I can see the shape of a man. He's tall with broad shoulders.

When he turns, I lean closer to the window to get a better look.

He does the same. His gaze locks with mine and a shiver of excitement runs through me.

He's gorgeous. He has dark hair and a chiseled jaw.

He slides his suit jacket off, and I long for him to open each of the buttons on his white dress shirt.

He does. He unbuttons them one-by-one and as he reaches the last, he stops and rests both hands on the glass.

I hold my breath wanting more, but then he turns abruptly, walks away from the window and leaves me wondering when I'll see him again.

Click here to continue reading THIRST

ALSO BY DEBORAH BLADON

The Obsessed Series

The Exposed Series

The Pulse Series

Impulse

The Vain Series

Solo

The Ruin Series

The Gone Series

Fuse

The Trace Series

Chance

The Ember Series

The Rise Series

Haze

Shiver

Torn

The Heat Series

Risk

melt

The Tense Duet

Sweat

Troublemaker

Worth

Hush

Bare

Wish

Sin

Lace

Thirst

Compass

Versus

Ruthless

Bloom

Rush

Catch

Frostbite

Xoxo

He Loves Me Not

Bittersweet

The Blush Factor

BULL

CRUEL

Starlight

SAINT

Sweetheart

Trust

Greed

Rook

Dreamboat

Honor

ABOUT THE AUTHOR

Deborah Bladon has never read a romance hero she didn't like. Her love for romance novels began when she was old enough to board the bus, library card in hand to check out the newest Harlequin paperbacks. She's a Canadian by heart, and by passport, but you can often spot her in New York City sipping a latte and looking for inspiration for her next story. Manhattan is definitely her second home.

She cherishes her family and believes that each day is a gift for writing, for reading, and for loving.

Printed in Dunstable, United Kingdom